Praise for Catherine Ma

The Blood Runs Cold

I think I've found a new favorite author! This is the first book that I've read from Catherine Maiorisi and I must say that she certainly has my attention because I'm a huge fan of her flawless and captivating writing.
- The Lesbian Review

Maiorisi populates her story with some much-needed diversity, but never strays into exhortative territory: these characters feel like individuals rather than stereotypes intended to fill a role (or purpose). The mystery is suitably complex, sure to keep readers guessing until late in the game.
- The Bolo Books Review

An excellent police procedural with twists, turns and surprises. Looking forward to other mysteries featuring Chiara Corelli.
- Map Your Mystery

Love page-turner thrillers? Pick these books up—then try to keep up with Chiara. It'll be a breathtaking ride.
- Kings River Life Magazine

A Matter of Blood

This book was a long time in the pipeline for Catherine Maiorisi, and it shows. The pacing is perfect, and there has clearly been a lot of work done over a long period on making sure that everything is just right. As a result, this is a really easy read that will hold your interest until the final page. The characters are well fleshed out and relatable, with terrific chemistry between the leads and a great story line. There is nothing in this book that doesn't need to be there, and it was a pleasure to read from start to finish. My only gripe is that number 2 in the series is not out yet!

- The Lesbian Review

This is an excellent mystery and whodunit with well-developed characters, an interesting backstory and great potential. The action is fast-paced but nicely interspersed with moments of stillness and humanity.

Well written, enjoyable reading. I literally can't wait for the next one to see where Ms. Maiorisi takes us with both the crime-fighting team and the prospective romance.

- Lesbian Reading Room

READY
for LOVE

Other Bella Books by Catherine Maiorisi

Matters of the Heart
No One But You

A Chiara Corelli Mystery Series
A Matter of Blood
The Blood Runs Cold

About the Author

Catherine Maiorisi lives in New York City with her wife Sherry.

While working in corporate technology then running her own technology consulting company, Catherine believed she was the only lesbian in New York City who wasn't creative, the only one without the imagination or the talent to write poetry or novels, play the guitar, act, or sing.

Catherine eventually found her imagination. And, when she's writing she feels as if she's meditating. It's what she most loves to do. But she also reads voraciously, loves to cook, especially Italian, and enjoys spending time with her wife and friends.

When she wrote a short story to create the backstory for the love interest in her NYPD Detective Chiara Corelli mysteries, Catherine had never read a romance and hadn't considered writing it. To her surprise, "The Sex Club" turned out to be a romance and was included in the *Best Lesbian Romance of 2014* edited by Radclyffe.

Another surprise was hearing the voices of two characters, Andrea and Darcy, chatting in her head every night, making it difficult to sleep. Reassured by her wife that she wasn't losing it, Catherine paid attention and those conversations led to her first romance novel, *Matters of the Heart.*

No One But You, Catherine's second romance grew from thoughts of a child on a beach into an exploration of what happens after the happily ever after.

Ready for Love, her third romance, started with an image of Renee watching Darcy and Andrea dance their first dance as a married couple and became an exploration of racism.

Catherine has also published mystery and romance short stories. Go to www.catherinemaiorisi.com for a complete list and while you're there sign up for her mailing list.

An active member of The Golden Crown Literary Society, Sisters in Crime and Mystery, Writers of America, Catherine is also a member of Romance Writers of America.

READY
for LOVE

Catherine Maiorisi

BELLA
B O O K S
2019

Copyright © 2019 by Catherine Maiorisi

Bella Books, Inc.
P.O. Box 10543
Tallahassee, FL 32302

All rights reserved. No part of this book may be reproduced or transmitted in any form or by any means, electronic or mechanical, including photocopying, without permission in writing from the publisher.

This is a work of fiction. Names, characters, businesses, places, events and incidents are either the products of the author's imagination or used in a fictitious manner. Any resemblance to actual persons, living or dead, or actual events is purely coincidental. The publisher does not have any control over and does not assume any responsibility for author or third-party websites or their content.

Printed in the United States of America on acid-free paper.

First Bella Books Edition 2019

Editor: Ann Roberts
Cover Designer: Judith Fellows

ISBN: 978-1-64247-075-8

PUBLISHER'S NOTE

The scanning, uploading, and distribution of this book via the Internet or via any other means without the permission of the publisher is illegal and punishable by law. Please purchase only authorized electronic editions, and do not participate in or encourage electronic piracy of copyrighted materials. Your support of the author's rights is appreciated.

Acknowledgments

Ready for Love started with an image of Renee watching Darcy and Andrea dance their first dance as a married couple. I'm not sure why that image popped into my mind since *Matters of the Heart*, which featured Darcy and Andrea, was published in 2016. Renee was a minor character and the only thing I knew about her was that she was a butch. Though I only saw her back in the image, she appeared sad and unhappy to me. My imagination did the rest.

When early in the book Renee casually announced she was biracial, I didn't give it much thought. But as I wrote and as Olivia, her therapist, questioned Renee's feelings about being biracial, I suddenly realized what I was writing and thought, holy shit, I'm in trouble. I never intended to write a biracial character, at least not consciously. And I seriously thought about changing her mother from black to white. But I couldn't. I was already in love with Renee, with her story and her struggle, so I continued writing. At the same time though, I began to read whatever I could trying to understand the feelings and experiences of mixed race and black people in our increasingly racist world. The stories are out there every single day but focusing and immersing myself changed me, sensitized me to racism. Of course, like Renee, I can empathize with the people who live with racism but I can't really *know* their experience. I did my best. I hope I got it right.

One interesting tidbit: As I immersed myself in Renee's feelings and conflicts I remembered talking to a guy at a party at a black friend's house, almost fifty years ago. At the time I was shocked that this white-skinned, blue-eyed, sandy-haired guy identified as black and he graciously spent about two hours discussing it with me. The character Ed is based on him.

This was a hard book to write and the support I received from friends and colleagues helped me continue writing when I worried that I would never get it right.

As always, thank you to my wife Sherry, my first reader and provider of support and encouragement throughout the process.

Thank you also to Annette Mori, a multi-published author, for taking time from her own writing to beta read for me.

Thank you to my friend Carol Glassman for taking time to read and comment from her perspective as a white mother of an adopted black son and a black grandson.

Thanks to my friend and editor Ann Roberts for putting up with my moaning and groaning about changes and for her continued support and encouragement.

Thanks to Jessica, Linda, and all the women at Bella Books for the work you do. I'm proud to be a member of the Bella family.

Special thanks to Cheryl Head, author of the Charlie Mack Motown Mystery Series, for taking time from her own writing to do a sensitivity read of the book. Cheryl's specific comments and criticisms made this a much better book.

Writing is a strange business. We solicit comments and suggestions and go off to our little hidey-holes to make (or not) changes that we think will address the issues identified. However, it's an imposition to ask the same people to reread the manuscript to make sure the changes hit the mark so the problem may still exist. Or we may have made it worse. And, it's likely in the process of making changes that we make other errors.

So, although I'm grateful for the feedback I've received, I want to make clear that the opinions in *Ready For Love*, the discussions of racism, the ideas the characters express, the feelings of the characters and any errors, omissions, or misstatements are mine and only mine.

Dear readers, I hope you enjoy reading *Ready For Love* and I hope it makes you think. Please let me know by contacting me at http://www.catherinemaiorisi.com or by message on Facebook.

CHAPTER ONE

The lights dimmed. A hush fell over the guests and all eyes followed the golden spotlight to the entrance of the tent. A drumroll. And the glowing brides entered to applause from the more than two hundred guests.

Tessa of The Tessa DeLong Band eased into "At Last," and Darcy and Andrea floated onto the floor for their first dance as a married couple. The brides were so beautiful together, so obviously in love it was painful to watch. Yet Renee couldn't take her eyes off them.

Except for a few pounds and a few laugh lines, Darcy looked the same as the young woman Renee had fallen in love with at first sight twenty plus years ago. But today's more mature Darcy was even more beautiful. The intensity of Renee's love and the power of her sexual attraction to Darcy were as strong today as they were then. Knowing it was her fault that she'd lost Darcy forever didn't make it any easier. If only she'd—

"She looks beautiful, doesn't she?" Tori's voice in her ear pulled her back to the wedding in a tent on the beach in Fire

Island. The guests were still cheering and clapping as the brides waltzed; waiters still circulated offering hors d'oeuvres and champagne, and candles still flickered on the tables decorated with bouquets of multicolored flowers, and white tablecloths and napkins. Renee blinked, trying to keep the tears blurring her eyes from overflowing. "That she does."

Tori, one of only two friends taller than her, draped an arm over Renee's shoulders. "And happy."

"That too." Flooded with memories of Darcy looking at her the way she was looking at Andrea, singing the words to the song in her ear the way she was singing to Andrea, Renee pressed her handkerchief to her eyes. Hopefully Tori and the several hundred other wedding guests watching the newlyweds would think Renee's tears were tears of joy. She *was* happy for them. And, at the same time, sad for herself. She'd expected today to be difficult, but she hadn't expected the lush romantic atmosphere of the wedding tent and the rituals of exchanging vows and dancing a first dance as a married couple to exacerbate her sense of loss and intensify her loneliness.

Tori squeezed her shoulder. "Are you ready to let her go?"

Renee stiffened. Was she misinterpreting Tori's question? Or did she know? Feeling exposed, Renee looked up at Tori. She didn't know what she was expecting, but she found love and warmth and sympathy. "How long have you known?"

"Since Darcy and I became a couple my freshman year in college. I could see the pain in your eyes. I knew you wanted to be with Darcy and I could feel you struggling to relate to us as a couple. I'd just come out with Darcy. I was light-headed with love and lust and excited about playing with the big girls, but I was barely eighteen, and though I wanted to reach out to you, I didn't know how. Or whether I should."

"And you didn't feel threatened by me hanging around?"

"Oh, but I did. I was pretty sure Darcy was still in love with you when she and I first got together. And your friends and other upperclasswomen were only too happy to tell me how you and Darcy drifted in and out of being a couple, that you never stayed broken up for long, that Darcy slept with other girls while she waited for you. I felt the ax could fall at any time. After all, Darcy was attracted to my mind but visually and personality-wise, I was like a butterfly in the caterpillar stage, shy, awkward, and not fully formed. Why would the sexy, gorgeous, brilliant, and sophisticated Darcy Silver choose me over her equally gorgeous, brilliant, sophisticated, and sexy French ex-lover Renee Rousseau? But Darcy was never anything but attentive, loving, and kind to me. And after a few months I began to trust that she wanted to be with me."

Renee dabbed at her eyes again, glad that the lights were low and focused on the brides. "How did you know I'm still carrying a torch for her?"

"Kindred souls? Remember, I loved her too. And I carried a torch too. Until I met Elle." She drifted off for a few seconds, remembering. "I believe you never fully let go of your first love. And maybe somewhere very far inside of me there's still a tiny ember burning. But I've let go of Darcy in a way that I believe you haven't. She was your first love, too, and, though you've dated hundreds of women over the years, it seems to me you've never moved on."

Renee flinched. Speaking to be heard over the band, Tori seemed to be shouting, announcing Renee's secret to the world. She eyed the people standing on either side of them at the edge of the dance floor, but everyone seemed focused on the brides. Everyone except *Maman*. Her mother's concern was apparent from across the room. Renee forced a smile and waved, hoping to reassure her. "How does Elle feel about you loving Darcy?"

"Elle doesn't doubt that I love her. She understands Darcy was my first and had a profound influence on the person I am today."

Renee scanned the crowd again. Tori must have picked up on her anxiety because she put her arm around Renee and lowered her voice. "If it makes you feel better, I don't think anyone else knows." She raised her eyes to the dancing brides. "Except maybe Darcy."

"*Merde*." Renee pulled away and glared at her. "You think she knows?" She couldn't keep the panic out of her voice.

Tori pulled her close again and spoke only for her ears. "I'm pretty sure she does. You know she's sensitive to all of us in the Inner Circle." Tori laughed. "After all, at one time or another just about every one of us has been her lover, and though I've never had the pleasure, your lover too. She's always tender and loving with you, as she is with me. Our history with Darcy is special and sometimes we see things in her and she in us that aren't apparent to others."

"It's true. I've always felt she could see into me." What made her think she could hide her love from Darcy? "Do you think Andrea knows?"

"I don't know. As an ER doctor she's tuned in to people. And she knows you and I are important to Darcy so she pays attention to us. But I wouldn't worry about her knowing. Remember she carried a torch for her friend Julie for twenty years after their relationship ended and was best friends with Julie and her wife Karin the whole time."

"I forgot that." Renee ran her hand through her hair. "What a sorry group we are."

Tori snorted. "Sorry, yet wonderful."

Renee smiled. "Did you ever try to get back with Darcy?"

Tori shook her head. "I was really raw when she dumped me. I eventually began to date, but it was Darcy I wanted. If the modeling contract hadn't brought me to New York City after I graduated, I probably would have moved to Chicago to avoid seeing her. But, with the clarity that years of therapy bring, I know it was anger rather than love that propelled me to ask Nancy to move to New York with me. I knew we'd socialize with the Inner Circle and I wanted to hurt Darcy like she'd hurt me."

Tori cleared her throat. "I'm not proud of myself but I barely noticed when Nancy got involved with someone else and left me. A few weeks later, I flew to the Caribbean for a two-week modeling job. Two days into the shoot, I was walking on the beach by myself thinking about Darcy and about my life and I realized my behavior was childish and self-defeating. Though Darcy was seeing someone, I decided to go after her when I got back."

Tori grinned. "But life is unpredictable. The day after my walk, the other model on the shoot arrived." Tori's eyes wandered to the statuesque woman talking with a group of their friends. "We were in sync from the first hello. The electricity between us on and off camera was magical. Elle, the sexy black warrior goddess and me, the Nordic icy white blonde, were together in almost every shot. By the time we flew back to New York City, I was crazy in lust for the first time since Darcy. And before I knew what was happening, the anger and the pain had dissipated and my feelings toward Darcy had changed. I was madly in love with Elle. When I finally talked to Darcy, she couldn't explain why she'd dumped me, so we had a good cry together and became great friends again. What about you, Renee, have you ever tried to get back together?"

She'd spent so many years loving Darcy. Yet she'd never broached the subject of getting back together. "The timing was always off. By the time I finally resolved to talk to her, she'd crashed her car, was bedridden with casts on her four broken limbs, and was already pursuing Andrea. Who could have predicted Darcy's heart would be so bad she would need a live-in doctor to monitor her? And, it could only be fate that sent the beautiful Dr. Andrea Trapani to sweep Darcy off her feet." She shrugged. "Maybe we weren't meant to be together." Her gaze flicked back to the dance floor where the brides were wrapped in each other's arms for another slow dance.

Tori followed her gaze. "It's been a long time, Renee. You were both so young and you've both changed over the years. Maybe you didn't try to get together because you understood how difficult it would be to re-create a relationship you had when you were both eighteen years old. And maybe a part of you has used Darcy as an excuse to avoid committing to anyone."

Renee had been in love with Darcy more than half her life. Had she been lying to herself all these years? "You think I don't really love Darcy?" She'd tried to tamp down the anguish in her voice, but judging by the guilt on Tori's face, she'd failed miserably.

"My bad." Tori slapped herself on the hand. "I probably shouldn't have said that, Renee. Only you know what's in your heart. But as wonderful as Darcy is, she's not the only wonderful woman in the world. You've been with so many women in the last twenty years it's hard to believe you haven't found another who touched your heart. Or maybe you have and I never heard about it."

Renee hesitated. She rarely talked about her feelings, and though she and Tori were good friends, their friendship wasn't in the bare-your-soul category. Until now. But as Tori said, their history with Darcy made them kindred souls. Besides, she trusted Tori and it was a relief to share all of this with someone. "Gina."

"Our Gina?" Tori frowned. "Really? I didn't know it was ever that serious."

"Yes, our Gina, in our senior year in college. No one knew because we pretended to be casual sex partners."

Tori scrutinized Renee's face. "Why?"

Renee's gaze skittered over the crowd standing around the dance floor and settled on Regina Octavia Gibson standing with her arm around her girlfriend Beth Braxton. She still had the grace and presence of the figure skating champion from the slums of Newark, New Jersey but she looked a lot more sophisticated in her sleek haircut and elegant pantsuit than she had in her dreads and jeans all those years ago. Gina, like all of the Inner Circle, had mellowed with age and her activist edges had softened. "A long story, Tori, and too painful to go into right now."

"But you've managed to stay best friends."

"*Oui, cheri*, that's what we lesbians do, *non*?"

"Oh, oh, you're slipping into French. It must be important. I'll drag it out of you another time. Only Darcy and Gina. No one else in all the years since college?"

Renee shook her head, opened her mouth to deny there had been anyone else, but the smiling face of someone she hadn't let herself think about in years, popped into her mind, followed immediately by a familiar longing and sense of loss. And just as she had since the day she'd been left without even a "fuck you," she refused to acknowledge the still vivid hurt and want. "There may have been one other." Saying it out loud made it real. She trembled, remembering.

Tori's put an arm around Renee's waist and pulled her close. "I've got you."

Renee gripped Tori's arm, steadying herself. "*Mon Dieu*, Tori, I can't discuss this in the middle of Darcy's wedding."

"I'm so sorry. I didn't mean to stir up bad memories."

"It's not you, Tori. The wedding awakened memories and feelings I thought I'd dealt with, memories and feelings I'd rather not think about now." *Or any time.* Renee loosened her grip and straightened. "I'm okay, thank you."

Tori met Renee's eyes. "So what are you going to do now?"

Renee shifted her attention back to the brides slow dancing to a fast song. Darcy always preferred to dance to the music in her heart, regardless of the music the band was playing. Memories of dancing like that with Darcy filled her with sadness. She needed to do something fast, before she became a weepy mess. "Right now I'm going to take you onto the dance floor and act like I'm having a good time."

Tori pretended to pout. "You mean I'm not good company?"

"You're wonderful company but I need to dance with the bride, so don't be insulted if I turn you loose to dance with Andrea."

"There are worse fates in this world." Tori threaded her fingers between Renee's. "Are you planning to celebrate New Year's Eve in Paris with Darcy and Andrea and the rest of us?"

The thought of being in Paris with Darcy married to someone else was nauseating. "If I hadn't promised my parents a visit, I'd probably skip it. I'll be there with you all New Year's Eve, but how much additional time I'll spend with the brides and the Inner Circle will depend on how I feel by then." She swung Tori around so they were facing each other.

Tori squeezed her shoulder. "I found love on an island in the Caribbean. Paris is the most romantic city in the world. Who knows? You might find the love of your life there."

Renee snorted. "I spent the first eighteen years of my life in Paris and never had a glimmer of a love life so I'm not going to hold my breath. But you never know. For now, I'm going to dance you over to the love of my life and claim her. At least for a dance." She whirled them onto the floor and at the first opportunity she tapped Andrea on the shoulder. "May I steal Darcy for a dance?"

Darcy smiled as Tori spun away with Andrea. "You were gazing into the distance for so long, I thought you'd never ask." Darcy moved into Renee's arms.

"Just remembering."

Darcy tilted her head back to see Renee's face. "Time for you to move on."

Renee spun them. "I'm working on it."

"Are you really?"

"Don't rush me, Darce. It's only been twenty or so years."

Renee's attempt at humor fell flat. Darcy's eyes glistened with unshed tears. "Oh, Renee, I'm so sorr—"

"No, you don't have anything to be sorry for. I'm the one who needs to apologize for using a joke to push you away. And for so much more. I promise to work on moving on. Soon." *God, what an ass. Causing Darcy pain on her wedding day.*

Darcy looked up again. "You know for years I thought we'd end up together, but our lives always seemed to run on parallel tracks with no way to cross over."

"I did too. I mean I thought we would end up together." Renee sighed. "More accurately, I hoped. I guess it wasn't meant to be. Tori just suggested that hanging on to you is my way of avoiding commitment. And she might be right."

Tessa burst into "I Will Always Love You." Renee laughed and brushed the tears from her face. "Ironic. Here I am baring my soul, saying out loud what I thought I'd hidden for twenty years, and this comes on. Did you tell her to sing it?"

Darcy flashed a mischievous grin. "I did. I told her to sing it when she saw me dancing with a tall, sexy, dark-haired butch with kissable lips and bedroom eyes, wearing a perfectly tailored black tuxedo."

"You still think I'm sexy?" Renee couldn't keep the surprise out of her voice.

"Hey, don't cry, sweetheart." Darcy tightened her arm around Renee's waist. "You're one of the sexiest women I know. I seem to recall telling you that often."

"Maybe if I hadn't been so selfish and self-involved, I might have been listening instead of running away. And I might not have—"

"Don't." Darcy put her finger over Renee's lips. "You were my first love and I'll always love you. But we've both wasted too many years wanting what we can't have. I don't mean to speak in clichés, but you have so much to offer someone, Renee. I hope you give up the ghost of our past love and find her soon."

Renee blinked back tears. "Thanks, Darce. I'm going to try. Andrea is a very lucky woman. And so are you. I hope you know that despite everything, I really am happy for you two."

Once again, Darcy leaned back to look into Renee's face. "I do, love, I do." She kissed Renee lightly on the lips. "Please come to Paris."

A tap on Renee's shoulder. "My turn." Renee dropped her arms and watched Darcy waltz away with Dr. Julie Castillo, Andrea's best friend and the cardiologist who had saved Darcy's life mere months ago. It wasn't until a couple danced in front of her, cutting off her view of Darcy and Julie, that Renee realized she was standing in the middle of the crowded dance floor, alone. *Merde.* She strode out of the huge tent erected on the beach in front of Darcy's Fire Island house and stood on the boardwalk. The roar of the ocean and the pounding surf always put life in perspective for her. It was a mild evening for October and the breeze off the Atlantic was chilly but refreshing, the taste of salt on her tongue and the fishy smell familiar and invigorating.

She'd spent so much time here with Darcy over the years it almost felt like a second home. She smiled, remembering all the good times. But there were some not-so-good times too. The first time they'd been here together was the summer after their freshman year before Renee went home to Paris. They'd tried to repair the relationship Renee had broken, and it had been a painful and tender two weeks. They'd made love in nearly every room of the huge house, on the wraparound deck, in the pool, on the beach and in every position they'd learned in their first six months of experimentation. By the time Renee went home to Paris, they were hopeful they could work it out and were both looking forward to spending time together in Paris later that summer.

Renee walked out on the large wooden platform built on the beach for the wedding, past stacks of folding chairs that the several hundred guests had sat in during the ceremony, and stood under the flowered canopy where Tori had led the brides through their vows earlier today. She gazed at the pounding surf and breathed deeply, filling her lungs with ocean air. Her shoulders dropped as some of the tension left. She was still sad but she felt lighter than she had for a long time. Why hadn't she talked to Darcy about her feelings before today? She actually was happy for Darcy and Andrea. What did that mean about her? About her feelings for Darcy? Was Tori right about her using Darcy as a shield? And what about...

A gust of wind pulled at her jacket and brought her focus back to the beach. She shivered. Music, laughter and the tinkling of glasses drifted out of the tent, reminding her she was here for the wedding of her best friend. Time to focus on celebrating and having fun. She took another deep breath, adjusted her tuxedo jacket and headed inside. As she moved through the tent, she noted women she'd slept with at one time or another. Some smiled and waved. Others cut her dead. She hated hurting the women she took to bed, or anyone for that matter, so she always discussed her no strings sex policy upfront, but inevitably some of her partners hoped for more. When at last she made it to the safety of the Inner Circle, she was surprised to see her mom and dad surrounded by her friends. Her dad put his arm around her waist and murmured in French, "I've never seen so many women in tuxes. Everyone looks marvelous, but you, my sweetheart, are the most gorgeous and sexy."

"Merci, Papa. Perhaps you're a little prejudiced?" They laughed together.

"What is this, you two?" Without waiting for an answer, Maman straightened Renee's bowtie. "It's all settled. Papa and I are hosting a gala New Year's Day brunch for Darcy and Andrea and all of their friends and family who come to Paris."

Renee repressed the groan that threatened. Her suspicion that her mom knew she was still in love with Darcy was confirmed during the exchange of vows when Maman had put her arm around Renee's waist and held her close. And though Maman had always adored Darcy, Renee suspected the brunch was Maman's way of forcing her to confront the fact that Darcy was now married to someone else. So much for her plan to limit the time she spent with her friends when they all were in Paris. "That sounds great."

"May I have this dance?" Renee turned. Dr. Laurie Feldman, once a lover, now a good friend and her physician, curtsied. Happy to be rescued from hearing all the plans for Paris, Renee bowed. "You may, madam." They danced a few fast numbers, then a slow dance. She hadn't been body to body with a woman in almost a year and holding Laurie close felt good. Laurie was a perfect example of what Tori had described—an intelligent, independent, attractive woman, wonderful in and out of bed. Yet Renee had felt no spark past the initial sexual attraction and after a couple of months had backed away. Gently. But away. Renee would have been sorry if Laurie had been one of the ones who chose not to remain friends.

When the music turned fast again, Renee released Laurie and bowed. "Merci, madam." She turned to see who had tapped her shoulder and was eye to eye with a grinning Gina. "May I?"

"My pleasure." Renee led Gina onto the dance floor. When the music slowed and they were in each other's arms, Gina spoke. "You looked sad earlier. Are you okay?"

Renee shrugged. "The wedding has brought up a lot of memories." She pulled Gina closer. "Of Darcy. Of you. Of us. And…things I haven't thought about in years. I was feeling sad about lost…opportunities. About seeing the women I most care about paired up with others." She tickled Gina's side. "I think I'm having a midlife crisis." No way was she getting pulled into this discussion here. Again.

"I'm not surprised at the memories." Gina touched Renee's cheek. "I've been remembering too. But you've seemed down for a long time. I figured you'd talk to me when you were ready, but let's get together soon, just the two of us, so I can get into that head of yours."

"Are you going to marry Beth?"

"She's ready but I'm not. I'm sure she's the one for me but I never thought marriage would be a possibility for us, the LGBT community, and it's not something I ever wanted." She stiffened. "You're not thinking you want us to get together again, are you?"

Renee kissed Gina's cheek. "I love you Gina but once was enough. I like us as best friends."

Gina sighed. "Me too." The song ended and they gazed at each other for a moment. "I'll be out of town next week but I'll call when I get back. We haven't talked in too long."

The fabulous cocktail hour was followed by a fabulous dinner but why wouldn't it be? Darcy had hired the best lesbian caterer in New York City and given her carte blanche to create the menu. Of course steak, Darcy's favorite, was an option but Andrea's touch was seen in the vegetarian and fish choices available. Wine and champagne and beer were served at the tables and drinks of any sort were available at several bars placed around the tent. Renee had heard that the lesbian waitresses were willing to work for nothing just to be at the lesbian event of the year. Of course, Darcy made sure they were well paid.

In between courses, Renee danced with her mom, her dad, Darcy's Aunt Maria, and her Uncle Carlos, as well as many old friends.

The reception was in full swing around midnight when Renee escorted her parents, Darcy's aunt and uncle, and Andrea's parents to the dock to get the next ferry to the mainland, where Darcy had a limousine waiting to drive the six of them back to New York City. Marveling at how good she felt after admitting her secret, she whistled as she walked back to the party, ready to really let go in a way she hadn't for almost a year. She didn't need to drink to have fun, but there was no need to watch her intake because, as usual, Darcy had thought of everything. She'd rented the ferries for the night and they were running every half hour; plus she'd hired a fleet of vans to drive guests from the ferry landing back to the City.

From the minute she entered the tent again until the music stopped, Renee danced with so many partners she could barely remember some of them. She left with most of the Inner Circle and the other dancing fools on the last ferry departing Fire Island at five in the morning. It was light when she tumbled into bed. Alone. She'd felt happy and free dancing, but she hadn't felt even a glimmer of sexual attraction to any of her many partners. Her libido had never failed her before. From the first time she and Darcy made love their freshman year until just under a year ago she had been full-steam ahead whenever a woman caught her eye. She was starting to worry.

She slept until noon. Now she lay in bed. Thinking. For more than twenty years she'd stood on the sidelines watching and longing for Darcy but she'd never spoken to Darcy about her feelings. Darcy was one of the kindest and most caring people in her life, so it wasn't as if she would have slapped her down or laughed if she'd tried to get back together. Instead, she'd jumped into bed with anyone who came onto her or any woman who attracted her. Tori's comment bounced around in her head. Was she right? Had Renee used Darcy as a shield to keep anyone from touching her heart? But why? She was sure that kind of hang-up usually came from some trauma in your family or childhood. But her parents were still very much in love and they'd always been loving and supportive of her. And she'd had a happy childhood. Hadn't she? Did it matter? She didn't need to know why she was holding on to Darcy. She needed to figure out how to let go of her.

She checked the bedside clock. Time to get ready for lunch with her parents before their flight home but she needed to figure this out and continued to mull over the issue in the shower. Almost twelve weeks to New Year's Eve but given she'd already committed to be in Paris with her family the weeks of Christmas and New Years, she really only had ten or eleven weeks to work through her feelings for Darcy. Not a lot of time but it had to be enough because she was determined to be free of Darcy when she saw her again in Paris.

Last night, thinking she needed to start putting herself out there to meet women again, she'd changed her mind about giving away the two tickets she'd purchased for the Gala at the Metropolitan Museum of Art next week. Instead, she'd invited her cruising buddy Maya to go with her, knowing they'd walk in together, then be free to circulate on their own and leave alone or with someone else. Were her feelings for Darcy holding her back? In any case, she would be forty soon. And Darcy was a married woman. Time to be done with her. If she was going to change her life she needed to do something different. And she knew just who to call.

CHAPTER TWO

Renee was shocked to hear Darcy's husky voice when she answered her phone the Saturday following the wedding. "Aren't you on your honeymoon?"

Darcy's silky laugh reminded Renee of things she was definitely trying to forget now that Darcy was married. "Technically, I guess. But we've been busy getting my aunt and uncle ready to fly to Italy with Andrea's parents tonight, and helping Francine and Jennifer settle into the downstairs apartment, so for me, the honeymoon will start when our plane takes off for Greece tomorrow night. Are you free for brunch tomorrow? Just the two of us?"

Renee hesitated. Was Darcy mad? Talking about being in love with her when she'd just married someone else was totally inappropriate. "Am I in trouble?"

This time Darcy's laugh was hearty. "No, sweetheart, I feel the need for closure with you and I hope you're willing to humor me."

Renee should have expected Darcy's call. Always so careful with the feelings of her friends, Darcy would want to make sure Renee wasn't hurting. A burst of love warmed her, love for the friend who probably knew her best of almost everyone in the world, the friend who took time away from her new wife to make sure her ex-lover was all right. To avoid the tears threatening, Renee sang, "I will always huuuumor youuuu" to the tune of "I Will Always Love You."

Darcy harmonized with her and they repeated the lines a couple of times, then she laughed again. "Pretty cheesy, Renee. It'll be quiet around here tomorrow afternoon so come about noon. If it's another warm day we'll eat in the garden. And don't worry, Gregg will cook, not me."

"And Andrea is all right with this?"

"She might object if I was planning to seduce you but she's fine with us meeting to talk about our torrid past."

Renee cleared her throat. "Um, sorry, I didn't mean to imply—"

"Damn it, Renee, I'm the one who should apologize. I didn't mean to make light of...us, of our past. I love you and I really want us to finally..." Darcy sniffed and was silent for a moment. "I hate being so emotional these days. I want us to put the past behind us. And, yes, Andrea is all right with it. She knows everything. She actually figured it out on her own that first weekend we were all at Fire Island. But she trusts me. And she knows what it's like to love someone from afar for years, so she encouraged me to meet with you alone to try to help you work it through. She won't be here. She's rented the apartment she owns on the West Side to a family from England and she's meeting with them to be sure everything is in order before we leave."

The next day was one of those cloudless, sunny October days that felt like summer but the cool blue of the sky, the red, yellows, and oranges of the trees turning and the smell of burning leaves signaled autumn. Renee strolled across Central Park to Fifth Avenue, then down several streets to Darcy's house, mansion really, that, with its walled garden, took up about two-thirds of the east side block. An only child, Darcy had inherited her dad's multibillion-dollar financial empire plus this huge house in the city, the one on Fire Island, another in Palm Beach and her mother's family villa in Italy.

Renee mounted the stairs and reached for the bell, but the door opened before she pressed it, and she was face-to-face with Andrea. The warmth of Andrea's smile and her hug dispelled Renee's doubts about Andrea's feelings toward her. "I'm so glad I got the chance to see you, Renee. We really didn't have much time to talk at the wedding. Let's be sure to spend some time together in Paris."

She kissed Andrea's cheek. "Maybe after you and Darcy have had a couple of months alone you'll have eyes for the rest of us." Though Renee had disliked or, at best, tolerated every woman Darcy had been involved with since Tori, she genuinely liked Andrea, separate from Darcy. "We'll definitely do something together in Paris."

"I have to run. Darcy is reading in the garden. Enjoy your brunch." Andrea dashed down the stairs and jogged toward the park.

Renee wandered through the house to the door leading out to the garden. Gregg, the young man Darcy's Uncle Carlo had rescued from a life of petty crime when he was a teenager, poked his head out of the kitchen. "Ah, Renee. Mimosa or Bloody Mary? Coffee? Or tea? And lemon ricotta pancakes, eggs your way, waffle, chicken sandwich or all of the above? Darcy is having the pancakes."

"Good morning, Gregg. Coffee and orange juice. No alcohol. And I'll go with the pancakes." She watched him pour her coffee. "I thought you were done here."

"I volunteered to cook until the newlyweds leave tonight. Tomorrow I start work with Tori at Buonasola. And then in January I'm off to the Culinary Institute." He handed her a mug of coffee. "Darcy is in the garden."

Renee walked down the ramp. She had lots of fond memories of time spent here with Darcy, reading, making out, and lazing about when they were still a couple or a sometime couple. And, many more recent memories of dinners and parties and quiet brunches like this one.

Darcy waved from the table under the now almost bare grape arbor. Renee wiped her sweaty palm on her jeans. What the hell was she nervous about? She'd already professed her enduring love to Darcy so what could be so bad? She kissed Darcy's forehead and joined her at the table.

"Hey." Darcy smiled. "I see you have coffee. Did Gregg get your order?"

"He did. He said brunch would be out in a few minutes." Images of Darcy in this very spot splayed in a wheelchair with casts on both arms and legs after her car accident, then later struggling on a walker as she recuperated from emergency heart surgery, flashed in Renee's mind. Darcy had been through a lot in the last six months but today she was strong and healthy and had that newlywed glow. "I don't have to ask how you're feeling. You look terrific."

"Terrific sums it up." Darcy gazed at her. "What about you?"

Another thing Renee loved about Darcy, no beating about the bushes. "I'm good. As we discussed while we were dancing, I want the kind of happiness you've found with Andrea and now I have to figure out how to get from here to there."

Darcy covered Renee's hand with hers. "I want that for you too. I was sitting here remembering the day we met. My first sight of you in front of the dorm, tall and gawky and so handsome in your suit and tie staring at me as if I was a goddess. You took my breath away. And I almost dissolved into a puddle later when I discovered you were my mysterious French roommate."

Renee closed her eyes remembering that first encounter. "It was magical. I felt like Cupid's arrow had pierced my heart. Maman had to tell me to close my mouth because my jaw dropped when I heard your voice for the first time. And when I got a look at you I was enchanted."

Gregg delivered plates and silverware, two glasses of orange juice, a platter of lemon ricotta pancakes, maple syrup, a large bowl of fresh strawberries, blueberries, and raspberries, a separate dish with sliced mango, pineapple, cantaloupe, and honeydew, and a large carafe of coffee. "Enjoy. Text me if you need anything else." He walked away humming.

Renee poured more coffee for each of them while Darcy served them pancakes and fruit. "Still eating healthily, I see. Do you miss the steak and chops and bacon?"

Darcy sighed. "Sometimes. But then I think about how close I came to dying from that heart attack. I'm trying to take responsibility for what I eat and to eat what's good for me. Andrea is my wife now, not my doctor, and I don't want to put her in the position of having to monitor my diet."

Renee dribbled a little maple syrup over her pancakes and took a bite. "I guess we're both growing up. You not eating what you know is bad for you. Me trying to let go of a lifestyle and, um," she cleared her throat, "a love that I know aren't healthy for me."

Darcy put more strawberries on her pancakes and added pineapple and mango to her plate. "We're both going to be forty soon so it's about time we grow up. But there's a lot to be said for youth, for first loves. I was so in love with you, Renee, that it was almost painful."

"And I was out of my mind in love with you, Darcy. I know I screwed us up, but I still don't know why. Or why we never got together again. Hopefully, forty will bring some insights."

"Yet all these years we both acted like this grand passion wasn't that important. Instead of definitively ending our relationship, we ignored the pain we'd caused each other and acted as if it hadn't mattered. But first loves are always important. I think talking about it will help you, and me, get some closure. I don't know if you realize how much you hurt me by deciding at the height of our passion that I wasn't enough."

"It wasn't—"

Darcy put a hand up. "Let me finish. Intellectually, I knew it wasn't about me. But I felt unworthy because you couldn't commit to me, and because you were always looking for someone else. I thought I wasn't smart enough, pretty enough, or sexy enough for you. Yet, I knew you loved me. It was confusing.

At first I thought you'd eventually realize it. When I walked away for the last time, I was battered and depressed as hell. Even when I first got together with Tori, you were the one I wanted. It took some months but I slowly fell in love with her and was able to let go of you, of the hope you would realize you wanted me, only me."

Deeply ashamed of the pain she'd caused the woman she said she loved more than anyone in the world, Renee was speechless. Finally she whispered. "I'm so sorry, Darcy. I've been thinking about you, about us, since the wedding. There's no defense for what I did to you. I was so self-involved that I didn't let myself know I was hurting you." Renee stood. "Can we walk and talk?"

She took Darcy's hand. They'd strolled the paths of this garden hand-in-hand like this many times over the years; some strolls were idyllic, some were painful as she tried to heal the wounds she'd inflicted on Darcy, and later all were companionable. "The depth of my feelings for you scared the shit out of me. Sometimes I wanted to crawl inside you or lock our dorm door and never leave. It was overwhelming. Our love woke me, woke my sexuality, it fed me and gave me the confidence I'd never had. It was that sexuality and that confidence that made me desirable to other girls, and, needy twerp that I was, I couldn't resist. Being wanted made me feel powerful. I believed you would wait for me, that you would be there when I'd had enough, not enough sex, but enough of the ego boost that was like a drug to me."

Renee took her handkerchief out of her pocket. She wiped the tears from Darcy's face and then her own. "When I tried to get back with you at the beginning of our junior year and you refused, I wasn't worried. In my mind Tori wasn't your type and you'd dump her in a month. But as the months passed and you spent more and more time with her, I felt you slip away."

Darcy squeezed her hand. "I wasn't looking to fall in love with Tori or anyone. I was waiting for you. But I was wounded and she healed me. I'm a lucky woman. I've had three glorious loves in my life. You, Tori, and now Andrea."

Renee wrapped her arms around Darcy. "I'll never understand why I let you go." Her sobs surprised her. Darcy pulled Renee's head down to her shoulder, gently rubbed her back and held her while they cried together.

Once again Renee used her handkerchief to dry both their faces. She laughed. "What a pair we are. Maybe it's better we're not together. We'd be crying all the time."

Darcy punched her shoulder lightly as they started walking again. "I'm more emotional since my heart surgery. What's your excuse?"

"Unrequited love?" Renee stopped to face her. "I'm curious. Did you ever think of getting back together?"

Darcy nodded. "I seriously considered trying again when you were at Stanford and I was at Harvard, but from your sporadic letters and our occasional phone calls, I got the impression you were still far from committing to anyone. Just the thought of going back to our ping-pong relationship made me sick, so I started dating others."

Her need for conquest, or was it affirmation, hadn't changed until recently. In graduate school she was still jumping from woman to woman, running from anyone who wanted more than a casual sexual fling—except for that one time when she'd wanted more but let her go, or, more accurately, had been let go without a word.

Darcy was right. Renee probably couldn't have made a commitment then. "We should write a book. Our relationship has had more angst than a Shakespearean drama. Talk about star-struck lovers. It really seems as if we weren't meant to be together."

"It does. Ironically, minutes before I crashed my car I'd decided to dump Gerri and call you to talk about trying to get together." Darcy shrugged. "Of course, thanks to Candace, by the time you all found out I was lying here helpless with all four limbs in casts feeling abandoned and spewing my rage at anyone who dared approach, Andrea had appeared and rescued me. And I was smitten."

Renee laughed, then doubled over laughing so hard she couldn't speak. Aware of Darcy's puzzled look, she fought to regain control. "You won't believe this, Darce. But I swear I had decided to call you to talk about the same thing, but you were supposed to be in Italy. I thought about flying there so we could talk about it in person but I decided it had waited so long another few weeks wouldn't matter. I had no idea you were right here feeling alone and abandoned."

Darcy hugged Renee. "I believe it. And, again, you're right. It definitely seems as if the universe thinks we weren't meant to be a couple."

Darcy shivered and pulled her phone out. "I'm getting chilly. After I text Gregg to bring us more hot coffee, let's go sit and talk about this unrequited love of yours." She led them back to the table and turned on the outdoor heater. They picked on the fresh fruit until Gregg arrived with a steaming pot of coffee and clean mugs. He poured the coffee, picked up the dirty dishes and the cold pancakes and left them alone again. Renee inhaled the rich dark brew before tasting it.

Darcy eyed Renee over her coffee cup. "So, my darling Renee, I know I'm special and wonderful and the most gorgeous, intelligent woman you've ever met, but I'm still having trouble understanding why you say you're still in love with me after twenty years."

Renee threw her hands in the air and shook her head. "I honestly don't know. I've never thought about why. I just am. Or I think I am."

Darcy sipped her coffee. "You and Gina were pretty serious for a while. Were you in love with her?"

"You knew about that? We kept it pretty quiet."

"I ran into Gina on campus right after one of your arguments. She was distraught and needed to talk. I got the impression you were both talking about the long term. And then, you weren't."

Renee flushed. "We were in love for sure. And it was wonderful. Except, she didn't want to be seen with me because her friends, the other activists in the Black Student Alliance, wouldn't approve of our relationship. We fought about race constantly. She couldn't see my point of view and I couldn't see hers. It was horrible. Right after graduation we realized that being together was more painful than breaking up, so we decided to try being friends."

"I'm puzzled. If you were in love with Gina after you were in love with me, why is it you feel you've been in love with me since freshman year?"

Renee wrapped her arms around herself and stared off into the distance. "Good question. I don't have the foggiest. I just know almost always when I felt myself getting close to someone, it was feelings of love for you that made me push them away."

Darcy's expression made clear what she thought about that. "I find it interesting that as close as we've been all these years, you never once mentioned the possibility of us getting back together." Darcy hesitated, as if unsure of what she was about to say but then continued. "Andrea thought she was in love with Julie for twenty years, but she was holding on because of some childhood trauma. You've never mentioned any trauma but there must be a reason you've been holding on."

Renee took Darcy's hands in hers. She gazed into Darcy's eyes. "I swear I'm going to figure out what the hell I'm doing with my life. Things are really bad when I'm not interested in sex. And, believe it or not, for nearly a year I haven't been. I'm ready to change. In fact, I'm starting therapy tomorrow."

Darcy pulled Renee into a tight hug and kissed her cheek. "Go forth and heal thyself. I expect to see a new woman in Paris."

CHAPTER THREE

At eight a.m. the following morning, Renee sat facing Dr. Olivia Cummings, the therapist who had kicked her out of therapy ten years ago after almost a year of listening to her moan about Darcy while rejecting any attempt to delve into her issues. Dr. Cummings had said come back when you're ready to change. At the time Renee had been angry and frustrated because she thought she was ready.

Now sitting across from the blondish, sixtyish woman, Renee knew Olivia had been right to kick her out of therapy and knew she'd made the right choice to come back. She was definitely ready to change.

Olivia sat in her therapist chair, legs up on the hassock, drinking her tea. She looked relaxed but Renee knew she was taking in her posture, her clothing, the movement of her fingers, her expression, everything and anything to get a reading on her. "It's nice to see you again, Renee. What brings you back?"

Renee ran her hand through her hair but conscious that Olivia would recognize that as nervousness, dropped her hand into her lap. Suddenly she had nothing to say. This was ridiculous. She'd gone over this in her mind a thousand times since she'd made the appointment last week.

Olivia smiled. "I checked my notes and I was surprised to see that it's been more than ten years since our last session. Does this visit mean you're ready to give up Darcy? Or have you already done that and are here about something totally different."

The warmth in Olivia's voice bolstered her confidence. She took a deep breath. "I'm ready to give up Darcy."

Olivia nodded. "It's been how many years?"

"Twenty or twenty-two, depending on whether you mark it from when I declared at eighteen that Darcy and I needed to have an open relationship or when I was twenty and she fell in love with Tori and walked away from me permanently."

"So why now?"

"I'm not sure. For almost a year I've felt like something was missing from my life. I've lost interest in dating and casual sex." She took a deep breath. "And Darcy got married last weekend. At the wedding, I admitted my feelings for Darcy to Tori, another ex of Darcy's, and Tori suggested I might be using Darcy to avoid making a commitment to anyone else. I also acknowledged my feelings to Darcy and she encouraged me to move on. Yesterday, for the first time, Darcy and I spent a couple of hours talking about what happened between us."

Olivia put her tea down on the table next to her. "Do *you* feel you've been using Darcy to avoid commitment?"

Renee sighed. "Maybe. I've dated a lot of women and never committed to anyone since. So it's plausible. I'm hoping you can help me with that."

Olivia made a note. "I'm flattered you chose to come back to me, despite the way we parted. But it's been a long time so we'll need to start from the beginning again."

Renee had hoped to skip some of that old stuff, but she was determined to do whatever it took. "I'm very serious. And I'd like to be free of Darcy by mid-December, which gives us a little over nine weeks."

Olivia laughed. "You hang on for twenty plus years and now you expect to work through it in nine weeks?"

Renee blushed. "I'm ready, Olivia. I'll see you five times a week if that's what I need to do. But I want to be well on the way when I meet up with Darcy, Andrea, and the Inner Circle on New Year's Eve in Paris."

"And the Inner Circle is?"

"Originally close college friends but expanded to include others over the years. We're each other's chosen family."

Olivia picked up her calendar and flipped the pages, nodding. "I can accommodate you three times a week, most weeks, and I'll try to squeeze in more sessions toward the end if we need extra time. If you'd like to start now, tell me about yourself."

It was stupid to think any therapist would remember details after ten years so moaning about it would just slow her down. In her management consulting work Renee always asked clients to start at the beginning. But where does her beginning begin? Her mind raced, tossing out and discarding opening statements. Focus Renee, this isn't a deposition. The beginning is where you decide it begins. "My African-American mom met and fell in love with my French dad while she was backpacking through Europe the summer after she graduated from college. They married and she moved to France to be with him. I was born and grew up in Paris, the youngest of five children. I have a sister who's eighteen years older than me, and three brothers— sixteen, fourteen, and twelve years older. All well planned and spaced. Though my mom denies it, I've always believed I was an accident. The photograph considered the official family portrait was taken years before I was born. As a child the picture made me feel like an outsider looking in on the happy family. It made me sad.

"My dad, Alain, is a famous sculptor and painter, and my mom, Natalie, a not-so-famous musician, composer, and author. We spent most summers and some years in Italy while my dad taught painting and sculpture and my mom taught music. I went to private schools in Paris and Italy, and I'm fluent in English, French, and Italian." Renee hesitated. "Is this what you want?"

Olivia lifted her cup as if saluting. "Go on."

"I was tall, skinny, and geeky with very long hair. In school we had to wear uniforms with skirts and I always felt awkward and ugly. As I got older my few friends suddenly focused on boys and I had absolutely no interest in talking to them, talking about them, or dating them. I didn't understand it then but I knew I was different from everyone. I buried myself in my studies and became more and more isolated until even my few childhood friends dropped away. My mom thought I was depressed and needed a change of scene, so when I was considering colleges, she suggested I go to her alma mater in the US and make a fresh start. I liked that idea. I applied and was accepted.

"My life changed for the better about a month after I graduated from high school. My mom and I were shopping for college clothes and we saw a woman dressed in a man's suit, button-down shirt, and a necktie. She even seemed to be wearing men's shoes. She was beautiful and sexy. I was enthralled. My mom noticed my goggle-eyed stare and figured it out. At lunch later, she asked whether I thought I might like to dress like that woman. I denied it and she let it go. But I couldn't stop thinking about the woman and a week later I admitted that I did want to dress like her, like a boy. Her only question was whether I wanted to start now or wait until I was at college.

"I didn't even have to think about it. I wanted the clothing immediately. I said I wanted to have it in enough time so I could get used to wearing it in the house. The next day we went to a tailor who took my measurements and suggested styles, fabric, and colors. I had a number of fittings but it wasn't until a couple of weeks later, when the first two suits, shirts, and ties were delivered that I was actually able to see myself dressed the way that woman was dressed. The clothing fit beautifully and I felt sexy and self-assured and more comfortable than I'd ever felt in skirts and dresses. The whistles and compliments from my brothers and sister made me blush but boosted my confidence. I felt comfortable and attractive for the first time in my life, and within a few days, I ventured out into the streets.

"The week before we were supposed to fly to New York, my mom and I went for haircuts. I surprised her and the hairdresser by pulling out a picture of a very short boy-style cut. After confirming I wanted that style, my mom nodded to the hairdresser. The hairdresser tied my long, wavy hair close to my neck then easily clipped it off, leaving me feeling light-headed from the sudden loss. As she styled the remaining hair, the hairdresser asked whether I wanted to donate the sixteen inches of hair to a place that made wigs for cancer victims. I was so anxious she had to repeat the question twice. Finally, she stepped back, made a few quick snips, and spun the chair so I was facing the mirror. I stared in wonder at the stranger looking back at me. It was the appreciative sounds from my mom, the hairdresser, and the other workers and customers in the shop that made me realize I wasn't the only one who thought I looked beautiful. I was ecstatic."

"Your mother sounds very supportive," Olivia said.

"She is. And so is my dad. She told me that they had been pretty sure I was a lesbian, that it was obvious I wasn't comfortable in dresses, but they felt it needed to come from me rather than them."

"We need to stop in a couple of minutes but how do you think feeling like an afterthought, like an outsider in your family, affected the way you are in the world?"

Renee stared out the window, gathering her thoughts. "I'm not sure. I know my parents love me. I think it's just because I was born so many years after my sister and brothers. And that damned family picture."

Olivia nodded. "So you feel rejected by your family."

"I wouldn't say…well maybe I do. They all have each other and sometimes I feel like I don't belong."

"Do your sister and brothers love you?"

Renee shrugged. "They've always been there, always been part of my life, but there's not the same closeness as with my parents."

"Do you think the distance is put there by them? Or by you?"

Renee thought about her visits. "It's hard to know. I only go to Paris for four or five days a few times a year, and when I'm there I try to spend time with my nieces and nephews so they know who I am. My sister and brothers invite me over but I'm generally focused on their kids and my parents. Maybe it's just a time thing. This year I'll see them when I'm in Paris for a couple of weeks over Christmas and New Years."

Olivia stared into her cup as if looking for the next question. "Because we have so little time, Renee, I'm going to be more active in your sessions than I usually am. When you are with your siblings, pay attention to how you relate to them and make an effort to connect. Also, have you ever asked to have a new family photograph taken?"

"You mean one with me in it?" Duh. Of course that's what she meant. What an idiot. Why hadn't she ever thought of it? "No, I haven't."

Olivia stood. "We're out of time now, but we can explore that next time if you want. I'll see you Wednesday, same time."

CHAPTER FOUR

Maya whistled softly when Renee arrived Tuesday night to escort her to the Metropolitan Gala. "My, my, you look stunning, Renee. Midnight blue is your color, though I do like your black tux and your gray tux and... Well, I love that you have so many tuxedos in so many colors."

"Merci, madame." Renee bowed. "And you look fabulous, as well. Green is definitely one of your colors and that gown brings out all your best features."

"Gallant as always." Maya smoothed her gown.

Renee helped Maya into her cape and followed her out of the apartment. The luxury car she'd hired for the evening was idling at the curb. Renee waved the driver off and eased Maya into the backseat before going to the other side and sliding in next to her.

The Metropolitan Museum was a brief ride across Central Park but Renee always preferred having a car waiting rather than having to fight for a cab at the end of the evening. Besides, the luxury car was much easier to get in and out of in formal clothing.

A few minutes later, the car turned onto Fifth Avenue and idled a few minutes as taxis and limos in front of them stopped briefly to dispatch elegantly dressed socialites, celebrities, business giants, and models. The museum was lit for the event and seemed to glow in the early dark of October, casting a warm light over the crowd of spectators. As Renee help Maya out of the car, they heard some in the group nearby wonder who they were amongst all the luminaries attending this prestigious event.

Maya took Renee's arm. "Let's give them something to think about, Renee." She moved closer and looked up at Renee with adoring eyes. The click of cell phones and the flash of cameras accompanied them and the other attendees up the sweeping staircase.

At the entrance, they walked past a row of ushers and the roped-off area where the press was confined, displayed their invitations and meandered from the Great Hall to the Egyptian collection. Heads turned as they entered the room already filled with hundreds of men and some women in tuxedos and women in elaborate gowns juggling flutes of champagne and hors d'oeuvres. Before Renee got her bearings, before she adjusted to the background classical music and the low roar of conversations, Maya was swept away by a woman who must have been waiting to pounce. Maya threw Renee a kiss as she was led away. Renee smiled. Maya was short, full-bodied, and attractive, not beautiful, but her voice, both speaking and singing, was deep and rich like warm chocolate and soothed like sultry nights of sex. Fold in her high energy, good humor, and fine intelligence and she was unstoppable. Women were drawn to her like bees to nectar.

Like Maya, Renee had no trouble attracting women, but now that the meeting and seduction game, the casual hookups, no longer interested her, she wasn't sure what she expected of tonight—or why she hadn't given her ticket away.

As Maya faded into the crowd, Renee wandered in the opposite direction, past the reflecting pool, past the Egyptian statues, past the Temple of Dendur, to the floor-to-ceiling windows overlooking Central Park. She gazed out into the semidarkness of the park for a few minutes then turned back to the room. The lavender and blue lighting cast romantic shadows on small groups of people standing or sitting on the ledge of the reflecting pool. Her eyes skimmed the hundreds of people who appeared deep in conversation. Was she the only one feeling lost and lonely? She turned back to the windows. She'd experienced these exact feelings when Darcy told her she was in love with Tori, when she and Gina decided to be friends not lovers, when she was dumped at Stanford, and less than two weeks ago at the wedding. What was she doing here? At the time she'd bought the tickets to the gala, she'd already lost interest in dating and casual sex, but she was still hoping if she put herself out there, she'd meet someone who captivated her and fired up her libido.

But while she was dressing earlier this evening, it occurred to her that dancing and laughing with so many desirable women at the wedding hadn't done a thing for her libido. The truth was, she'd been putting herself out there since the end of the first semester of her freshman year in college and she was still single. She laughed at herself. Even though she wasn't remotely interested in going home with a woman, she'd come here tonight. Wasn't the definition of insanity doing the exact same thing over and over again and expecting a different result? She fingered her bow tie. Maybe she *was* insane. She took a deep breath. The five thousand dollars she'd paid for the two tickets were a business expense, so she'd do the honorable thing, chat up some business contacts and then go home and curl up with her book. That was another perplexing thing. Why was she suddenly addicted to the lesbian romances she'd always poked fun at? Was it the satisfying happily ever after? Damn. She needed a drink. Avoiding eye contact, she moved back through the room and found a bar with no line. Keeping her back to the crowd, she ordered.

As the bartender poured her glass of sauvignon blanc, Renee planned her circuit around the room. No more than an hour and out. Suddenly slender arms wrapped around her waist from behind, lovely long-fingered hands clasped her abdomen, breasts pressed to her back, and a familiar fragrance filled the air around her. She recognized the perfume but strained to remember who wore it.

"Renee Rousseau, as handsome and sexy as ever, I see."

Renee shivered at the whisper in her ear. No question about that sultry voice with the high-class English accent. It had reverberated in her head for years and still had the power to touch her in places usually inaccessible. The woman tightened her arms and breathed in Renee's ear. "I've missed you more than you'll ever know."

The warm breath traveled through her like liquid fire. How many years had it been? Sixteen? Seventeen? And she could still do that. Renee swiveled and locked onto impertinent green eyes sparkling in a lovely face framed by a cascade of luxurious, wavy blond hair. She leaned back, needing to see more of the only woman, other than Darcy, who'd lingered in her heart and mind and senses after their affair had ended. The elegant black gown clung to her still lovely figure and displayed just enough cleavage to get the imagination going. Renee needed no help imagining sex with this woman. Her body definitely remembered. "Constance Martindale. Long time no see."

"That's Lady Constance Martindale to you, bub."

"Ouch. Still angry after all these years?"

"I don't take being dumped lightly." Constance dropped her arms and stepped back as the bartender put a glass of wine on the bar behind Renee. She tilted her head toward the drink. "Your wine is ready."

Forget the wine. She wanted Constance close to her again. But instead of pulling her back into an embrace, Renee turned, picked up her wine and faced Constance again. "Odd. I seem to remember you dumping me."

"That was a preemptive strike, Renee. I'd seen you with enough women to know what was coming." She met Renee's eyes and smiled, taking the sting out of the words.

That preemptive strike had hurt Renee more than she'd ever admitted. She'd responded by consciously pushing any thoughts of Constance and their relationship away. But she'd never totally excised Constance from her mind, and, based on the throbbing she was experiencing, not from her body either. It was true she was poised to hurt Constance back then, like she'd hurt so many others, but she never got the chance. She owed her the truth now. "I wasn't ready for commitment. But if I had been—"

"And now? Are you ready for commitment, Renee?"

She drank some wine to give herself a few seconds to respond. "Let's say, I'm more ready than I was when we were at Stanford and I'm working on it. Actively."

"Does that mean you're single or, since you're working on it, somewhat involved?"

"I'm single. What about you, Constance?"

Constance looked away and Renee braced for a rejection, but when she met her gaze again, she smiled. "What a happy coincidence. I'm single too."

Renee sipped her wine and eyed Constance. She'd really been into their no-strings relationship—until she realized they were no longer just having sex. They were making love. She was in love with Constance. Acknowledging it had terrified her. And she'd immediately started her usual gentle ballet of withdrawal. Constance must have sensed it because she abruptly disappeared from America and Renee's life the day following their fourth night of intense love making—without a word, no tears and no goodbyes, leaving Renee feeling empty, longing for something she didn't want to name.

Renee was intrigued. Was Constance flirting? Was she visiting? "So what have you been doing, where are you living these days?"

"I relocated to New York City about six weeks ago. As to what I'm doing, I paint."

"Really? Lady Martindale is a house painter?"

"You're a sly one, Renee. I have a studio. I paint canvases. And people actually buy them."

Renee made a show of looking at the museum walls.

Constance elbowed her. "I'm not as famous as your dad yet so you won't find any of mine hanging here, I'm afraid. But if you go downtown a bit you might see some of my work at a Chelsea gallery."

Renee frowned. "How could I not know you painted? I didn't even know you thought about painting."

Constance rolled her eyes. "As I recall, Renee, it wasn't my hobbies that interested you."

Renee ran her fingers through her hair. "True. But I'm interested now."

Constance removed a postcard from the evening bag hanging on her shoulder and handed it to Renee. "I hope you'll come to my opening at the Fine Gallery in two weeks."

Renee examined the postcard. "Awakening. Nice title. Nice painting. It looks bold and confident. There's a feeling of openness and freedom."

"As smart as ever, I see. You got it immediately." Constance touched her arm. "Come to the show and we'll talk after." She nodded at a young man waiting patiently nearby, held up a finger and mouthed, "One minute."

"Going younger and male these days, Lady Constance?"

"Ha, ha. Not quite that desperate yet. I'm a guest of the embassy and he's been assigned to escort me to meet the ambassador and other dignitaries. But you're distracting me. I'd really love to see you again. Will you come to the exhibit?"

"I'll be there." But it had been sixteen years and she wasn't willing to wait another two weeks to see Constance. "Are you free for dinner tomorrow night? I'd like to see you again, if you're willing to take a chance on me."

"Only if you promise not to break my heart again."

"As I said, Lady Constance, I'm working on it but I can't promise."

"I would love to have dinner tomorrow." Constance touched Renee's cheek and stared into her eyes. "You may call me Constance." Her lips brushed Renee's. "This has my cell phone number on it." She handed Renee a business card. "Call me tomorrow to make arrangements."

Renee studied the card. "You live—"

Constance shook her head. "On the Upper West Side. That's the address of my studio."

"We're neighbors. I'm also an Upper West Sider." She kissed Constance's cheek. "I can't wait to talk to you tomorrow." She bowed slightly. "Lady Constance." As Renee moved away, she glanced back hoping for another glimpse of Constance. She was surprised to see her still standing there, gazing at her. Their eyes locked. Constance smiled, a slow, sexy smile, and a thrill shot through Renee's body. She grinned. Her libido wasn't dead after all. Constance took the arm of her young escort and they turned away. Renee stared long after they were absorbed into the crowd.

Later, in the car traveling across Central Park to her apartment, Renee mused about the evening. She'd flipped, almost instantaneously, from lonely and hopeless to excited about spending time with Constance. Was the universe toying with her? Or was it a coincidence that Constance had popped back into her life after all these years? Constance was as intriguing as ever, still playful and sexy and mysterious. And Renee was still attracted to her. For the first time in nearly a year her body was voting yes for sex. But while the thought of sex with Constance was tantalizing, she hoped there was the possibility of something more between them, the more that had frightened her all those years ago, the more she'd been wanting. So rather than go for the easy score, she'd work on freeing herself from Darcy while letting things unfold with Constance.

CHAPTER FIVE

Renee lowered herself into the hot seat, the chair she sat in during therapy. She'd had an erotic dream about Constance and considered talking about meeting her again but with limited time to accomplish her goal of freeing herself from Darcy, she chose to stick with the plan. "Should I continue?"

Olivia waved a hand. "It's your session."

It was more than twenty years ago but Renee had no trouble remembering.

"I fell in love with Darcy on the curb outside our dorm the first day of our freshman year at college.

"We were unpacking the limousine when the sound of Italian being spoken in a very sexy voice by someone in a nearby car brought me up short. The petite blonde standing on the curb caught my eye but the tall, dark-haired girl who backed out of the car and looked into my eyes, took my breath away. She handed a box to the blonde, offered her hand to an older woman getting out of the front seat, then, as if she felt my eyes still on her, looked up and smiled.

Later, I imagined I saw cherubs floating above her, pointing their bows at me. A few arrows must have pierced my heart because I was smitten. Instantly.

"I'd probably still be standing there gaping at her if my mom hadn't elbowed me and told me to close my mouth and get a move on because she had a plane to catch.

"I picked up the guitar my mom gave me when she started teaching me to play, grabbed the handle of my rolling suitcase and started walking. I glanced back at the beautiful dark-haired Italian speaking girl who'd captured my heart and felt a stab of disappointment. She was carrying things into the next dorm.

"At the entrance to my dorm I asked for directions from a woman who seemed to be in charge. She looked me up and down. "This is a girl's dorm. What dorm are you looking for?"

"I told you not to wear a tie today." My mom whispered in French. She was okay with me being a lesbian and she loved my boyish haircut and masculine clothing, but she worried about the reactions of Puritan Americans.

I was already used to being mistaken for a boy. I smiled. "Sorry for the confusion, Madam, but I assure you I am a girl." I took my mother's hand. "And my mother is here to testify to that."

The woman blushed. "I am so sorry. Things are hectic today and I made an assumption."

I bowed slightly. "Many have made the same error." I held out the letter with my dorm assignment. "I am Renee Rousseau and I'm assigned to room 212 with Ms. Darcy Silver." The woman pointed. "Up those stairs."

The chauffeur Maman had hired, helped us carry my things up then went downstairs to wait in the limo to drive her to the airport. I selected a bed and we made it together. "I'll unpack later or I'll never find anything." A crash in the hall interrupted Maman's weepy list of things I needed to do to take care of myself.

Giggles and the sound of something being dragged followed. When the beautiful dark-haired girl backed into the room pulling a huge carton, I gasped. She turned. Her eyes widened. "Is this two-twelve?"

I shivered hearing that sexy voice up close. "*Oui*. I mean, yes."

She stuck her hand out. "*Je suis*, Darcy Silver."

I couldn't speak. The poke from my mom started my motor. "I am Renee Rousseau." I took her hand. "Very pleased to meet you, mademoiselle." Our eyes locked and for a breathless few seconds neither of us spoke. Maman cleared her throat.

Darcy broke the connection. "I've been practicing my French but your English is very good."

I blushed. "Um, you must meet my mother, Natalie."

"*Bonjour Madam Rousseau*." Darcy turned toward the door. "My parents, William and Francesca Silver. And my sister, Candace, who is in the dorm next to this one."

Mr. and Mrs. Silver greeted me and Maman, but Mrs. Silver's eyes jumped from Maman to me and back. I couldn't tell whether she was reacting to my black mom or biracial butch me. She said something in Italian to Darcy. Darcy opened her mouth, but before she could speak, I responded in Italian and explained I was a girl and I'd chosen to wear boys clothing because I liked the style. Mrs. Silver looked stunned at my Italian but she nodded and smiled as if she got it. I left my mom and Mrs. Silver chatting in Italian and went with the two girls and their dad to bring in the rest of Darcy's things.

"Your mom doesn't like the idea of you rooming with me?"

"Wait." Darcy grabbed my arm and pulled me aside. "She didn't understand why I was rooming with a boy. After you explained she was fine." She started moving us toward the stairs, then stopped. "And I like it a lot."

The blood rushed to my head and I knew I had a stupid grin on my face but I couldn't help it. In the back of my mind, I wondered if Mrs. Silver's second objection would have been to Darcy rooming with a black girl, but it didn't come up then or any time after, and I forgot about it.

When we returned, Maman said her goodbyes and I escorted her down to her limo. She pulled me close. "Call me whenever you want to talk, Renee. Take care of yourself." She grinned. "And, don't get into too much trouble with Mademoiselle Darcy."

"*Merde*, how did you know?"

Maman hugged and kissed me again. "A mother knows these things, my dear."

I watched until the car disappeared from sight. I was sad to see my mother go, a little scared to be on my own so far from home, excited about getting to know Darcy, and feeling free for the first time in my life. I was sure I was a lesbian, but in reality, at eighteen, I'd never kissed anyone. Thinking I might come out soon made me light-headed. And, very, very anxious.

By the time Darcy and I were alone in our room, I felt more comfortable in her presence but I couldn't help peeking at her as we moved around each other, putting things away and talking about classes and ourselves. Every once in a while our eyes met. It seemed Darcy was also peeking at me.

I floated through the next three weeks. I felt intoxicated most of the time, even though I wasn't drinking. It was Darcy. Not only was she beautiful and sexy, she was intelligent and funny and warm.

We spent all our free time together. We talked and discussed and challenged each other. We laughed and took long walks and long runs. We went to the gym, ate almost all meals together, and studied together.

One night in our third week we were alone studying in our room. I was on my bed reading. I looked up and Darcy was staring at me with a look that caused a blast of heat to burst through my body. Everything tightened and tickled. I held her eyes while I tried to take in air. She seemed to float as she moved from her desk to sit next to me on the bed. She took my hand and I noticed her eyes were dark and her dark complexion was even darker. She gently touched my face. My body felt like liquid. I leaned in. She leaned in. We stared into each other's eyes. The rasp of our breathing was the only sound. She kissed my eyes, my nose. Our lips touched. Such softness. I put a hand on her waist, pulled her closer. She put a hand on either side of my face. Her tongue brushed my lips. My lips parted of their own accord. Oh my God, I never knew kissing could be so erotic. After a long while, lack of oxygen forced us to separate.

Darcy cleared her throat. "Well, I'm glad we got that out of the way."

"Are you upset?" I knew I'd die if she didn't want to do it again.

"No, I've never felt better. What about you?" She ran her finger down my arm.

I gulped. "I can't wait to do it again."

Darcy grinned and leaned in. We stretched out on the bed kissing and exchanging stories. I was thrilled to find out that she had kissed plenty of women but had never gone all the way. We were both virgins.

For the next few days it was impossible to be near each other without touching and kissing. We were constantly ducking into empty classrooms, broom closets, and bathrooms. I felt as if I had a fever. My skin was on fire all the time. I couldn't think about anything but Darcy. We went to class but I barely heard a word, and I got caught out a few times by questions directed at me. I usually answered in French, pretending I hadn't understood.

On the fourth night, we decided it was time. We locked the door to our room and undressed. I confessed I wasn't sure of what to do. Darcy shot me a mysterious and very sexy look and said, "I have a lesbian sex manual." We kissed, then kissed some more. We were both so turned on, so anxious to touch each other, that we began to explore, found the right spots and figured it out ourselves. Oh, what a night. Hot and sweaty, smelling of sex, giggling and awkward, we bumbled around bumping heads, trying to figure out how to arrange arms and legs. But we were both so turned on it didn't take too long to figure out how to bring each other to orgasm. We didn't get out of bed for two days, except to pay for food deliveries and relieve ourselves. We never did look at the manual.

We were still in heat six months later. I don't know whether it was because I was giving off a sexual vibe or because my self-confidence had soared, but suddenly no matter where I went, women were coming on to me, asking me out. I wanted them all. I wanted to be free to bed anyone I felt like whenever I felt like. Darcy was hurt. She didn't understand. She thought I didn't love her. I did love her, but I felt like I'd hardly lived. I wanted to experience life to the fullest. I insisted we could be lovers and still see other women.

We tried it for the last few months of our second semester. I was exhilarated. Darcy was depressed. We spent two lovely weeks at her parents' house on Fire Island, and then I went home to Paris for the summer. We wrote and talked on the phone every day and Darcy came for a two-week visit in August. My parents were away for most of the two weeks so it was just the two of us. We walked. We talked. We made love. I thought Darcy had come around to my way of thinking about an open relationship, that we'd healed the wound. It wasn't until the day before I arrived back at school for our sophomore year at the end of August that Darcy told me she couldn't continue as before, that it was too painful for her, and she needed to separate from me. She'd made a unilateral decision that we shouldn't room together and had arranged for both of us to have singles.

I was stunned. I was heartbroken. I was angry. I was hurt. I loved Darcy. But I wasn't ready for monogamy.

We avoided each other for a few weeks. Then one night we were leaving the library at the same time and we ended up in Darcy's room. Our lovemaking was tender and passionate. We both cried. The anger seemed to dissipate and we were together for a few weeks until I met someone I wanted to sleep with and Darcy broke away. That was our rhythm for that entire year. We'd each date other women but then we'd end up back together for a month or so, until my eye wandered again. Thinking back, it's clear to me I was afraid to admit even to myself how deeply in love with Darcy I was."

Olivia tapped her fingers on the cup in her hands and seemed lost in thought.

Renee glanced at her phone. Just a few more minutes. What was going on with Olivia?

Olivia took a deep breath and focused on Renee. "As I said in our last session, because we have limited time to achieve your goal of freeing yourself from Darcy, I'm going to be more direct than I would ordinarily be with a client."

"Okay."

"Practically the first thing you said in our first session was that you are mixed race. And earlier in this session you brought up the racial issue again in relation to Darcy's mother. How do you think being mixed race has influenced your life?"

Renee laughed. "I hardly think about it." She blinked, pushing away the image of Gina that flashed through her mind.

"Yet you've brought it up in the two sessions we've had. I want you to think about how you feel about being biracial before our next session."

"Why?" Renee couldn't keep the annoyance out of her voice.

"Because it's apparently important to you, and it likely has framed your self-image and how you place yourself in the world." Olivia stood. "I'll see you, Friday."

CHAPTER SIX

Renee hadn't gotten much reading done last night after the gala because her thoughts kept going back to her twenty-four-year-old self in graduate school at Stanford. And to Constance.

Constance was an undergraduate so they didn't have any classes together, but Renee had noticed her walking around campus and thought she was one of the most beautiful women she'd ever seen. Normally she would have pursued Constance despite the group of male and female students always surrounding her, but she assumed Constance was straight. And, following her own rule to never get involved with straight women unless they initiated and pursued her, she looked but didn't touch.

One Saturday right before Renee left for a party, Darcy called, which she rarely did, and they chatted about this and that, but neither mentioned the elephant in the room, their relationship. Bits and pieces of the conversation, places where she could have asked Darcy to try again, played over and over in her mind. Distracted, she wandered aimlessly through the party. In the middle of the crowd of high-spirited graduate students, she felt lonely.

Not ready to be alone but not wanting to socialize, she found a quiet corner, played her guitar and sang sad songs. As she succumbed to the music, the noise of the party faded and she sank into her pain. The sound of clapping pulled her back from her dark place. She blinked and lifted her gaze to find emerald eyes staring at her with an intensity that warmed her blood and tickled all her sensitive places. She locked onto those eyes, and forgetting her loneliness and her sadness and her pain, sang French love songs to the beautiful blond straight woman whose name she didn't know. The woman was a rapt audience, and from time to time Renee looked up and their eyes locked for a few seconds. When she'd exhausted her repertoire and her voice, Renee played an intricate guitar solo that built to a dramatic crescendo then ended suddenly. There was a brief pause, then the small audience that had gathered began to clap. But it was the awed look on the blond woman's face followed by her enthusiastic applause that made Renee smile. She took a bow then knelt to put her guitar in its case. When she turned back to introduce herself, the woman had disappeared. Had she misread the look in her eyes? Had she projected her need for connection onto the beautiful stranger? The possibility of sex with her was tantalizing. Desperate to know whether there was something there, Renee circulated through the rooms seeking the blonde connected to those eyes, asking people if they'd seen her. Finally she found someone who'd seen her leave with her group of friends. Feeling sad and lonely again but determined to track the blonde down in the morning, she said her goodbyes.

Strolling along the dimly lit path in the quiet of the late-night campus, musing about the interaction, she stopped short. Not only had the blonde captivated her at first sight as Darcy had, but the sexual longing burning through her was even stronger than she'd felt for Darcy. She shivered, anxious all of a sudden. The intensity of her response to the young woman brought up painful memories of losing Darcy. She couldn't go through that again. Maybe it was better the blonde had left without speaking to her. Maybe she wouldn't track her down. Maybe she'd leave it be. She started walking again and swiveled as she became aware of someone running behind her. The campus was generally safe but she was always careful. She waited to deal head-on with whoever was racing toward her. "Oh."

Face-to-face with the blond, green-eyed beauty, Renee, the suave lover of women, called Doña Juana by the women in her class, was tongue-tied. Was it her imagination or did the woman glow and did her smile brighten the path?

Seeming unaware of her effect on Renee, the woman touched her arm. "Hi, I'm Constance Martindale. I wanted to tell you how moved I was by your singing. I love your voice and your guitar playing is fantastic." She took a few breaths and not getting a response continued. "Is it all right if I walk with you?"

In the thrall of that smile Renee forgot her anxiety. Who could resist that gorgeous, upper-class English accent combined with something like a cat's purr? She glanced behind Constance. No entourage. She opened her mouth and hoped her voice wouldn't fail her. "Thank you, Constance, I'm happy you enjoyed my self-indulgent concert." She bowed slightly. "I'd love for you to walk with me. I'm Renee Rousseau."

"I know," Constance said, her voice so low it was almost a whisper.

Renee was thrilled Constance had made the effort to find out her name. *So maybe she's not straight. Or not so straight.*

It had been an hour, but it seemed like only a few minutes had passed when Constance stopped in front of her apartment building. For the first time since they'd started walking, there was an uncomfortable silence between them. Renee didn't want the night to end. "So…"

Constance stared at the ground and then met Renee's eyes. "So I'm having a wonderful time with you. I'd prefer to keep walking unless you're tired."

"Sure." Renee struggled to contain the part of her that wanted to shout and jump up and down. She adjusted the guitar on her back. "I'd like that too." She took Constance's hand.

They ambled for hours, talking, teasing, and laughing. Dawn was breaking the second time they stopped in front of Constance's apartment building. She took both Renee's hands in hers and looked into her eyes. "Meet me for brunch later?"

Renee felt a slight tremor in Constance's hands, saw the vulnerability in her eyes and heard it in the softness of her voice. Constance's shy and uncertain invitation in that sexy voice touched Renee. She felt protective of her. And anxious again. Her attraction to Constance, as with Darcy, was intellectual as well as physical. She'd enjoyed their exchange of ideas enormously. Constance made her think and laugh and feel things she hadn't felt for a long time. Part of her wanted to run. "I'd love to. Where? When?"

Constance flashed a brilliant smile. "Here at noon?"

That smile was dangerous. She was sure it could launch the proverbial thousand ships, and if a woman wasn't careful, it could cause her to fall in love. She couldn't help smiling back.

It was strange. Women came onto Renee all the time, but usually all they wanted was sex. And she was usually happy to oblige. When she initiated contact, the only invitation she issued was for casual sex. Meals were spent with friends or the occasional casual affair that lasted more than a week or two. Yet she'd accepted Constance's invitation to brunch, really enjoyed the time at an off-campus café, and not ready to separate from her after, proposed they walk to digest. That walk morphed into a walking and talking marathon. Renee was again amazed at how quickly the time passed, how easily the conversation flowed, how many issues they discussed, and how much she enjoyed the connection. She was so totally into Constance, she barely thought of sex, except, of course, for the many times the touchy-feely Constance held her hand, ran a finger down her arm, squeezed her thigh, rubbed her shoulder or brushed her cheek.

She took Constance to dinner at her favorite Italian restaurant, Guido's, a homey place she reserved for friends because it felt too personal for casual sexual partners. The lighting and music were soft but not romantic, there was enough space between tables to ensure a private conversation, and the food was delicious. The dinner felt intimate and connected. Later, in front of Constance's apartment building, Renee was uncharacteristically indecisive. She wanted to kiss

Constance, but it would mean an end to the night. And what if kissing Constance scared her off? It might mean an end to their connection. Surprising herself, she blurted out an invitation. "I'm planning to study in the library tomorrow. Would you like to join me?"

Constance touched Renee's cheek. "Only if you'll have brunch with me again."

Renee bowed. "I'd love to, Lady Constance."

"How do you know?" Constance frowned. "Is that why—"

Renee placed a finger on Constance's lips. "When I was looking for you at the party last night, someone told me you're the daughter of an Earl so I should call you Lady. Believe me a title means nothing to me. It's you, Constance the person, who means something. I love being with you. You're brilliant and fun and lovely and sexy and so much more." Renee stopped, surprised to hear herself say those things to Constance. They were true but she felt exposed.

Constance stared at Renee as if trying to see into her soul. "All right, brunch tomorrow."

Walking back to her apartment, Renee replayed the events of the last twenty-four hours. What was she doing with Constance? She was on fire with desire yet she hadn't made a move to get her into bed. She told herself it was because of her straight woman rule, but deep down she knew that wasn't it. She was enjoying getting to know Constance, and to her surprise, enjoying the delayed gratification. Being with Constance was exhilarating. She hadn't been this into someone for a very long time. Her impulsive invitation to study in the library came out of fear, fear of losing Constance if she let her go without definite plans to see her again soon. That she was afraid to lose Constance after just one day was scary. Maybe she should cut her losses and run now. On the other hand, maybe she should give them more time to… She grinned where her mind took her, more time to *come* together. Damn she could be a pig sometimes, but, happily, she rarely had to deal with delayed gratification, so it didn't happen too often.

Constance's vulnerability around the title issue touched her and confirmed her instinct to let Constance take the lead. It must be awful not being sure why someone befriended you. She'd told Constance the truth. She didn't give a rat's ass about her title. It was her mind and her body she was after.

Late the next morning, Renee led them to another of her private places, a restaurant she usually went to when she wanted to be alone. The food was good and the open, bright atmosphere conducive to thinking or studying. It was a perfect backdrop for the challenging discussions she and Constance had been having. As they ate their waffles, eggs, and fruit, they debated the English vs. American political system and the role of the royal family. The exchange of ideas flowed easily from topic to topic and continued on the leisurely walk to the library after brunch.

In a brief moment of silence, Constance cleared her throat. "I've heard stories about you. With women." Renee leaned in close to hear. She'd noticed that when they discussed ideas and issues, Constance's voice was strong, but when she was feeling unsure, her voice was soft, almost a whisper.

Could it be Constance didn't know she was a lesbian? Renee steeled herself for rejection. "All true, I'm sure. I'm a lesbian. I prefer sex with no strings. And, I date a lot of women but only one at a time. Most of my, um, encounters last a week or two." She always put it out there up front and Constance needed to hear it.

"Let's sit." Constance pulled Renee to a bench under a sprawling tree. She looked into the distance and cleared her throat again. "I've kissed a few guys and two girls but I've never wanted to have sex with any of them. I'm very attracted to you and I was wondering…"

Renee imagined it was embarrassing for her to be this direct. "Are you asking me whether I would like to have sex with you?"

"Yes." Constance met her eyes. "Do you find me at all attractive?"

Renee took hold of Constance's hands and swiveled so they were facing each other. "I find you gorgeous in mind and body. I'm not only attracted, I'm fascinated and intrigued by you. And to say I'm dying to take you to bed is a gross understatement."

Constance's eyes widened and her body relaxed. "Really?"

"Really." Renee squeezed Constance's hands. "But did you hear the part about no strings? And many short-term sexual partners?"

Constance smiled her glorious, brighten-up-the-day smile. "I heard every word you said and it fits perfectly with my needs. I'll be going back to London after I graduate at the end of this semester so short term is good."

Renee's gut told her she wouldn't get her fill of Constance in a week or two, but Constance's schedule imposed a time limit. At most two months. It fit perfectly with Renee's desire for sex with no strings. "Why do you want to have lesbian sex?"

Constance fidgeted with Renee's fingers. Then she lifted her eyes and captured Renee's gaze. "I don't want lesbian sex. I want sex with you. I can't seem to get you out of my mind. I'm on fire just being near you. Like right now I'm dying for you to kiss me."

Renee only got involved sexually with women she liked, women she would like as friends. She always made the terms of the arrangement clear up front to avoid hurting them, but, nevertheless, she often suffered through tearful, painful endings. Some women became friends. Others needed distance. Constance was a virgin. And vulnerable. There was a fine line between giving Constance what she clearly wanted and the damage Renee might inflict if only a week or two of sex with Constance was enough. The last thing she wanted was to cause Constance pain, so she had to be sure Constance understood the terms of any sexual encounter. "So you want a casual relationship. Short term. No forever. Just great sex?"

"Yes, Renee. No forever. Just great sex." Her lips quirked.

Constance was humoring her but this was serious business. Should she go with her desire for Constance or her fear of hurting her? Wait. Why was she thinking she should make this decision for Constance? She was an adult so let her decide. "What if I break your heart?"

"What if I break *your* heart?" Constance kissed the tips of Renee's fingers. "I know exactly who you are, Renee. I'll gladly take the risk." She caressed Renee's face. "I appreciate your concern for me, but trust me, I know what I want. And I think you want it too. Can we skip the library?"

Renee stood and bowed. "At your service, Lady Constance." Renee's apartment was closer so that's where they went.

In her bedroom, Renee cupped Constance's face between her hands and gazed into her eyes. "Remember we can stop any time."

Constance stroked Renee's face. "I'm nervous, but I want this with you, Renee."

Renee took Constance's hands and kissed both palms. "I want you too." And she did. But she was aware that her desire for sex was overshadowed by something she had not felt for many years: a desire to cherish. Above all, she wanted to make Constance's first time beautiful and memorable, as hers had been.

She kissed Constance tenderly and slowly undressed her, taking time between each garment to caress and kiss the soft skin and sensitive places she uncovered. Constance was shy, but responsive to Renee's touch and her lips and tongue. When she was naked, she didn't flinch as Renee gazed at her body, appreciating her. "Still okay?"

"Yes."

Renee undressed quickly, led Constance to the bed and covered her with her body. Constance moaned softly at the skin-to-skin contact and wrapped her hands around Renee, pulling her closer. Renee gazed into her eyes, and finding no fear or anxiety, kissed her forehead, her eyes, her cheeks, her nose, and lightly brushed her lips. Then she kissed her deeply for a long time while running a hand down her side.

Constance moaned as Renee slid off her. "I'm not going far, sweetheart," Renee whispered in her ear. "I want to touch you and make love to you, if that's still what you want."

"Yes. Please. I do." Constance turned her head to find Renee's lips.

Renee's hand brushed Constance's breasts, and surprised to find them so sensitive, she broke their kiss to place her mouth on a nipple. As she gently sucked, Constance arched a few inches off the bed and moaned appreciatively. Renee grinned. One erogenous zone identified. While Constance writhed in response to Renee's mouth and lips and tongue loving her breasts, Renee's hands roamed over Constance's body, rubbing circles on her stomach, teasing her inner thighs, and squeezing her butt cheeks. It turned out Constance was one big erogenous zone. She was also a fast learner. Before long her hands were in Renee's hair and her mouth and tongue and lips were returning the favors. The easy transition from passive to active participant surprised Renee and stoked the already high flames of her desire. But this was about Constance. And fearing Constance would orgasm before she had time to properly make love to her, Renee backed off to check in again. Glassy-eyed, Constance clutched her. "Please don't stop."

Renee kissed her, then slid down and parted her legs. Constance raised her head and locked onto Renee's eyes. Renee slid a finger in. Constance's eyes widened. Renee slid a second finger in. Constance gasped. "Renee," she whispered, and threw her head back on the pillow. Renee lowered her head and used her tongue, lips and mouth to pleasure Constance while easing her fingers in and out. Constance's breathing, her escalating moans, and her writhing body signaled she was close to the edge. It didn't take long for her to fall over the cliff, screaming Renee's name. Renee's orgasm followed quickly, and then she crawled up and cradled Constance in her arms while they both dozed.

When Renee opened her eyes, Constance was staring at her. "Thank you, Renee. I… That was even more wonderful than I imagined." She touched Renee's face. "And believe me, I have a vivid imagination."

Renee smiled. "So you like lesbian sex?"

Constance looked beautiful and sexy and turned on. "If that was lesbian sex, I love it. And, I want to do it again and again. As often as I can."

Renee traced Constance's eyebrows, her cheek, her jaw, her lips. "You are a very sexy woman. Are you sure this was your first time?"

"It was embarrassing to admit that, Renee. Why would I say it if it wasn't true? Why do you ask?"

"I've been with women with tons of experience who are so guarded they barely allow themselves to come. But you were so open and responsive the sex was a joy."

"Thank you." Constance flushed. "But I haven't made proper love to you and I'm not sure what to do."

"You turn me on so much that I came making...listening to you come." Renee put two fingers under Constance's chin and lifted her head. "There are no rules, no right or wrong, Constance. What you were doing before was wonderful. Touch or do whatever you want, wherever you want and if I need something else, I'll let you know." And they were off. They spent the next day and night in bed, then went to classes, then came back together in the evening. And that was how they spent most evenings and weekends for the next two months.

Knowing the relationship was time limited had set Renee free. She didn't check her feelings at the door as she normally did. She relaxed and enjoyed Constance. To her surprise, the relationship was intense, her feelings for Constance deeper than any she'd had before. And, the relationship lasted right up to Constance's departure. Oddly, as Constance had predicted, she broke Renee's heart.

Thinking back to their younger selves, Renee acknowledged she had fallen for Constance early on but hadn't let herself know it. When she realized she was in love with Constance, she got scared and was ready to run. But Constance beat her to it. Now they had a second chance and she planned to get to know Constance again, to see whether there was still more than the sexual connection between them.

CHAPTER SEVEN

On the way to the restaurant to meet Constance, everyone Renee passed smiled at her. She thought it was strange until she caught a glimpse of herself in a store window and noticed the huge grin on her face. No question she was excited about seeing Constance again. Despite what Constance had intimated about Renee only being interested in her for sex, it was her intellect, her well-thought out arguments, the ideas she expressed, and her rapier wit that had drawn Renee to her in their twenties. Of course, her gentleness, her beautiful face, her curvaceous body, her enthusiasm in bed, and her low-thrummed voice and British accent didn't hurt.

Now Constance was in her high thirties and Renee was almost forty but their electric connection hadn't dimmed. It was tempting to act on it and jump right into bed, but she really did want to change. She really did want more. Not only would getting involved sexually while she was trying to work out her feelings for Darcy be a diversion, it might ruin any possibility of something more with Constance. She hoped Constance wanted more too and was willing to wait. So, rather than the super romantic place she would normally have taken a date, she met Constance at Trattoria Montero, her favorite Italian restaurant, a little place in her Upper West Side neighborhood run by a family she'd become friendly with over the years. The lighting, table arrangement, and the atmosphere were conducive to talk and the food was delicious. The restaurant was filled with neighborhood people—families, loners reading a book, couples and larger groups enjoying themselves.

When they entered, Mrs. Montero greeted Renee like the old friend she was. Constance surveyed the restaurant as Mrs. Montero led them to a table. She seemed puzzled but then she looked at Renee with one of those light-up-the-room smiles of hers. "The first time you took me to a homey Italian restaurant you were trying to seduce me. Should I be on my guard?"

Renee was pleased she remembered that intimate, connected dinner at Guido's in Stanford. "You keep getting our history wrong, Constance. I distinctly remember you seducing me." She smiled. "But you can relax. No seduction planned tonight."

"Phew. What a relief." Constance pretended to wipe sweat from her brow but she also seemed to let go of some tension.

Had Constance feared Renee would try to get her into bed tonight? Maybe. But she seemed at ease as they settled into the comfortable family atmosphere. Maybe they would be all right.

Renee ordered the pasta with mushrooms special and Constance the lemon sole. Both ordered salads, and they agreed on a bottle of sauvignon blanc.

When the waiter brought the wine, Renee indicated they'd both do the taste test. He poured. They sipped and nodded at each other, then at him. After he walked away, Constance smiled again, a more intimate smile this time. "You've changed, Renee. You seem, I don't know, less cocky, more open, more vulnerable, more available."

"I'm trying."

"What is it? Age? Heartbreak? Boredom? Loneliness?"

"All of the above." Renee felt exposed but she wanted to be honest. "I'm in therapy trying to figure out who I am and what I want out of life. I'm trying to change things that aren't working for me anymore." She cradled Constance's hand. "You're as beautiful and as sexy as you were the first time I saw you, Constance, and I'm as attracted to you now as I was then." Renee squeezed her hand. "I would love to spend time with you and get to know the person you've become, but this time I'm not interested in a purely sexual relationship. Sex is the easy part for me. I don't want to move right into bed. If that's not what you're looking for, let's enjoy the evening and move on."

The waiter arrived with their salads, fussed with black pepper, and then refilled their wineglasses before leaving. Renee hoped the fact that Constance's eyes hadn't left her face and she hadn't pulled her hand away were good signs, but the long silence made her uneasy.

Constance took a breath. "I'm not interested in picking up where we left off either. I'm also in transition and taking time to get to know each other again sounds right. For me, our connection was deeper than just sex and I've wondered over the years what our relationship might have become given other circumstances." She flushed, apparently embarrassed by the admission. "It will be nice to see if there's anything other than a great sexual vibe between us. That's not to say that great sex isn't of interest." She lifted her glass. "Here's to long walks, long talks, great cuddles and many laughs."

"Sounds like a plan." They clinked glasses, drank and smiled at each other. That moment felt more intimate than the sex with the last woman Renee had taken to bed months ago.

Constance put her glass down. "I'm starving. What about you?"

The tension was gone. Dinner was lovely. They reminisced some but mostly they discussed art, the news, and people they knew in common. They laughed a lot.

Renee was pleased to find that Constance was living quite near her on the Upper West Side. "You seem like an Upper East Side kind of person, being royalty and all. How did you come to live on my side of the park?"

Constance sipped her wine. "When I decided to move to New York City I called an old friend at the embassy who has lived here many years to ask him about visa arrangements and apartments. He helped with the paperwork and gave me the rundown on the East versus the West side of Central Park. He recommended a couple of places on the Upper East Side because people in our social circle live there. But I moved here to get away from the royalty thing and all the social life that goes with it. So I asked him to look for something on the West Side and he put me in touch with a woman who was getting married and wanted to rent out her apartment. It's large and lovely in a doorman building on Seventy-Fifth Street on Riverside Drive, facing Riverside Park and the Hudson River. Best of all, she wanted to rent it furnished, so I was able to move right in when I arrived."

"That's great. I live on Central Park West and Eighty-Eighth Street, about a fifteen-minute walk from you."

Mrs. Montero interrupted to offer dessert on the house. She sat with them as they shared a slice of Italian cheesecake, the house specialty. The restaurant owner seemed quite taken with Constance, who charmed without effort, and she encouraged them to come back soon.

Renee didn't want the evening to end so she suggested she walk Constance home. They strolled downtown, from Montero's on Eighty-Ninth Street and Broadway to Constance's apartment, talking easily as usual. Even the silences were easy. Constance steered them to a bench on Riverside Drive facing her building. They chatted a while longer, then she took Renee's hand and kissed her cheek. "This has been lovely, Renee. I'm so glad we found each other again. The ball is in your court. I'll go as slow as you want, but I definitely want to go, so don't wait too long to call."

Renee had forgotten how much she loved Constance's frankness.

They crossed the street and Constance greeted the doorman standing at the entrance to her building. She turned to Renee. "Thank you for a lovely evening. Goodnight."

Much too soon, the night was over and she was walking home with that smile still on her face, thinking about when she could see Constance again.

Take it slow. How does one do that? She had absolutely zero experience with slow. She'd always gone fast—meet a woman, get her into bed and leave—usually after one night, occasionally it lasted a week or two. She needed help figuring out how to do slow. Gina was out of town so she called and made a reservation for dinner the next night at Buonasola, Tori and Elle's restaurant.

* * *

She'd made the reservation for late in the dinner hour so Tori would be able to join her while she ate. She was just digging into her Lamb Tagine when Tori kissed the top of her head, dropped into a seat at the table and poured herself a glass from the bottle of Malbec Renee had ordered. "Hey, good to see you." She searched Renee's face. "You're looking better."

Tori plucked the spoon from Renee's place setting and fished a piece of lamb out of Renee's dish. She chewed slowly, savoring the tasty meat. "Delicious, if I say so myself."

Renee laughed. "I second that." Tori looked tired but Renee knew she loved cooking and feeding people. The combination of Tori's fabulous food and Elle's incredible ability to remember names, likes, dislikes, and personal things about their regular customers made everyone feel special and welcome. The restaurant was the go-to place for fashionable New Yorkers.

Tori waved to Elle, then focused on Renee. "How are you feeling, sweetie?"

"Better. I started therapy this week."

She squeezed Renee's shoulder. "Good for you."

"I need some relationship advice." Tori cocked her head and waited for Renee to speak. "Do you remember I mentioned there might have been one woman besides Darcy and Gina who touched my heart?"

"I do." Tori sipped her wine.

"At the Metropolitan Museum Gala the other night I ran into her, an old, um, someone that I had a thing with when I was at Stanford. I still find her attractive, and this time I want to get to know her before we jump into bed. She's okay with that but I'm not sure how often I should see her since I want to go slowly."

Renee could see Tori trying to hold back her laughter. She pretended to be annoyed. "So is it the going slowly, or getting to know her, or not wanting to jump into bed that you think is laughable?"

Tori cracked up. "You have to admit, Renee, given your history those statements are hilarious coming from you."

Renee joined in the laughter and each time one of them stopped, they looked at each other and off they went again. Elle strolled over. "What's with you two? You're disturbing our guests."

Renee looked up. The customers at the few tables left in the restaurant were staring with huge grins. "I just said I—" She cracked up again.

Elle stood with her hands on her hips trying in vain to hide a grin.

Tori took a breath. "Renee said she's interested in a woman and wants to go slow, wants to get to know her and doesn't want to jump into—" She was overcome with laughter again. "Bed," Tori snorted.

Elle shook her head. "You two are hopeless." She walked away, commenting to the guests watching, some themselves laughing in sympathy. "Sorry, please forgive them for disturbing your dinner. It must really be funny but I have no idea what they're laughing at."

When they finally regained control, Renee dried her tears.

"There must be a word to describe something so out of character that it's ridiculous," Tori said, wiping her tears with the clean napkin on the table. "Where's Darcy when we need her? She always knows the right word."

"How about incongruous? Strange? Bizarre? Outlandish?" Renee was trying to sound annoyed but her broad smile showed her true feelings. "Okay, I'll admit those words are kind of unusual coming from me. But I swear I mean it. How frequently should I see her if I want to go slowly?" She picked up her fork and started eating again.

Tori put a hand on Renee's shoulder and waited until Renee looked at her to speak. "I hope you know I was teasing."

Renee put her hand over Tori's. "Didn't you notice I was laughing as loud and long as you?"

Tori ran her finger around the rim of her wineglass. "She must be pretty special."

Renee thought of Constance, her wit, her intelligence, her beauty and sexuality, and the strength of their emotional and physical connection after all these years. "She is. Very special. And, I don't want to screw it up this time."

"Tell me about her."

"Her name is Constance Martindale. She's British and just moved to New York City from London. At Stanford we had a two-month, I want to say fling, but really, though I never admitted it to myself then or since, it was a relationship. She's a blond, green-eyed beauty with a wicked wit, brilliant intelligence, and intense sexuality. She's strong and independent. In fact, the minute she sensed me pulling back years ago, she dumped me before I could dump her."

"Ah, a woman with backbone and self-respect." Tori helped herself to some more of Renee's dinner. "She sounds perfect for you. Is there something special about Constance or would you feel the same about any of your many old flames if you met them today?"

"It's Constance. She's the only one, other than Darcy and Gina, with whom I've ever wanted more than sex."

"Interesting coincidence that she shows up now when you're dealing with your feelings for Darcy. I gather you're still attracted to her and it's not just a get her into bed kind of attraction?"

"It's strange. I haven't seen her in sixteen or so years, and we've both changed but it's like there's been no break. Being with her again has been wonderful but this time I want more than casual sex. I want a real relationship."

"Wow, I have to meet this woman." Tori buttered a piece of bread. "But since you're also dealing with your feelings for Darcy, you need to be careful that it's not just a rebound thing.

Taking it slow seems like a good idea. You need to judge, of course, but it seems to me if you're serious about changing and she's willing to go along with what you need, seeing her once or twice a week will give you time to reflect in between. And it's a good idea to leave sex out of it as long as you can so it doesn't complicate things or bring up old feelings that make you want to run."

Renee considered the advice. "Sounds right to me."

"Just so you know, I haven't forgotten you owe me the story of you and Gina. But I don't want to overload you so it can wait." Tori poured them both more wine. "The Inner Circle is not for the fainthearted, but if she likes music and you think she can handle being with all of us, bring her to the next songfest."

"She used to sing but I don't know whether she's still into music. I'll have to give it some thought. Songfest feels like bringing someone home to meet the parents."

Tori laughed. "Well, Mama Darcy won't be there so it shouldn't be too bad."

Renee looked around and they were the only two people still at a table. Elle was at the register and the waiters and busboys were cleaning up. Apologizing for keeping Tori from cleaning up, Renee hugged and kissed her, then moved to pay Elle.

Tori called out. "I ate half her dinner and drank her wine." Elle waved her off. "The chef says I can't take your money. Sorry I didn't join you but I didn't want to intrude."

"I'm sorry about disturbing your customers, Elle, but it's been a long time since I've had such a good laugh."

Elle looked back toward the kitchen. "It's Tori, I know. Once she starts it's hard to stop her. I guess it's better laughing than crying."

"It felt good. Thanks for dinner. And thanks for respecting my privacy. But I'd never ask you to keep secrets from one another. If you're interested, Tori can fill you in." Another hug and a kiss on the cheek, and then for the second night in a row, Renee went home with a smile on her face. Her smile got even bigger when she called Constance and she agreed to drive upstate Saturday morning, have lunch, take a hike then stop for dinner on the way home.

CHAPTER EIGHT

Renee felt uneasy as she followed Olivia into the room. She wasn't sure why thinking about being biracial made her so uncomfortable but she found she couldn't concentrate on it and didn't want to talk about it. "Olivia, can we table the biracial discussion for now?"

"This must be really important, Renee, if you can't deal with it. We'll skip it but don't expect me to forget about it. What do you want to talk about?"

Renee didn't want to get sidetracked but she wanted Olivia to know what was happening. "Mainly, I want to finish talking about Darcy but before we start, I wanted to tell you that Constance, the only woman besides Darcy and Gina who was important to me in the past, has resurfaced in my life and we're dating."

Olivia sighed. "But you don't want to talk about her either?"

Renee smiled. "I want to talk about Darcy." Olivia didn't say anything else so she launched into her story. "The summer between our sophomore and junior years, Darcy and I traveled throughout Europe. It was a wonderful trip and by the end we were close again. So when we returned to school, to our single rooms, I was confident that Darcy would be there when I was ready to settle down sometime in the future.

"I hadn't counted on Darcy meeting someone else. I wasn't threatened by Tori when Darcy started seeing her in September of our junior year. She was absolutely brilliant, but she was a very tall, scrawny, naïve seventeen-year-old farm girl from an ultrareligious family, and in my mind, no competition. Yet, suddenly Darcy was unavailable, unwilling to get together with me. I was puzzled but not worried. I figured it was her mind that interested Darcy and we would bounce back together, as usual."

"By the end of the first semester of our junior year, Darcy and Tori began to look like a couple. I was nervous but still believed she would be there when I wanted her. It wasn't until Darcy told me she was in love with Tori that I allowed myself to feel the depth of my love for her. It was then I realized what I'd thrown away.

"Darcy asked that we remain friends. I still hoped I could win her back so I forced myself to spend time with them, always with a date as a buffer, hoping to make Darcy jealous. But she only had eyes for Tori. Though Darcy and I forged a deep friendship, I never again mentioned my true feelings for her.

"My senior year, I fell in love again. Gina was the first girl I'd slept with after I decided Darcy and I needed an open relationship freshman year. We'd had sex off and on after that, but she spent two weeks with me in Paris the August before our senior year and something shifted. We got serious. We were good together in so many ways, but she was a black activist and had problems with me being biracial. She—"

"Stop." Olivia nearly levitated. "Why is this the first time I'm hearing about you being in love with someone other than Darcy? And how that someone had an issue with you being biracial? If you're going to withhold information, Renee, I can't work with you."

Renee flushed. "I…" She ran her finger around her collar and loosened her tie. "I didn't mean to withhold. I don't know how to explain it. When Darcy and I had lunch, she asked why I claim to have been in love with her since we first got together when I loved Gina after her. I'm embarrassed. But I don't know."

Olivia sat back. "Tell me about Gina."

Renee gazed out the window. Gina was important to her, yet she'd spent years denying their relationship. "Gina and I were in love and things were wonderful in Paris but once we were back on campus she wanted to hide our relationship. She was a black activist and she was embarrassed to be seen with me because her activist friends thought I was passing. She also felt I was passing, that I had no idea what it meant to be black, no understanding of how a black person is looked down upon. I protested that I did know. I'd read about it and heard her stories. My mom had described the racism she'd faced growing up black in America, and though it was better in France, she and my darker-skinned brothers and sisters had encountered racism there too. Gina insisted that hearing about it or reading about it was not the same as living it, and she pointed out that when I read a book or went to a movie, I could see myself in the characters and that wasn't true for her. I couldn't understand what she wanted me to do. I couldn't change my skin color or how people saw me. If we weren't fighting over my alleged racism, we were fighting over class—my family being upper class, while she was a scholarship student from a poor working-class family. It got so that the only time we weren't tearing each other apart was when we were making love.

"Then the day after we graduated, Darcy, to everyone's surprise, broke up with Tori, who she adored, leaving all our friends bewildered and Tori heartbroken. Darcy was in pain and I rushed to comfort her, ignoring everything and everybody else. That was the last straw for Gina. We were both so battered and demoralized by our fighting over race and class, by her shame at being with me, and finally, my sudden focus on Darcy when I'd said I was done with her, that it became too painful to stay together. We both caved and gave up on the relationship. Though we'd planned to remain a couple while I was in the Peace Corps and she was at MIT working on her PhD, we agreed to take some space, try to be friends, and see where we were in a couple of years.

"I understood Darcy was by no means done with Tori, but I wanted to be there for her so I changed my scheduled early June departure for my Peace Corps assignment in Africa to early August. We spent some time at my family's country home in southern France, some in Fire Island and some in New York City. I kept in touch with Tori, giving her updates and trying to help her deal with her loss, all the while feeling like a traitor because a large part of me fantasized Darcy would get over Tori and come back to me." Renee stopped to take a deep breath. "Shallow bitch that I am, somewhere in all the caring for Darcy, my feelings for Gina and my relationship with her got lost."

"I know you said you don't know why you buried your experience with Gina and went back to Darcy, but take a minute and see what floats up." Renee closed her eyes and tried to free her thoughts. After a minute, she opened her eyes. "I don't know."

"She accused you of being a racist, of passing, of denying half your heritage. She was ashamed of you. Don't think, just tell me how that made you feel."

Renee flashed on Gina in tears screaming at her while she cried helplessly. "Hurt, worthless, a coward, rejected. Sad. Unloved." She blew out a breath. "And guilty."

"And Darcy? How did she make you feel?"

"Even though I hurt her, I always felt loved by Darcy. Important to her. Accepted by her. She never questioned my racial identity. I was who I was."

Olivia let her sit with that a minute. "Renee, it's really important that you talk about your mixed-race heritage and what it means to you, what it's meant to you."

Renee nodded. "All right but not until our next session. Should I talk to Gina about this?"

Olivia seemed surprised. "Gina is still in your life?"

Renee laughed. "She and Darcy are my best friends. She's mellowed over the years. You know when you're young and militant everything seems black and white but as you get older you start to see the grays."

"It's up to you whether you want to scratch the scabs off old wounds and possibly hurt your friendship. Have you ever talked about it?"

"Not since we broke up."

"I'm seeing a pattern here, Renee. You say you wanted Darcy back but you never brought it up, never tried to make it happen. And now you say Gina hurt you and made you feel worthless but you never discussed it with her after you were no longer locked into your positions. These are your two closest friends? How close can you be if, in both cases, you allow these unspoken issues between you to fester? You and your friends seem to live in a fog of denial."

"But they never brought it up either." Crap. She sounded like a whiny five-year-old. "I've talked to Darcy, so I guess I should talk to Gina, but that makes me nervous. What if I find out she still feels that way? What if she hates me?"

"Do you think that's how she feels?"

Renee considered Olivia's question. She would have sensed it if Gina hated her, wouldn't she? "No, I doubt she hates me but I'm not sure if she resents me or still believes…those things." She looked Olivia in the eye. "I guess it's time to find out."

Olivia leaned forward. "In our first three sessions, you've given me mostly the facts of your life, but the next phase of therapy will be the in-depth exploration of the things you don't want to talk about. Are you ready for that? Do you want to continue with therapy?"

She opened her mouth to answer but Olivia raised a hand. "We have a session scheduled for Monday. I want you to think about it over the weekend. Obviously the feelings beneath your actions are painful or you wouldn't have avoided dealing with Darcy the first time you were here, and you wouldn't be afraid to talk about your racial issues. So decide whether you're ready to take those feelings out and examine them in the light of day. If you are, I'll see you Monday morning at our usual time. If not, leave a message on my machine."

Renee looked Olivia in the eye. "I'll definitely see you Monday morning." She left her sitting there with what could have been a satisfied smile.

CHAPTER NINE

It was a glorious October Indian summer Saturday morning and Renee hummed as she put the top down on her BMW convertible. She hummed as she drove to Constance's building and waited for Constance to come down. And she hummed when she saw Constance exit the building with a huge smile, looking fabulous in close-fitted jeans, a long-sleeved blue T-shirt, and ankle boots. After a brief greeting, she put Constance's jacket and hiking shoes on the backseat, opened the passenger door and handed Constance a scarf.

Once settled in the car Constance poked Renee. "Still a butch in good standing, I see, driving a proper butch fancy convertible."

Renee responded to the playful tone. "I've heard some ladies like a proper butch."

"Hmm. Maybe some do." Constance turned her attention to the streets as they drove out of the city.

She'd been so thrilled by the idea of spending the day with Constance that she hadn't stopped to think that this was a peak weekend of fall foliage season so the heavy traffic on the New

York State Thruway was a surprise. But erudite and witty as usual, Constance was charming company. In between teasing and telling funny stories they discussed serious topics like Brexit and the current US political situation. And when things got too heavy they switched to their favorite flavor of ice cream, favorite color, favorite place in the world. Renee hardly noticed the stop-and-go driving.

They arrived in the town of Phoenicia in the Catskill Mountains later than projected but stopped, as planned, at Sweet Sue's for brunch before driving to the hiking trail a little further north. It was still warm enough to sit outside. Renee ordered the pancake sundae—two inch-thick, plate-sized buttermilk pancakes topped with yogurt, fresh strawberries, blueberries and peaches, and a tasty raspberry sauce. Constance ordered the huevos rancheros, two sunny-side eggs on tacos with black beans, cheese, guacamole, salsa, and fresh coriander. They moaned over the delicious food, shared bites, and continued their nonstop conversation. As they were relaxing with their coffees, Constance touched Renee's arm. "There's something I should have told you the other night."

Constance was nervous so suddenly Renee was nervous too. "What?"

Constance took a sip of water. "When I said I preemptively dumped you to avoid you dumping me, I didn't tell you the whole story. Remember, you were in your first year of graduate school and I was in my last year of undergraduate school and the dumping occurred just before my graduation."

Renee nodded.

Constance fiddled with a packet of sugar, then looked at Renee. "Sex with you at Stanford was meant to be just playing around before I married a man and my real life started. I don't know how it was for you but our last few days and nights together were intense and incredible. I felt we were making glorious love, not just having sex. Until then I hadn't let myself know the depth of my feelings for you, but lying together after making love that last night, I sensed you gently pulling away from me and the possibility of losing you forced me to really look at my feelings. And, for the first time, I understood I wanted you in my life forever. I totally freaked. That wasn't how my life was supposed to play out. So immediately after I left you the next morning I changed my flight home to a flight that evening, notified the university I wouldn't be at graduation, packed a few things, and ran back to the safety of England. I couldn't even say goodbye because I knew if I saw you again I wouldn't have the strength to leave."

Renee eased her chair away from the table and Constance. "How could I not know you were thinking about marrying a man? We'd said we'd be casual, nothing long-term, but we'd been so close, talked so much about everything, I assumed I knew you, assumed your life would be with women, only in London. And I had no idea your feelings for me were so strong. I thought I was the only one who felt we'd made love those last few nights. Believe me, it scared the hell out of me. I hadn't felt that intimate, that connected, that loving, with anyone for many years. My gut reaction *was* to ease myself out of the relationship immediately, even though I knew you'd be leaving for London in a week or two."

Constance laughed. "How could you have any idea about any of it? I never talked about what waited for me in London because I didn't want to think about it. I can explain it to you now, but then I had no idea what I was doing. I was just acting on instinct. It took me a couple of years to figure out why I ran."

Renee pulled her chair closer to the table. "Thank you for sharing but I'm not sure what this means. For us? Now?"

Constance squeezed Renee's hand. "What I just told you was in the interest of full disclosure. I like our plan a lot. You know, going slow, talking, walking, cuddling." She put her hand on Renee's knee. "What a pair we are, eh?"

Were they a pair? Did Constance still feel that way about her? Renee pushed the questions aside. "You don't know how right you are. So how about we move onto the hiking part of this excursion."

"Righto."

Renee smiled. She used to love when Constance said that. She moved behind Constance and helped her up. And then it hit her. Lady Constance Martindale's real life was to start when she married a man. Was Constance into men? Maybe the plan wasn't such a good idea after all. The last thing she needed was to let go of Darcy and fall in love with someone straight, someone who would ultimately be unavailable.

Renee tried to shake the sadness as she drove them to Haines Falls where they would pick up the trail for the Kaaterskill Falls hike they'd decided on. Neither of them had hiked in years so they'd picked a short trail with some challenges. According to the guidebook, the trail climbed steeply and there were many slippery rocks, roots, and other obstacles, but the view was well worth it. It also said there were a number of deaths on the trail each year. Did being unlucky in love transfer to having bad luck on dangerous trails? Should she cancel the hike?

She was aware of Constance's puzzled glances as they drove but she pretended to focus on finding the trail's parking area. They changed into their hiking boots in the lot and started up the trail. It was gorgeous. Constance took her hand. "I've seen pictures of the fall foliage in this part of the States, but the real thing is so much more. The canopy of red, yellow, gold, and green leaves arching over us make me feel as if we're in the middle of a glorious painting or a box of sixty-four Crayola crayons." She inhaled. "It smells lovely." She dropped Renee's hand and pointed to the trail ahead of them. "I think we'll need two hands from this point on."

It was steep, and as the guidebook warned, the slippery rocks and roots required their full attention, leaving no opportunity for conversation. But from time to time their eyes met and Constance smiled. She looked happy. Renee was happy too, happy to be here with her, but she couldn't rid herself of the fear that Constance wasn't who she'd thought she was, that she wouldn't stay this time either. How foolish to think they could pick up after sixteen years.

When they reached the base of the Kaaterskill Falls, they found a rock to sit on and admire the two-tiered falls while they drank the water they'd carried in.

After a few minutes of silence, Constance reached for Renee's hand. "You've disappeared. Have I offended you? Did what I say about wanting more from you back then scare you? Are you afraid of what I want now?"

Renee squeezed Constance's hand, not sure if she had the right to ask the question, not sure she wanted to know, not sure of what she wanted from Constance this time around. She could be a coward and lie, but she really wanted to change. And Constance deserved her honesty. She was starting to understand why she didn't stay around long enough to care for someone, why she didn't do relationships. This was hard. And she could get hurt.

Renee shifted slightly to face Constance. She tried to smile but it felt more like a grimace. Constance's smile was tender. Renee took a deep breath. Her eyes went to the higher of the two waterfalls. All the signs warned about trying to climb to the top of the waterfalls from here. There was no cleared path from here to there and it was dangerous. People died trying. She needed to know if there was a clear path between her and Constance. If not, as painful as it would be, she would say goodbye at her door tonight.

She cleared her throat. She was about to take her first step on a path she didn't think was there and was resigned that she might make a misstep and die trying. "You shocked me when you said you were supposed to marry a man. I should have known, I guess, but I thought of you, still think of you as Constance, not Lady Constance. When we talked at dinner the other night I had the impression you wanted to work on being friends but might be interested in pursuing a relationship with me. A real relationship this time, if I can get my shit together. I've been trying to reconcile that with you having to marry a man. I know I have no right to ask—"

"Oh, my sweet girl. I'm so sorry. I gave you half the story, no wonder you're confused." She brought Renee's hand to her lips, kissed her palm, then enclosed the hand in both her hands. "I've already done it."

Renee pulled her hand away and jumped to her feet. "You're married?"

Constance put her head in her hands. "For someone who prides herself on being articulate, I'm making a bloody mess of this." She looked up. "Please sit next to me and let me blather, and hopefully, clear things up."

When Renee was seated, Constance took her hand again. "My parents allowed me to go to Stanford with the understanding that after I graduated, I would come home and marry Nigel, my childhood friend who would inherit his dad's title one day. That I wasn't in love with him or, he me, mattered sod all to our parents. So when I realized I was in love with you, I panicked. You must understand. The responsibilities of being the daughter of an Earl were pounded into my head from the moment I was born, and turning my back on what was expected was unthinkable. I was miserable but I knew what I had to do. And I did it. I flew home and married Nigel three months later. On our wedding night I was extremely agitated. I couldn't stop crying. Nigel held me and promised I could tell him anything. We'd been friends all our lives. I trusted him. So I told him I was a lesbian. He dropped his arms and stared at me. I thought I'd made a horrible mistake telling him, but then he doubled over laughing. Turned out he didn't want to marry me any more than I wanted to marry him. And for the same reason. He was gay. So instead of having sex, we sat up all night and hatched a plan to live separate lives but stay together a couple of years and then quietly divorce."

Renee perked up. "Oh, so you're divorced?"

"Please let me finish, Renee. I want to get it all out this time." She kissed Renee's knuckles. "With the pressure off, our honeymoon turned into a wonderful vacation. We were at a beautiful resort in Greece having fun playing together. But you were always on my mind. I even thought about calling you, but what would I say? 'Hi, come and join me and my husband on our honeymoon?' So instead, I decided I'd return with you someday. I even made notes about things I thought you'd like to do. One night Nigel and I got smashed and he proposed we have sex once so we would at least know what it felt like between a man and a woman. It seemed like a brilliant idea at the time.

And, you can probably guess what happened." She tightened her hold on Renee. "I got pregnant."

"You have a child?"

"Two."

Renee tried to pull away. "So you had sex—"

"Once. Twins. Two girls. Chloe and Cara. We were devastated when we found out I was pregnant. Neither of us was keen on an abortion but we were considering it until we learned I was carrying twins. We just couldn't do it. At first we thought we'd go through with our plan of divorcing after a couple of years, but once we held them, we knew we'd do what was best for them. Our new plan was to stay together until they turned eighteen and went off to college or got married or were out on their own."

"So, now you...no wait." Renee did a quick calculation. "They can't be eighteen yet. What happened?"

Constance stared at the waterfall for a few seconds before continuing. "You've heard the saying, life is what happens when you're making other plans? Seven months ago Nigel intervened to save a woman being raped in an alley and was stabbed to death."

"How horrible for you and the girls."

"It was and it is. They miss him terribly. And so do I. He was my best friend. We weren't lovers, we weren't in love, but I loved him and I believe he loved me. Our lives hadn't turned out the way we wanted, but our daughters were our priority and we made the best of our situation. For the most part, we were happy."

They were silent, listening to the rushing water, each lost in their thoughts. Suddenly overcome with the need to be home, in familiar surroundings, Renee glanced at her phone. Four o'clock. "Rather than hang around here, what would you think about driving back and having dinner in the city?"

"That's a great idea. Let's go back to Trattoria Montero if it's not too boring for you."

Downhill over the slippery rocks and gnarly roots required careful attention to maintain balance and avoid a tumble and injury. So grunts and warnings to watch out or be careful were the only conversation on the tense descent. Once they were settled in the car, Constance put her hand on Renee's thigh. "So what do you think about what I told you?"

Was that a tremor in Constance's voice? Did she think Renee would run at the first sign of discomfort? Yeah, well, that wasn't so farfetched, was it?

Before Renee could respond to the first question, Constance punched out another. "Do you still want to—"

"Yes." Renee met Constance's eyes for a second then quickly turned back to the road. "I still want to. But it's a lot to process. You've lived a whole life that I know nothing of, a life so different that I can't even imagine it, while I've continued to live the same life as when we were at Stanford. I need to think about that. I still want to go ahead with exploring our friendship, but I have some questions."

"Such as?"

"You're free legally now but are you free emotionally? Are you ready to consider another relationship so soon? Possibly a relationship with me, someone who hasn't changed at all?"

Constance smiled. "I've grown up since Stanford and I believe you have too. We've both changed. I never expected I would come to New York and find you again. And find you in a state of mind very similar to mine. Like you, I can't make promises about a relationship. We both have issues to work out and our plan to work on being friends before we complicate things still sounds like a good idea to me. Other than my daughters, my priority now is figuring out who the hell Lady Constance Martindale is. No. It's actually Constance Martindale I need to figure out. And I would very much like your support doing it."

"I'm here. What about your family?"

"I expect you mean Mum and Dad and the royal issue, rather than Chloe and Cara. Before I left London I came out to my parents and to Nigel's. I told them I'm done with pretending to be someone I'm not. Thanks to Nigel, the girls and I are financially independent so they can't use that as a stick. But they're still pressuring me. My moving to New York City makes dealing with them easier."

They listened to NPR for a while then Constance changed to an easy listening jazz station. The silence was companionable. They dropped the car off at Renee's garage and strolled to Trattoria Montero. As they waited for their food, Renee asked the question that kept coming up in her mind. "Why did you come back to the US?"

"Nigel's death gutted me. I was in shock but I had to keep it together because I had two devastated thirteen-year-olds to help through the funeral and the first weeks after. But once the girls were back in school and appeared to be dealing with the loss of their father, I had a lot of time to think. About the past. About the future." She paused while the waiter poured their wine. "By marrying when we didn't want to, Nigel and I had put the needs of our parents ahead of our own. Then we'd stupidly had sex neither of us really wanted and ended up with two beautiful babies. And, perhaps rightly so, we put their needs above our own." Constance flashed a rueful smile. "In effect, we'd put our lives on hold, put our needs and desires aside, with the intention of starting our real lives after we'd given the girls a secure beginning. Because of his kindness to a stranger Nigel never got to have his real life. But I realized I could have mine, if I dared."

Renee touched her shoulder. "And is this your real life?"

"I hope so. I needed to get away from England, from my title, to really be free, but it's not only me I had to consider. Luckily, the girls are kind of a self-contained unit so they were actually excited about moving to a new school in a new city in a new country. I've always felt an affinity for the States. I chose New York City because of the culture and the art scene."

"Not because you expected to find me?" Renee tried to wiggle her eyebrows but failed.

Constance laughed. "Sexy move. Not."

"I don't understand. It always works in lesbian romance novels."

"Really Renee? You read lesbian romance novels?" Her lips twitched. "Wait. I'd rather not know." Her expression became serious. "I did think of you when I made the decision. I've thought about you a great deal over the years but I had no idea where you were. You could have been living in California, or on a sheep farm in Australia, or, more likely, in France. And I had no idea of how your life had changed, whether you had a wife and five kids or had entered a convent. I never dreamed you were single and living in New York City. I never dreamed I'd find you again." Constance seemed mesmerized by the wine she was swirling in her glass.

Renee followed her gaze. Reflected in the candlelight, the deep red cabernet looked like liquid rubies. Renee's feelings swirled like the wine. Lit by the dancing flame and the splashes of red, Constance looked mysterious and unattainable. Was she? Suddenly Renee needed to know. "You could have found me through my parents anytime."

"I suppose I could have. But I wasn't interested in an affair with you. Nigel and I had decided as long as we were discreet and practiced safe sex, occasional casual affairs were all right. From time to time we went away for a weekend together. He usually hooked up. I tried casual sex a couple of times but I need more. It was easier for me to be celibate, so I'd stay in our hotel room reading while he went out. Once Nigel was dead it seemed important for me to be independent and not base my life on someone else." She met Renee's eyes. "Do you understand?"

Renee considered the question. Their lives had been so different, yet here they were both dealing with similar issues. "While you were married you wanted more than you could have, then when you were free you wanted to manage your life the way you wanted and not go chasing after some fantasy woman you'd had a sexual relationship with sixteen years ago?"

"Close enough, I suppose, though you were very real to me."

"And now?"

"Now I'm happy to have found you. And I truly hope we can explore who we can be to each other in the present."

Their dinners arrived. They'd both ordered the Branzino and they focused on it for a few minutes. But Renee was intent on getting answers so between bites she asked another question. "Do Chloe and Cara know you prefer women?"

"They do. Cara asked recently if I thought I would marry again. I tried to talk around it, but ultimately I decided they were old enough for the truth. So I said I wasn't sure I would ever marry again, but if I did, it would most likely be to a woman. They nodded and said cool but who knows how they'll react if it happens."

At least there would be no reason to hide. Renee relaxed. "Why didn't I read about your wedding or about the birth of your twins?"

Constance laughed. "You bloody Americans are only interested in royals close to the crown, like William and Harry. Or those who go from one scandal to another. Nigel and I didn't fit into either category."

Renee laughed. "Hey, don't forget I'm just as much French as American."

Constance held Renee's gaze. "I've never forgotten a single thing about you, Renee. Whatever happens between us now, I'll always remember and be grateful for your gentle and tender introduction to sex, for the intense sexual and intellectual experience throughout our almost two-month relationship, and the mind blowing love making of our last few nights together." Her eyes filled. She blinked back the tears.

"I apologize for not telling you the whole sad story of my life right away. It wasn't intentional." She looked away and took a deep breath, then another before meeting Renee's eyes again. "Or maybe it was. I was afraid if you knew, you'd run. Being free is new and I'm just learning who I am now. That's why I'm happy to take things slowly. I don't want to make promises I can't keep."

CHAPTER TEN

Renee sat in her usual chair facing Olivia but avoided her eyes. Now that the easy part, talking about her history with Darcy, was over, she didn't have the vaguest idea where to start. She'd been here before. Ten years ago she'd spent four sessions without uttering a word before Olivia told her to come back to therapy when she was ready to change. Well she was ready to change. But what magic words would make it happen?

She loosened her tie, ran her fingers through her hair and leaned forward. "I'm afraid you'll kick me out again if I don't talk."

Olivia blew on her tea and watched Renee through the steam.

"I don't know why this is so hard." Renee chewed the cuticle on her thumb, then dropped her hand into her lap. "It's strange, but I've hardly thought about Darcy this week." She frowned. "Actually, I haven't thought about her at all."

"Is that so unusual?"

Olivia's gentle question pulled Renee from her introspection. "Very. Though there have been periods in the last twenty years when I haven't been preoccupied with thoughts of Darcy, she's always been there in the background like a low-grade fever. Then when I lost interest in casual hook-ups, she moved front and center again."

Olivia made a note on the pad she kept on the table next to her chair. "So what changed recently?"

Renee gazed out the window. Good question. What changed? An image of Constance laughing flashed in her mind. Was that it? Had the reappearance of Constance in her life been enough to blot out Darcy? Was she so shallow? Would Olivia think she was shallow? What the hell? If she couldn't be truthful here, she might as well kick herself out of therapy this time. "Maybe a convergence of things. Talking to Tori about Darcy. Talking to Darcy. Talking to you." She cleared her throat. "Constance?"

"Constance?" Olivia said. "Are you asking or telling me?"

Renee turned from the window. Olivia was smiling. She relaxed. "Telling you. Is it all right if I don't talk about Darcy? Will you think I'm shallow if I talk about Constance?"

"Tell me about her."

Renee took a deep breath. "I was involved with Constance when we were graduate students at Stanford. She's the only woman, other than Darcy and Gina, who I've ever thought I could have a future with. Of course having those thoughts scared me so I told myself *she* was getting too involved and I needed to dump her. But before I could scamper away, she left. She disappeared, went back to England without even a goodbye. We reconnected recently after almost sixteen years and the feelings are still there for me. And from what she says, it's mutual."

"How did you feel when she left you without a word?"

"It was so long ago." She knew Olivia would wait for the answer so she closed her eyes and thought back to that day. They hadn't had classes together but they knew each other's schedule and usually managed to touch base several times during the day. So when she hadn't seen or heard from Constance by dinnertime, she called. Getting no answer again, she decided something was wrong and went to her apartment to check on her but she wasn't there. She tracked down Constance's closest friend and was stunned to learn Constance had booked a flight first thing that morning and had flown to London that evening. It wasn't a family emergency; she'd just decided to go home to London earlier than scheduled and wouldn't be attending her graduation the next week. Reeling, Renee had stumbled back to her apartment. She was devastated. Constance had abandoned her, tossed her away like a used-up tube of toothpaste. She cried for hours, moped for weeks in Paris, then pushed Constance to the back of her mind. Remembering that day, the emotions, still raw, still as painful as they had been then, flooded her. Her eyes popped open. "Shocked. Confused. Hurt. Devastated. Angry. Lonely. And sad, overwhelmingly sad." In fact, tears were threatening right now.

"How did you explain it to yourself? Did you try to contact her?"

"She's the daughter of an Earl so my first thought was that my being biracial wouldn't fly with the Queen. Later, I thought she just wasn't as into me as I'd thought." Renee rubbed her eyes. "I never tried to contact her. I was hurt and I was too proud. I'd never had to pursue a woman. Besides, we'd agreed upfront on a short-term, no-strings affair."

Renee watched Olivia study her over her teacup again. No doubt she saw a butch lesbian. But was it a strong, determined butch or a sniveling, helpless, floundering butch?

"So Constance had a problem with you being mixed race?"

"Not that she ever said."

"And yet, it was the first thing you thought of when she abandoned you. Did it ever occur to you that the Queen might not have liked her bringing a woman home?"

Had it? "No."

"So how did you feel about being left because you're biracial?"

She gripped the arms of the chair fighting the impulse to run as the feelings bubbled up. "Rage at feeling less than. Hurt that Constance thought I was less than, and even more devastated because I felt unlovable, that no one would ever truly want me."

"What about Darcy? Do you attribute her unwillingness to love you to your being biracial?"

Renee's breath caught. She doubled over, as if Olivia had punched her, and struggled to push back the hurt. Gulping for air, breathing deeply, covering her mouth, or tensing her body didn't work, and the pain erupted with a wail and sobs burst from somewhere deep inside her. Convulsing, she struggled to regain control. After what seemed like hours, she became conscious of Olivia's hand gently rubbing her back and she started to breathe. She raised her head. "Sorry."

Olivia handed her the box of tissues and moved back to her chair. "How do you feel?"

"Embarrassed. Relaxed. Lighter."

"One way or another, you've casually mentioned your racial heritage in every session we've had. Are you ready to talk about what being biracial means to you?"

Was that the elephant in her life? Always there but never confronted? "To answer your question, my being biracial never seemed to be a problem for Darcy. Or Constance, for that matter. But it was for Gina and I think somewhere in the back of my mind I believe that was why they all left me."

"So your mother is black and your father white. You have four older mixed-race siblings so I'm assuming you didn't have problems in your family."

"Not in my immediate family but my dad's mother never accepted me. My mom's mom was fine, the lighter the skin the better as far as she was concerned. But my aunts, my mom's older sisters and their daughters who were older than me, made fun of me, called me ugly and said no man would ever love me. From articles I've read, my experience was a stereotypical biracial experience—I wasn't white enough for my French grandmother because I might have black children, and I wasn't black enough for some of my American relatives. Maybe because my siblings are all darker than me, clearly not white, they didn't have the same problem. Besides they had each other. I was so much younger I was like an only child.

"The other night I remembered an incident in fourth grade. My mom and dad came to school to see me sing in the spring pageant, and my classmates thought she was the maid. When I said she was my mom, they accused me of lying. When I insisted she was, they followed me around and asked over and over, 'What are you?' I didn't know how to answer. I was miserable, ashamed of my mom, and feeling that I was bad for some reason I didn't understand. It went on for a couple of months, until the end of the school year. That summer we went to Italy so my parents could teach and we spent the next two years there.

"But after those months of shaming, I felt I was different, lesser than. For a while, I tried to avoid being seen with my mom, but it was hard because we were, and still are, really close and I was particularly needy. I retreated into my studies and rarely made friends. It probably didn't help that I expected to be rejected so I closed everyone out."

Olivia looked like the proverbial cat who'd swallowed the canary. Renee imagined she could see feathers in her mouth. She stared at Olivia, puzzled. What had she said? "I don't know what…oh, I get it. You think I rejected Darcy and Constance because I was afraid they'd reject me like Gina had, because I'm mixed race?" She knew she sounded incredulous but she'd never actually verbalized it in that way to herself.

Olivia peered at Renee over that damned teacup. Did that cup even contain tea? Maybe she was a vodka drinker or maybe it was hot Saki.

"It's what you think that's important, Renee. Our time is up but it's time we explored your feelings about race. I'd like you to give it some thought before our next meeting."

CHAPTER ELEVEN

Renee had spent the time since her previous therapy session struggling with the issue of her identity. Because of her white skin and blue eyes the world treated her like a white woman even though she was as black as she was white. In reality, she didn't feel black. Or white for that matter. She felt like herself. As usual, when she tried to think about being biracial she ended up with many more questions than answers. What is she? Could anyone truly love her? What did it mean to be black? How did it feel to be black? Did she need to carry a sign or hang a picture of her with her parents around her neck? Was she a fake? Was she passing? She told everyone she was biracial. Did that make it all right? Did her black friends think she was a traitor? Did her white friends think she was passing? What the fuck did any of it matter?

She rubbed her eyes, gazed at her hands clasped tightly in her lap, then looked Olivia in the eye. "I don't hide that I'm biracial, but I reject who I am every single day. I have all the privilege that comes with white skin, and by remaining silent, I'm rejecting the black part of me. Yet I don't feel authentic saying I'm black because I don't have to deal with any of the hate and fear and insults that dark-complexioned people face on a daily basis. And saying I'm black feels like I'm rejecting the white part of me." She grabbed a tissue and dabbed at her eyes. "I'm half white and half black. What do I need to do so I'm not lying to the world and rejecting half of myself?"

Olivia nodded. "It's difficult. You can't change society or even other people. All you can do is learn to celebrate both sides of who you are. Have you talked to Gina yet?"

"She's a senior officer at IBM so she travels a lot and I haven't been able to get her to commit to a date. Next week, hopefully. I've thought a lot this week about our relationship, and it seems to me it wasn't my being mixed race that was the problem. It was my white skin. She accepted that I was as black as I was white, but she was frustrated by my inability to understand her daily experience of life as a young black woman insulted and devalued by white society."

"Hindsight is a wonderful thing, Renee. But the issue isn't what you understand today, but what you felt at the time."

Digging up these old feelings was too hard. Renee suppressed a moan and then caught herself. Isn't that why she was in therapy? "At the time, while we were together, I felt rejected by her. It was as if my life experience didn't count because of my skin color. And no matter what I did, I could never be black enough or poor enough for Gina, the black warrior."

"Do I hear underlying anger?"

Renee sighed. "You asked what I felt at the time. I guess I was angry as well as hurt."

Olivia let her sit with that thought before continuing. "And the two of you have never talked about this. Are you still angry?"

Renee didn't have to dig deep on this. "Absolutely not."

"Really?" Olivia raised her eyebrows. "Besides Gina, are any of the other Inner Circle members black?"

Renee flashed on Elle, the bronze-skinned model who must have been an African queen in another life, and Gina's lover Beth. "Only Elle, Gina and Beth are in New York City. Oh, Erik and Joel, two guys new to the Inner Circle. Why?"

"Perhaps it would help you to have a group to talk to about race rather than to keep it, as I believe you do, locked up inside yourself."

"I don't know. Elle is with Tori, a white woman, and I'm not super close with the guys. I'd feel better talking to Gina alone, then maybe do a group thing later. I have to say, though, the idea of a group sitting around discussing my feelings about anything, especially being mixed race, makes me very nervous."

Olivia raised her eyebrows and leaned forward, a signal she thought what she was about to say was important. "However you decide to do it, all together or one-on-one, as a general discussion or one about your experience, I believe you need to start talking about this issue with people you trust. People who live this and obviously know more about it than I do."

Each time the race issue came up, Renee felt like a dog chasing its tail. There didn't seem to be a solution. The last thing she wanted was to drag this out into the open and involve her friends. "I'll think about it, okay?"

Olivia gazed at her a few seconds, then nodded. "So how are you and Constance getting along?"

Renee's head shot up. "What do you mean?"

"It's a simple question, Renee. You started the week saying you wanted to talk about her, then we got sidetracked into your feelings about being biracial, so I'm checking in to see whether there was something in particular about Constance that you wanted to discuss."

"We went hiking last Saturday." After hearing about the secret husband and two children she'd spent Sunday in a panic. "And Constance casually mentioned some things that I found upsetting."

Renee dropped her gaze to her phone. Damn, not as late as she hoped. She raised her eyes.

"Don't worry, we have plenty of time." Olivia's smile looked like a gotcha. But it could be she was projecting her feelings onto Olivia. She'd felt blindsided by Constance.

And, for some reason, the situation embarrassed her. Twice she'd opened herself to Constance in a way she hadn't to anyone except Darcy and Gina and twice Constance hadn't been totally honest with her. But this was what she paid Olivia for, so she accepted the inevitable and leaned back. "It had never entered my mind that she was married and had children. Did I mention she was Lady Constance Martindale when we were at Stanford? Remember I said she dumped me? She left Stanford and ran home to fulfill her family obligation…to marry a man, Nigel, a childhood friend and also the child of an Earl. On their honeymoon they discovered they were both gay and didn't consummate the marriage. Then one night under the influence of alcohol they decided to see what heterosexual sex was like and Constance ended up pregnant. With twins. Being good people they decided they'd stay in their sexless but loving marriage until the girls were eighteen. But about seven months ago Nigel intervened to save a woman who was being raped and he was killed. So now it's just her and her twin fourteen-year-old-daughters."

Renee hesitated, hoping Olivia would react but no such luck. "The good news is she came out to her parents and moved to New York City to make a fresh start. She asked me if, knowing her history, I still want to see whether there's anything worth exploring between us." *Did I? Is there?* She gazed out the window, suddenly not sure.

Olivia's voice brought her back into the room. "Where did you disappear to, Renee?"

Was Olivia responding to her body language or was the sudden onset of sadness visible? "I don't…" Renee shrugged. "I told her I wanted to continue exploring, but I can't get my mind around the fact that she chose him over me, and now she comes with two daughters. I haven't seen her since Saturday. I haven't called her. And I haven't returned her calls. She apologized Saturday for not telling me sooner, but she was afraid I would run. I assured her I wouldn't. But…."

"You're running." Olivia finished her thought for her. "And longing for Darcy."

It took Renee a few seconds to realize what Olivia had said but she couldn't hide her shock. "What? No." She bit her lip.

"Yes. How did you know? Not only has Darcy been on my mind every day since but I've also been dreaming about her."

"Why, Renee? Do you know?" Olivia said, her voice gentle.

For some reason the caring in Olivia's voice touched the sadness filling Renee. Fighting for control, she took a deep breath. "Sharing my thoughts and feelings, letting myself really care, scares me. I did it with Darcy and she left me. I did it with Gina and she left because she despised me. And, then I cared about Constance and she dumped me for a man. Why should I believe she'll stay now? What if her daughters hate me? What if I disappoint her? What if I feel trapped? What if she realizes she'd rather be with a man?"

Olivia frowned. "Do I need to have my hearing checked? I could have sworn you told me you left Darcy, not just once, but over and over again for almost two years. Perhaps I also misheard when you said you and Gina agreed to separate. And, I could swear you said you were in the process of dumping Constance when she left." She sipped her tea. "Oh, did I imagine that you told me Constance wasn't into men?"

Renee stared at Olivia. Damn. Throwing her own words in her face wasn't fair. "All right. I left them." She didn't try to keep the annoyance out of her voice. "But I'm really scared."

Olivia repeated the question. "Why did Darcy suddenly become front and center for you again, Renee? Do you know?"

"Maybe Tori was right. I use Darcy to keep from committing myself, that I use her as a shield."

Olivia let her sit in silence for a few minutes. "What are you running from? You say you want what Darcy has with Andrea, and Tori has with, um, her wife. By your own account, you've been running since you found yourself deeply in love with Darcy. What's the worst thing that could happen if you love someone and they love you?"

Renee sniffed. "They'll leave me and I'll be hurt and alone."

"And so?" Olivia sipped her tea and watched Renee fight her tears.

Damn how does her tea stay hot for the whole hour? She took a deep breath. "And so I leave them before they can leave me. And I'm hurting and alone. Is that what you want?"

Olivia's eyes widened, probably reacting to the anger in Renee's voice. "I want the truth, Renee. And so should you. Think about this and let's pick up here Monday."

Renee stood. "Sorry for being crabby, Olivia." She turned toward the door then stopped. "Should I see Constance over the weekend?"

Olivia put her tea down and stood. "Being crabby, as you put it, Renee, means you're getting close to something painful. As for whether you should see Constance, only you know what you're feeling." She grinned. "Though I'd love to hear about what you decide on Monday."

CHAPTER TWELVE

Renee stared at the phone in her hand. She'd walked for an hour after her therapy this morning trying to figure out what she wanted. And what she wanted was to see Constance. She was relieved, though, when her secretary reminded her of her plans to take a client to *La Bohème* at the Metropolitan Opera that evening. But now that client was snowed in at the airport in Chicago and had just canceled, leaving her with an extra ticket. Did Constance enjoy opera? Was three o'clock too late to call?

It had been almost a week since their last contact and she was torn between her desire to see Constance and her dread of facing Constance's anger. And, Constance would need time to get someone to stay with her daughters who, she'd confided, much to their chagrin, she refused to leave home alone. Maya was the safer bet for tonight. But not dealing with her feelings for Darcy had cost her a lot of years. Time to stop being a coward. Constance could say no and tell her to go fuck herself. But angry or not, she might say yes. What the hell?

She pictured Constance immersed in her painting and slowly becoming aware of her phone ringing. Ha. She had no idea when Constance painted or whether she forgot everything else when she did. Though she knew the young Constance, she only knew facts about the Constance of today, like she had a dead husband and two teenage daughters and had fled England and come to New York to live. Time to find out whether she liked opera. Time to find out whether she would forgive her for backsliding.

"Hello, Renee." A good sign. Constance had answered despite seeing Renee's name displayed on her phone. Her voice was low, tentative. "Nice to hear from you."

She thought of a thousand ways to explain why she'd disappeared after Constance opened up to her, but she sounded so vulnerable only the truth would do. "I got scared. And, as you predicted, I ran. I'm sorry, Constance. I can't promise it won't happen again but I'm working hard on it." Renee could hear Constance breathing into the phone while she was holding her own breath, waiting for the ax to fall.

Finally, Constance laughed. "I guess six days is an improvement over my disappearing for sixteen years."

A smile splitting her face, Renee took in air. She flopped back in her desk chair and spun around to face the windows. "You mean to say that my being gone for six days didn't feel like sixteen years to you?"

Constance laughed. "If I'm to be honest, it did in some ways. But since we've talked about things and since I know where to find you, it didn't feel so...so final. I'm glad you called."

Feeling ridiculously happy, Renee spun her chair. "Are you free tonight? I know it's last minute but the client I was supposed to take to *La Bohème* is stuck in Chicago and I was hoping you could make it. That is, if you even like opera."

"I do like opera and *La Bohème* is one of my favorites, even though it always makes me cry. I'd love to go. The girls are at a friend's house doing homework and they've been invited to stay for dinner. Maybe they can have a sleepover. Let me check."

Constance called three minutes later. "All set. I can meet you at Lincoln Center after I drop pajamas and a change of clothing off to the girls. What time is good?"

"Why don't we meet at six o'clock for dinner at Boulud Sud. It's right across the street from Lincoln Center and I already have a reservation."

Constance hadn't sounded angry but Renee was uneasy. She finally gave up on the report she was analyzing and left her office early. Hoping to calm herself, she walked to Sixty-Fourth Street and Broadway. She arrived ten minutes before their reservation and was seated immediately. She attempted to focus on the menu in front of her but couldn't keep her eyes from the entrance. She must have blinked or dozed because Constance seemed to have appeared from out of nowhere. Though she wasn't the most traditionally beautiful woman Renee had ever been with, Constance was the most striking. Motherhood, or perhaps age, had softened the once angular young body Renee had thought extremely sexy, to the voluptuous body of a woman. Constance had the carriage, confidence, and grace of a royal but none of the coldness or distance Renee associated with their stiff-upper-lip approach to life. Strolling through the restaurant, chatting with the maître d' escorting her to their table, she seemed to glow from within. Renee was reminded again of why she was attracted to this strong, warm, and caring woman. Their eyes met. Constance smiled and Renee relaxed. Why had she doubted her? What you saw was what you got. No artifice. No games.

Renee hesitated, then hugged her. "Hi. I'm thrilled you could make it tonight. Please sit." Renee cleared her throat. "Constance, I'm sor—"

"No apology necessary. I'm glad to be here with you. Let's enjoy dinner and the opera. We'll have plenty of time to talk about it later." She picked up her menu. "I tend to forget about eating when I'm painting, so as usual, I'm starving." She scanned the menu. "Everything looks delicious. Why don't you order for both of us?"

"Sure." Renee nodded at the waiter hovering nearby. "Bring us two glasses of the Yves Martin Sancerre." She studied the appetizer and dinner options and when the waiter arrived with their wines she said, "To start, we'll share the Sicilian Sardine Escabèche, the Octopus À La Plancha and the Arabic Lamb Flatbread. For dinner, we'll split the Lemon Saffron Linguine and the Seared Maine Scallops." Her gaze went to Constance. "Okay?"

Constance raised her glass. "Sounds delicious." She sipped her wine. "So tell me about the woman I'm standing in for. Is she someone you date?"

"Definitely not a date." She put her glass on the table. "She's a client. The CEO of a fairly large company who likes to be wined and dined, so when she's in New York, I take her out to dinner and to the theater or the opera. She's a lesbian in a long-term relationship, and I consider her and her wife my friends. When I'm in Chicago, I take them both out and often have dinner with them at their home."

"Sounds lovely. But I'm glad for the snow in Chicago so I get to spend the evening with you and I get to hear *La Boheme*."

"I'm glad I get to be with you after being my usual cowardly self."

"Stop apologizing and don't be so hard on yourself. I dumped a lot of stuff on you with no warning. You're not a coward. You and I are both dealing with some scary issues in therapy. Sometimes I feel like I'm on a roller coaster, but I stay on hoping there's a prize at the end of the ride." Constance waited for the waiter to arrange their appetizers. "So tell me about your work."

"I'm the senior partner in Millford, Cooper and Anderson, Management Consulting. We identify and solve financial, personnel, technology, and procedural problems, mainly for large corporations. Mostly these days I manage the work of others but occasionally I get to go into the field." As they ate, they shared stories and laughed a lot about the everyday comedy of life. They each finished with an espresso but neither had dessert. When the check arrived, Constance insisted on paying for the dinner since Renee had provided the tickets. Understanding Constance needed to be independent and in charge of her life, Renee didn't fight her.

Caught up in the rush of people headed for an opera, a play, a concert, or a ballet in one of the Lincoln Center venues, they strode briskly across the street and up the few steps to the plaza. Constance gasped and grabbed Renee's arm as the Metropolitan Opera House appeared in front of them. Renee really looked at it for the first time in a long time, trying to see what Constance was seeing. The five huge, glass-filled arches of the grand building seemed to glow. The gorgeous Marc Chagall murals filled an arch on either side of the building and framed the red-carpeted lobby, the crystal chandeliers, and the staircase leading into the house. It was truly breathtaking. "Thank you, Renee. I've seen pictures of this of course, but it's even more fantastic in real life."

They followed the crowd and filed into the entry. Renee handed over their tickets, Constance opened her bag for inspection, and they were directed to the orchestra section. Once they were settled in their center seats, surrounded by the low excited rumble of the audience, Constance remarked on the beauty of the hall and then studied the program for tonight's performance. As the lights dimmed and the hanging crystal chandeliers slowly moved up to the ceiling, Constance gasped, and grabbed Renee's arm. She along with many others in the audience was spellbound. Her eyes shining, she turned to Renee. "So beautiful."

Constance's pleasure thrilled Renee. Sixteen years later, her beauty still enchanted Renee.

Renee wasn't sure when Constance had gripped her thigh, but now that she was aware of it, she couldn't concentrate on *La Boheme*. Constance, on the other hand, was totally engrossed. By the death scene, tears streamed down her face and she seemed to be mouthing the words to the famous duet. Renee was charmed and fascinated. This was a side of Constance she hadn't seen before.

After the performance, they moved outside to the plaza with the crowd, and though the fountain wasn't shooting into the air as it did in warm weather, the pulsing of the water and the beauty of the lights were mesmerizing. Constance slipped her arm through Renee's arm. "Let's walk home."

It was only ten blocks and Renee was happy to prolong the night. "Of course."

Neither spoke for the first few blocks, then Renee became aware of Constance softly singing and it sounded like she was repeating the end of Mimi's dying aria, no fireworks or soaring orchestra, just a very quiet expiring of her life. It was gorgeous. "I didn't know you sang."

Still with tears in her eyes, Constance stopped and looked up at Renee. "We have a lot to learn about each other, Renee." She stood on tiptoe and kissed Renee's cheek. "Thank you for tonight. I haven't been out like this since before Nigel died. And to be honest, since he died I've had no desire to hear music or be entertained. I just wanted to be alone in my studio with my brush and paints and canvas. I feel…"

When it became obvious that Constance wasn't going to finish her statement, Renee asked. "You feel what?"

Constance tucked her arm back under Renee's arm and propelled them forward. They walked another block in silence. "I'm afraid I'll scare you again if I say, but if we're going to be in each other's lives, I want us to be honest." She took a deep breath. "I feel you're bringing me back to life."

"I'm glad." Renee pulled Constance's arm closer. For some reason that statement didn't scare her. Instead, it made her want to do more to make Constance happy. "I like you like this, singing and smiling and very alive. I imagine Nigel's death was a tremendous blow."

Constance slid her hand down Renee's arm and entwined their fingers. "Yes, his death did me in, but in therapy I realized recently that I'd put myself into a state of suspended animation after we married. Though I was happy with him and the girls and our life, only a part of me was there, the rest was hidden, waiting. It's hard to explain."

Renee thought about it. Only being partly in your life. She'd been doing that for as long as she could remember. Real or imagined, her feelings for Darcy had served to keep her from living fully just as Nigel and the twins had done for Constance. "I think I understand. I feel like I've lived most of my life like that. And, I believe you're the one bringing me back to life, as scary as life is."

CHAPTER THIRTEEN

"Delicious as always, Renee." Gina arranged her fork and knife on her plate and then folded her napkin. "I've wanted to get together, just the two of us, for a while but work has been crazy. Thanks for taking the initiative."

"I've missed you too." Renee stood. "And I need to talk." She pulled Gina up. "I'll clean up later. Let's sit in the living room." Gina wrapped her arms around Renee. "I meant what I said at the wedding. I've been worried about you for quite a while. And then at the wedding you looked devastated watching the brides." She leaned back to see Renee's face. "Talk to me, honey."

Renee had invited Gina here to talk, but holding her, letting herself feel her love for Gina, she panicked. Would she be opening old wounds and lose her? But then feeling the love in Gina's embrace, the caring in her voice, Renee trusted they would be all right.

"Bring your wine." She led Gina to the sofa and swiveled to face her. Forgetting she had changed into a T-shirt and jeans she reached up to loosen her tie.

"No tie." Gina laughed. "But that gesture means you're nervous."

They really did know each other well. "I *am* nervous because I need to rehash old history and I'm afraid of losing you."

"Just spit it out. You can't shock me. And even if you do, you won't lose me so easily."

Feeling the need to connect physically, to hold on, Renee clasped Gina's thigh. "I've been unhappy with my life for a year and seeing Darcy and Andrea so in love and so happy brought up thoughts of what might have been with her. Thoughts of what might have been with you, thoughts of us. After the wedding, I went into therapy to figure things out, so I've been thinking a lot about the past, about the women who have been, who are, important to me. I know we were headed for a breakup but I feel I owe you an apology for bailing the minute Darcy needed me."

Gina waved her hand. "No apology needed. We were both so raw from the constant fighting. Our relationship was already teetering. It was clear we both needed to escape. You running to comfort Darcy gave me the excuse I needed to break up." She squeezed Renee's hand. "Are you finding the therapy helpful?"

"Yes." Renee sipped her wine. Damn she was really nervous about bringing this up. "It seems my being mixed race has been more important for me than I let myself know. I was hoping we could talk about it."

Gina pulled away. "Are you sure? I was pretty harsh back then. I'm afraid rehashing will ruin our friendship."

Renee took Gina's hand and held their two hands in front of them. "One white, one a deep tan. A few shades lighter or darker makes all the difference doesn't it?" She locked onto Gina's eyes. "I need to talk about it Gina, please. And I hope you'll be honest."

"You know I've changed my opinion since then, right?" Gina bit her lip. "You promise it won't come between us?"

"I promise, though I might bitch a little along the way."

Gina punched Renee's arm lightly. "How else would I know it's you?"

"You obviously have white blood somewhere in your family. And, judging by the color of her skin, so does Beth. Am I wrong to assume rape by a master way back?"

Gina reached for her glass and sipped. "As far as either of us knows that's a good guess. And your mom and her sisters are probably mixed race for the same reason."

"And they, like you and Beth, are obviously African-American. Have you only dated dark-skinned women since me?"

Gina drank some wine and put the glass back down on the coffee table. "When we were a couple, I felt as if we lived in two different worlds, mine black, yours white. I had to constantly explain myself to make you understand my world. So yes, I've only dated obviously black women since you. It's just easier. Because our life experience is similar it's not necessary to explain certain things like what it feels like to be the only black person in the room or how people assume you must be the hired help not the top executive, or why the many small slights we call micro aggressions these days are racist. We don't have to struggle to communicate the anxiety, the ever-present fear of random violence from white men, and recently, white women. Even if white-presenting blacks like you make a point of identifying as black the assumption out in the world is that they are white and are entitled to be treated accordingly. So when they go into a store nobody follows them around thinking they're there to steal."

She hesitated, seeming indecisive, but then continued. "It doesn't happen that often but it happened when I was in Chicago a month or so ago. I ran out of moisturizer so I dashed into Macy's wearing an expensive business suit and carrying my expensive leather briefcase. As I wandered around looking for the counter with my brand, I became aware I had an escort, a store security person, a black woman. I confronted her and flashed my IBM ID. She got flustered and walked away. Without an apology. I am a fucking senior vice president at a major American corporation, Renee, not a dirty street person dressed in rags, and yet I still have to deal with that kind of thing. It hurts."

The rage and the hurt in Gina's voice broke Renee's heart. She knew these things of course; she read the papers and watched TV news but it always seemed distant, never personal. She was shocked to hear that even Gina was subjected to this blatant racism. "I'm so sorry you have to deal with that, Gina. I feel as stupid and confused as I did as a freshman in college. I still don't know what to say or do to make it better."

"Nothing you can do or say will make it better, Renee. I just want you to understand. That would never happen to you or any white-presenting black. No one will call the police if they see you struggling with the lock on your apartment or car. You're less likely to be stopped and harassed by the police. And, let's not forget, less likely to be killed by police on your own property while minding your own business. That's why we live in Harlem."

"What?" Renee couldn't help the shock in her voice. "I thought it was because it was easier for you to drive to work in Armonk, for Beth to take the subway to midtown and because apartments are less expensive?"

Gina laughed. "That too, my gullible friend. But, it's easier. And we feel safe. Of course, we're probably kidding ourselves because NYPD cops in Harlem aren't necessarily less racist than those in midtown, and who's to say some black criminal won't rob us or worse?" Gina shrugged. "But we feel more comfortable, less like targets. Nobody pays attention to us in the supermarket."

"Wow. I never guessed." Renee thought about what Gina had just revealed, and tried to understand. "I'm so sorry. I guess you're right. It's impossible for me to understand what your life feels like if mine is so different."

Gina blew out a breath. "You're an empathetic person. Maybe you didn't want to know?"

Renee considered the question. Did she not want to know? Could it be related to her not wanting to deal with being biracial? "You used to accuse me of being racist. Do you still think that's true? Maybe that's why I avoid knowing?"

"No." Gina leaned forward. "I've realized over the years that you have no choice because people see you as white and they treat you as white. As I did." She looked uncomfortable but rushed on. "But I still believe your white skin affords you a life of white privilege that makes it difficult for you to grasp what having brown or black skin means."

"I can't change my skin color, Gina, and I may never really get it, but I really do want to try. I'm sorry I was so insensitive when we were together. But every time we tried to talk about race and racism we ended up screaming at each other. I think I felt under siege and I didn't know how to be different. Obviously, I still don't know but I'm ready to grapple with who I am in the world."

"You're not the only one with problems, Renee." Gina shifted so they were face-to-face again. "I owe you a couple of apologies. I apologize for having the hubris to assume I knew what being you felt like and for accusing you of being a racist. I now believe The Black Student Alliance, me included, was racist for rejecting you because you didn't fit what we thought of as black. And I'm sorry that at the same time I was rejecting you as not black enough, I was putting a lot of energy into seducing you. I especially cringe remembering that I was so ashamed of being involved with you that I insisted we hide not only our casual sexual encounters, but even what we thought was going to be a long-term relationship in our senior year. Sometimes I felt crazy because I loved you and I hated you at the same time." She squeezed Renee's hand. "I hope I'm not the reason you're in therapy."

"No. It's me." Renee considered whether she should share the reason with Gina. She was tired of secrets. "Actually, I've carried a torch for Darcy more than twenty years. No let me correct that. I thought I carried a torch for Darcy but I'm learning that I used imagined feelings to keep myself from committing to anyone."

Gina laughed. "Thank God. I've worried that you swore off anything permanent after me. Interesting that you used Darcy and not me. Maybe it's because we were both so wounded by our relationship that deciding to end it was a relief. I know I couldn't think about you at all for the first year. It took a few years to heal, to remember what I loved about you. But you never had a chance to end your relationship with Darcy. Didn't she get together with Tori while you were still thinking you could get back together at some point?"

"True. But I'm starting to see that it's not Darcy but something deeper I need to deal with. Self-hate is part of it. I go into every relationship expecting to be rejected because I'm biracial."

"Self-hate because you're biracial?" Her voice dropped to a whisper. "Oh lord, did I contribute to that?"

"You might have fanned the flames a bit, but believe me, it started long before I met you. I've just become aware of it in therapy so I'm still trying to get a handle on it."

She could feel Gina pulling into herself, probably feeling guilty. "You didn't cause it, Gina, I promise. Don't withdraw. We were young and we were who we were then. And now I need you to help me deal with my own racism." She leaned in to hug Gina and kiss her cheek.

Gina relaxed. "Thanks, Renee. I'm here."

Time to talk about something happier. "On a lighter note, call it fate or the universe laughing at me, the week after Darcy and Andrea's wedding when I was feeling down, I reconnected with the only woman besides you and Darcy who I could ever see a future with. Her name is Constance. We were involved at Stanford when she was a senior undergrad and I was a first-year graduate student. She's single and the attraction still seems to be there for both of us. We've agreed to take things slowly and see how it goes."

"I'm really happy for you. I hate seeing you so down, and though you always put up a good front, I could see how lonely and unhappy you've been." She glanced at her phone. "I wish I could stay and hear all about Constance, but I have a seven a.m. meeting tomorrow. Can we do this again very soon?"

Renee pulled Gina up into a hug. "Thanks for listening, for being honest, and for always supporting me. Have you ever wondered if we could have made it together?"

"I used to think about it from time to time but not since I've been with Beth. She's definitely my future. But if you and I met today as the women we've become, we'd have a much better chance of making it than we had as college students."

Renee helped her into her coat and they hugged again.

Gina whispered in Renee's ear. "But between you and me, I sometimes miss being with the most perfectly gentlemanly woman I've ever met." She kissed her lightly on the lips. "I'm always available to talk, even when I'm on the road. Call me."

Renee watched her until the elevator doors closed.

CHAPTER FOURTEEN

"So I decided I wanted to see Constance. I took her to the opera Friday night. It was wonderful."

Olivia didn't comment so she continued. "It turned out she knew exactly why I'd run and she wasn't angry. We talked a little about…us. She said she'd been in a state of suspended animation all those years with Nigel and I was bringing her back to life." Renee felt herself getting emotional and took a moment to breathe and stay in control. "I've done the same thing. Lived in a state of suspended animation all my life, trying to protect myself but actually isolating myself and only half living. For a long time I only felt alive when I was having sex or when women were coming on to me. And yet, when things got too intense and the women wanted to get inside my wall, I used my love for Darcy to shut them down." Renee held her breath trying to hold back the sobs pushing up from deep inside, but eventually she had no choice but to let go. She covered her face with her hands, doubled over in her chair and let the pain out. When she had no tears left, she looked up into Olivia's sympathetic face. She sat back. "Sorry."

Olivia smiled. "I'm not." She shifted back in her chair. "How do you feel?"

"Better. But I didn't know I felt bad." She pulled a tissue out of the box on the table next to her and blew her nose. "It's painful to think I've willingly spent most of my life in an isolated bubble."

"Do you understand why you made that choice?"

She considered the question. "It felt safer?" She thought that was it but she wasn't sure and it came out as a question. She looked at Olivia for confirmation. Olivia nodded.

"I think I expect to be left so when I care for someone enough to be hurt by their leaving, I leave first." She stared out the window, trying to work out why she was who she was.

Olivia let her stew for a minute then pulled her back to the session with questions. "Are you loveable, Renee? Do you think you deserve to be loved?"

She swiveled to Olivia. "Loveable? Isn't everyone?" Her gaze went to the window again. She took a deep breath. "Maybe not." The voices were so clear they could have been right there in Olivia's office. But they weren't. They were in her head. And had been for as long as she could remember. "The voices in my head don't think so."

"The voices?" Olivia sounded surprised. "What do they say?"

"One of them says, 'Ugly white girl. Nobody will ever love you.' The other says, 'Nobody will love a white girl who's really black.'"

"Whose voices are they?"

"Mine, I suppose." She shrugged. "I've heard them forever."

"Think, Renee." Olivia leaned toward her. "This is important. Who could have put those thoughts in your head?"

She stared at her hands clasped tightly in her lap and let her mind wander, hoping it would find the answer. She closed her eyes, shutting the world out and listened. Pictures flitted through her mind. The voices echoed in her head. She sat straighter and looked at Olivia. "Remember I said neither side of my family was thrilled about my parents' marriage. All my siblings have the same or lighter skin tone as my mom but I have my dad's blue eyes and white skin." She stared at her hands still clenched in her lap and made no attempt to dry the tears streaming down her face. "When I was about five years old I spent a day with my mom's two sisters in New Jersey while she took care of some business. I overheard them talking about me. 'Poor baby, looks white but is black. She won't fit anywhere.' And my three girl cousins who were older than me, followed me around saying over and over. 'You aren't black. You don't belong in our family. Nobody will ever love an ugly white girl like you.' When I told my mom, she said my cousins were jealous because I was so beautiful. But after less than forty-eight hours with her family, we left and moved to a hotel. That was the first and last time I saw my mom's family other than my grandmother who visited us in Paris."

"Did your grandmother disparage you?"

"She was great. She believed as most of her generation did, that the lighter the skin the better. On the other hand, my white skin and blue eyes troubled my paternal grandmother. Whenever we were alone she would act like she was sad for me but she would say, 'Poor baby. Who will love you knowing your babies might be black?'"

"And how did your parents deal with this?"

"I was about seven when they realized what Dad's mom was saying to me and we never visited her again." Renee started to drift off.

"Renee." Hearing Olivia say her name, she looked up. "I know this is hard but try to stay focused. Did your mom and dad ever talk to you about it?"

"Yes, they did. But the words were already engraved in my mind. I've heard them many times since, but until today I thought they were my thoughts, not voices from the past. I'm starting to see that being mixed race was a big factor in my life. Being rejected by both sides of my family not only made me feel unlovable but it led me to expect everyone to reject me. So even though I was the one who rejected Darcy, I felt left by her when she got involved with Tori. And even though I knew Gina loved me and we decided together to separate because we couldn't communicate around race and class, I felt she rejected me. I didn't know why Constance rejected me, so, based on nothing at all, I decided it was because I'm biracial."

"How do you feel, Renee?"

"Drained. Exhausted. Brain dead." She summoned a weak smile. "I guess that sums it up."

"We have to stop now." Olivia stood. "Remember, you can call me if you need to talk before our next session."

CHAPTER FIFTEEN

Saturday morning Renee called to invite Tori and Elle to dinner at her apartment Monday night when their restaurant Buonasola would be closed. Cooking for a chef could be intimidating, but Renee had cooked enough lunches and dinners when they'd all been at Darcy's Fire Island house to know that Tori was never critical and always enjoyed having meals prepared for her. She decided Maman's recipe for Beef Bourguignon would allow her to cook ahead of time and the stew would taste even better when reheated. Saturday afternoon she shopped for the ingredients. Sunday she relaxed at home, cooking the stew while prepping the salad and fresh fruit for dessert, reading, listening to music, and thinking about Constance. A lot. She'd enjoyed their evening and felt close to Constance, who hadn't even brought up Renee's almost weeklong disappearance.

The meal was a success. Elle insisted on helping Renee clean up after dinner while Tori, happy to be off her feet, sat and kibitzed. "Have you decided to go to Paris for New Year's Eve?"

Renee had been thinking about inviting Constance to come with her to Paris, but what to do with the girls stymied her.

Maybe if Constance didn't want to come to Paris with her, she'd stay in New York City. "I promised my mom and dad I'd spend two weeks in Paris over the holidays. The weeks I planned include New Year's Eve, but, I'm not sure yet." She placed the demitasse cups and the fruit salad on a tray. "Thanks for helping me clean up, Elle." She poured the espresso. "Let's sit in the living room."

Tori helped herself to some fruit. "You were definite about New Year's Eve two weeks ago and now you sound unsure. What's up?"

Renee dropped the lemon peel into her espresso, collecting her thoughts. "How did you feel when you first realized you were no longer in love with Darcy?"

Tori thought for a minute. "It wasn't so much realizing that I stopped loving Darcy as it was realizing that Elle was the one I was thinking about constantly. Elle was the one I wanted to be making love with. Elle was the one I wanted by my side all the time. It took me a while to understand that as much as I still adored and admired Darcy, I wasn't in love with her any more."

Renee nodded. "I've been thinking a lot about Constance. And not so much about Darcy." She sipped her espresso. "Actually, other than in therapy, not at all about Darcy. But there are complications. She's a widow with fourteen-year-old twin daughters." Renee laughed as the eyebrows on Tori's porcelain white face and Elle's darker face shot up at the same instant. "Yes, while I was jumping from bed to bed with hundreds of women, Constance entered a planned marriage and had an unplanned pregnancy. I won't go into the details. If you meet her you can wring the story out of her."

Tori snorted. "What do you mean if? You are obviously so into this woman that I have no doubt we will meet her, and I, for one, will definitely get the story." She popped a grape into her mouth.

Renee glanced at Elle. She shrugged. "Don't look at me. You know I have absolutely no control over Tori." She reached for a piece of pineapple.

As usual, Tori went to the heart of the matter. "So now you have strong feelings for Constance and you think you're not in love with Darcy?"

"Yes. I discovered in therapy that I expect to be rejected, so I reject women before they can reject me." Renee blushed. "It sounds stupid I know. I believed I was in love with Darcy all these years. But, as you suggested, Tori, it seems I was using Darcy to protect myself from rejection. In fact, I was in love with Constance in graduate school, but she dumped me and I was so hurt I could never admit it or let myself think about it."

"Wow. All these years and you never let yourself know. You must be the queen of denial." Tori waved a hand. "But I interrupted. Please go on."

"Very astute, Tori. My therapist said essentially the same thing. But, back to Constance. I would like to spend New Year's Eve with her, if possible, but she can't just run off to Paris and leave the girls here. I'm not sure whether she already has plans or even whether she'd want to be with me on New Year's Eve, but it's possible I would go to Paris and then come back to the city and spend it with her. Or I could stay here for New Year's Eve and then fly to Paris later to be with my family."

Tori took Renee's hand. "I know you're brilliant because Darcy, whom we both love dearly, could only get serious with brilliant women like you and me."

Elle snorted but Tori ignored her. "But you are definitely overthinking here. Millions of people manage to have relationships with teenagers in the picture. Yes, it's more complicated, but as they say, where there's a will, there's a way. You have another five plus weeks to figure this out, but remember New Year's Eve isn't a make-or-break date. Life, and dating, will go on after January first. I suggest you try to relax and enjoy your time with Constance. Songfest is coming up. Bring her. And her daughters. Erik and Joel and their two teenaged daughters will be there. And, if you're so inclined, feel free to invite the three of them to our Thanksgiving dinner."

CHAPTER SIXTEEN

Constance sounded anxious when Renee called to wish her luck early in the day. This was her first show in the United States and she wanted it to be a success. She was also anxious because the paintings she'd done since Nigel's death were very different than those she'd done before and she had no idea how they'd be received. Renee tried to reassure her, but she knew from her parents that every artist, even one as successful as her dad, had pre-show nerves.

Yet Renee was nervous as she approached the gallery. What if she didn't like Constance's work? Should she lie? That wouldn't be fair to Constance. She deserved the truth. Damn, she'd hate their budding friendship to end because of art. Damn, damn, this is what happens when you let yourself care about someone. But she did care so she'd have to figure it out. She stopped short. With all their artist friends, her mom would know how to handle this situation. She checked the time. It was after midnight in Paris but her parents were night owls so she stepped into a doorway near the gallery and called. "Maman, I need help. I'm about to enter a gallery where a very close friend, a painter, is having her first American show. What do I say if I don't like the work?"

"Who is this artist?"

"She's English. Her name is Constance Martindale and I believe she's had shows in London."

"Martindale? The name is familiar." Renee listened to her mom switch to French to speak to her dad. "As I thought, we've seen her work in London and we believe you'll like it but it's always difficult. Even if the work doesn't speak to you, try to find something to praise. And, of course, don't offer any criticism unless she asks for it. Most of all, be honest. A true artist will understand not everyone will love everything they do."

"Thank you, Maman. I have to go now, love to papa, good night." Happy that the question of whether she would be there for New Year's Eve hadn't come up, and feeling more confident about dealing with Constance's art, she straightened her tie and entered the gallery.

It was packed. She was impressed. Constance must have a following to have a solo exhibit in such a prestigious gallery and to draw such a huge crowd. Good for her. Renee scanned the room, and not seeing Constance, politely shouldered her way to the rear where the paintings were hung. She moved along until she found what she thought was the starting point, the earliest dated painting. Constance's earlier works expressed sadness and rage through the use of dark, aggressive colors with an occasional slash of a bright color. It was contained yet strong, with glimpses of wildness. Then after the twins were born her palette became softer, the paintings were lighter, happier. That period stopped abruptly when, judging by the date, Nigel was murdered, and a series of melancholy and darker canvases followed. The last three painting were done in the last four months and Renee was stunned by the transformation. These paintings were bold and exciting and so beautiful her breath caught. She smiled. She should have known Constance would never have shown her work if it wasn't brilliant. Each painting in the exhibit made a statement about the life of the artist, but taken together they showed her resilience and strength. Constance's art declared, "I survived. I am here. I am alive. I am free."

She couldn't wait to discuss the work with Constance. Renee moved to a corner with a flute of champagne and scanned the room again but still no sign of Constance. She blinked. No, she wasn't seeing double. That must be Chloe and Cara huddled together looking lost and sullen and ready to run. She flashed back to herself standing alone and gawky at so many of her dad's openings, wishing she could disappear but forced to be pleasant to well-meaning adults who tried to engage her. At least they had each other. She was surprised to see the girls raise their phones, obviously taking pictures of the crowd, and even more surprised when they seemed to focus on her. Interesting. Had they noticed her staring?

The twins had inherited Constance's beauty but were too young to have acquired her grace and self-assurance. Something about their vulnerability reminded her of the young Constance she'd known at Stanford and her heart filled with a feeling she didn't recognize. Hoping they wouldn't resent her, she headed over to try to make them comfortable.

But Constance hadn't mentioned introducing her to Chloe and Cara. The girls were probably still fragile from the loss of their dad and Constance would probably want to protect them, not expose them to women who may or may not stay in their lives. Would she be angry? Maybe. But they were here in public and obviously distressed so she went with her impulse to rescue them. "Hi, you must be Chloe and Cara."

The girls looked at each other. "And you are?" one of them said, in Constance's poufy English accent. "It's not fair that you know us but we have no idea who you are," the other twin said. "You might even be a serial killer." The first one spoke again.

They not only looked like Constance they sounded like her. And they both had definitely inherited her spirit. Renee laughed. "I promise I'm not a serial killer. My dad is an artist too so I had to stand around at a lot of openings like this when I was your age. Bor-ring."

"Tell us about it. We thought it would be more fun, didn't we, Cara?"

"Yes," Cara said. "But if you're not a serial killer, who are you?"

The look Cara gave Renee was so like Constance, Renee almost laughed. What must it feel like to have miniature versions of you running around? "Actually, I'm an old friend of your mom's. From her days at Stanford."

The girls exchanged a glance. "Ooh, so can you tell us some stories about her wild youth?"

Renee grinned. "Maybe when I know you better. I'm Renee Rousseau. So which one of you is Chloe and which is Cara? And don't try to trick me, please."

"I'm Chloe," they said at the same time. They giggled.

Renee laughed. "So two bodies, one person? No individuality?"

They looked insulted. "We started out as one egg but we're definitely two people. I'm Chloe and she is Cara."

"For real?" They both nodded. She studied them looking for something that would allow her to tell them apart.

"Hey, you're being weird." Chloe spoke again while Cara snapped a picture of Renee. "It's only right we get a picture for proof in case you're evil. Why are you staring at us?"

"Just trying to see if I can tell you apart, Chloe. It's difficult without really knowing you, but I'll learn."

"Mummy can, but no one else…except Daddy could." The girls seemed to deflate at mention of their late father.

Renee took one of each of their hands. "I was so sorry to hear about what happened to your dad. It sounds like he was a hero. You must miss him terribly."

Each of the twins put an arm around the other's waist, as if needing to hold on when thinking about their loss. "Yeah, he was," Chloe said, "and we do miss him. So does Mum." She pulled her hand away to wipe her eyes. "But we shouldn't be sad tonight, Cara." She scanned the room. "We should be happy for Mum." Cara nodded and wiped her tears.

Renee followed Chloe's gaze. Her heart did a little flip. Her daughter had located Constance in the crowd, talking with a group of people. She was glowing and her audience looked totally enchanted. No surprise there. Who wouldn't be enchanted by Constance? "This is a big night for your mom. Her paintings are wonderful and judging by all the red dots next to them, it looks like the show is a success."

"She's been painting like a madwoman." Cara sighed. "Maybe now we can have some fun and see some of New York City besides school and home."

"Ah, has your evil mom kept you two locked up while she painted for the show?"

They eyed her, not sure how to take her remark, not sure to trust her with their feelings.

"Hey, I was kidding. I know she's not evil. What kind of things would you like to do?"

The twins exchanged one of those glances that probably meant they were silently checking in with each other. Apparently she'd passed some test and the two girls began to list the things they had in mind. "We'd like to go to Broadway musicals, and some off-Broadway shows too. We want to ice skate in Rockefeller Center and see the Empire State building, the High Line, the Statue of Liberty, the UN, Radio City Music Hall, Coney Island, the World Trade Center museum, the opera, the World Financial Center, Brooklyn, eat ethnic food in Queens—"

"Whoa." Renee held up her hand to interrupt. "I get the picture. I can help you start on your list but some things should wait for warmer weather. "You like music? Do you sing like your mom?"

"We used to when Daddy was…before he died."

She thought it was Cara who answered but it didn't matter. She'd made them sad again and for some reason it was important that they be happy. "We'd have to ask your mom's permission but if she's all right with it, I could do some of those things with you. We could walk on the High Line, tour the UN, and eat in Queens any time. Other things like skating in Rockefeller Center, the theater and opera require reservations and planning, so they couldn't be done right away. And some things would be better in spring or summer."

"Really?" They smiled, moved closer to her, and without any discussion each of them touched one of her arms.

Touchy, feely, just like their mother. Renee didn't know how she could be around three of those smiles without losing her heart. She wanted to connect with them. "You know when I was your age and forced to go to openings, I would make up stories about the people who were there."

Chloe brightened. "We do that too. In fact, we watched you study each of Mum's paintings and not pay attention to all the chattering fools so we made up a story that you would ask Mums out. At first we thought you were a man, but then we decided you were too beautiful."

Renee flushed. She bowed slightly. "Thank you." She considered saying something about her intention to ask their mom out but decided it wasn't appropriate.

"Renee Rousseau, are you seducing my daughters?" Her voice ran through Renee's body like a lightning bolt. Maybe she'd already lost her heart. But more likely that voice was fanning the embers of lust that had been burning all these years. "Constance." She hugged her. "Congratulations. The show is wonderful. I love the paintings. And so does everyone else, obviously. I'd love to discuss your work when you have some time." She looked up at the clicks of a camera.

Renee tried to step away but Constance wrapped her arm around Renee's waist and kissed her cheek. "Thank you, Renee, that means a lot coming from you. I see you've met Cara and Chloe." More clicks.

Before Renee could respond, the twins jumped in all excited about Renee taking them sightseeing. When Constance didn't comment, Renee hurried to explain. "With your consent, of course."

The three of them tensed, waiting for Constance's approval.

Constance cleared her throat, started to speak, then had to clear her throat again. "Only if I can come too." Her voice was almost a whisper. She dug her fingers into Renee's side.

While the girls talked to each other, Constance whispered in Renee's ear. "I was so afraid you wouldn't..." She took a breath. "I was afraid you wouldn't want to be around children, especially teenaged girls."

Renee didn't know what to say without saying more than she was ready to say. But she had to respond. She glanced at the girls. They were still discussing whether the High Line could be combined with a tour of Queens, so she spoke softly. "How could I resist two miniatures of you?" The tension between them was intense. Time to inject a little humor. "Maybe I'm a masochist. As if one of you wasn't enough, now there are three of you to torture me. So am I a glutton for punishment or what?"

Constance punched her arm lightly. "You'll live." She grinned. "Maybe."

Click, click.

Rather than a tiny ember, it seemed like a roaring fire, and humor was stoking it, not tamping it down. She needed to cool down. A change of the subject was in order. "Hey, what's with the pictures? I'm beginning to feel like a movie star."

"They're for the Grandees." Only one of the girls spoke but they both snapped pictures.

"Grandees?" Renee was puzzled. "Dignitaries?"

Constance laughed. "Yes, the word means dignitaries but I doubt they knew that at two-and-a-half-years-old when they surprised me and Nigel by referring to our parents collectively that way. Anyway, they promised their grandparents they would record our lives in New York City for them. So if you're going to hang around with us, you'd better get used to it."

The twins leaned on Constance. "Can we leave, Mum?"

"In a while, Cara. Remember, I said no whining." Constance turned to Renee. "Can you come home with us? We'll order something for dinner. I'd like to discuss the show with you and we can come up with some sightseeing dates."

"Sure." She couldn't wait to discuss the paintings. Besides, she was curious about Constance's apartment, and to her surprise, she was looking forward to spending time with her and the girls.

"I have to be here at least another hour until the gallery closes. So please be patient, girls." She turned to Renee. "Can you keep them occupied?"

"I'll try." But the girls were antsy and muttering about starving and she could see Constance glancing anxiously in their direction. Renee decided to take the situation in hand. She pulled Constance aside. "The girls are hungry. How about I take them up to Trattoria Montero and you meet us there when you're done? Or if you'd rather, give me a key and I'll pick up some takeout and take them home."

Constance glared at her. "Are you trying to worm your way into my bed by being nice to my girls, Renee?"

Renee rocked back, away from Constance, and searched for words to explain. Constance laughed. "You should see your face, Renee. Don't worry. I know you don't have to resort to tricks to get women in your bed. Besides, I'm sure you would never use Chloe and Cara that way."

"You're evil, Constance. I don't know why I want to spend time with you."

"Because you like me? Yes?" Constance's smile was a thing of beauty.

Click, click.

"Yes, you infuriating bitch. Now, what about dinner?"

"Trattoria Montero is perfect; they love Italian. But are you sure you want to be alone with them?"

"I wouldn't have asked if I didn't want to. So we'll see you there. Do you remember where it is?"

"I do. It'll probably take longer than an hour for me to get out of here and then I need time to get uptown, so don't wait for me to order." She touched Renee's shoulder. "Thank you for doing this."

Mrs. Montero immediately recognized the girls as Constance's daughters. She fussed over them, discussing what they liked to eat and suggesting appetizers that might challenge their tastes.

Chloe ordered first. "Chicken parmesan, please."

"I'll have spaghetti and meatballs, please," Cara said.

"And linguini in white clam sauce for me," Renee said. "Also we'll share stuffed clams, *scungilli* salad, stuffed peppers, and grilled octopus."

"Octopus? Eew." The girls made a face at each other. "What's a *scungilli*?" Cara said.

Renee laughed. "It's conch. You should try everything and decide whether you like it after you taste it." She turned to Mrs. Montero. "I'd also like a glass of pinot grigio."

Click, click.

"Can we have wine too?" She thought it was Chloe who asked.

Renee was pretty sure little English girls didn't have wine with dinner. "Does your mom allow you to drink wine?"

Chloe and Cara eyed each other. It was probably Cara who answered. "No, but we're old enough."

Renee had grown up drinking wine from the time she wanted it, watered in the beginning of course. She looked at Mrs. Montero and spoke in Italian. "Since it's their first time please give them a little wine mixed with a lot of seltzer."

"Will it be all right with Constance?" Mrs. Montero answered in Italian.

Renee didn't know how Constance would feel but she felt it was important to establish trust with the girls. She answered in Italian. "I'll take responsibility. Better they learn to drink in a safe environment." She turned to the girls. "When I was your age I had wine mixed with sparkling water and that's what I'm ordering for you."

"Three wines coming up," Mrs. Montero said. Chloe and Cara were wide-eyed.

When Constance arrived, they were laughing hysterically at a story Renee was telling them about her college days. Renee saw her standing in the doorway to the dining room watching them. What did she see? The girls had enjoyed their wine but they seemed normal. They were having a good time and so was she.

Click, click.

Renee hardly noticed the cameras.

Constance sat. She still had that glow but she was clearly exhausted. Mrs. Montero appeared with a goblet of red wine. "Your lasagna will be out shortly, Constance."

"Thank you, Mrs. Montero. What wonderful service." Mrs. Montero was all smiles. "Your daughters are *bellissima*, just like you."

"And thank you again." Her eyes wandered around the table as she drank some wine. "All right you three, what's going on?"

Renee opened her mouth but the twins spoke over her, their excitement evident. "Renee let us have wine with dinner."

Constance looked at Renee, her eyebrows raised. "Wine? Is that why you're all so happy?"

Renee cleared her throat. "They had wine but they're not drunk. We've been having a good time telling stories."

"Yes, Mums, we've been having a jolly time with Renee." She thought it was Cara speaking.

The other twin jumped in. "We're not drunk, Mummie. Renee let us have wine mixed with sparkling water so we'd know what to expect when someone offers us a drink."

"And how are you feeling, my darlings?"

Was Constance as calm as she appeared? Or was she just waiting to explode? Renee hoped she wouldn't attack her in front of the girls.

They glanced at each other. "Good," they said in unison. "We didn't really like the taste of the wine so we won't drink it until we're older."

That was interesting. They hadn't told her they didn't like it. But at least they know. She felt as if she was waiting for the ax to fall.

Constance's lasagna was delivered and she turned her attention to eating. The girls excused themselves to go to the bathroom. Renee was relieved to see that neither was stumbling as they walked across the room. She turned to Constance and found her staring. "Are you all right with them having wine? It was mostly sparkling water but they asked for it and I thought it was better for them to try it in a safe environment."

"You thought?" Constance didn't raise her voice but it was clear she wasn't happy. "Where do you come off making those kinds of decisions for *my* daughters?"

Renee bristled. "I'm sorry. They were here with me and you weren't. I was given watered-down wine when just a few years old and I rejected it until I was twelve. In my family and in France it's not such a big deal. Anyway, I didn't mean to overstep my bounds. Or usurp your authority."

Renee focused on her wineglass, leaving Constance to eat and relax without having to engage. When the girls didn't return, she realized they had figured out she and Constance were arguing and were giving them privacy to discuss it. She looked toward the bathroom and Mrs. Montero pointed to the kitchen. So she'd seen it too and was keeping the girls away.

She glanced at Constance. Her hands were in her lap, her eyes were focused on her plate, and tears were trickling down her face. She reached for Constance's hand expecting to be pushed away. Instead, Constance gripped her hand tightly. Eyes still down, she spoke softly. "I'm so sorry, Renee. You didn't do anything wrong. I agree it's best for them to learn about alcohol under adult supervision and I trust that you made sure they had enough to taste it but not enough to get sick."

Renee leaned, in straining to hear.

Constance shifted to face her. "Since Nigel died, I've had to do everything and make every decision for the three of us. I've been deathly afraid of screwing up, of hurting the girls. Bringing them to New York City so far from everybody and everything familiar petrified me. I've had us all on a tight leash and it's difficult to let go. I would never have guessed you'd be so good with them. In fact, I wavered about bringing them tonight because I wasn't sure I should introduce you. But I was thrilled to see you with them at the gallery and even happier that you seemed to like each other.

"When I watched the three of you from the doorway my heart split open. The girls haven't laughed like that, seemed so much like themselves, since we got the news about Nigel. But when they told me about the wine, I felt totally out of control. Only a bad mother would let a stranger make that kind of decision for her daughters. All my feelings of inadequacy rose up. It really had nothing to do with you." She raised their joined hands and kissed Renee's knuckles. "Please forgive me for acting like you would do something to hurt Chloe and Cara."

Renee squeezed Constance's hand. She admired her fierce love for her daughters and her willingness to do anything to shield them from hurt. It reminded Renee of her own mother.

"It's all right, Constance. I really do enjoy them. And whatever happens or doesn't happen between you and me, I hope you'll let me spend time with them." She could feel Constance relax.

Constance kissed Renee's knuckles again. "So you prefer the younger models to the older tried-and-true one?"

Renee grinned. "I do like the younger models and I think I'm even starting to be able to tell them apart. But give me tried-and-true every time." She didn't hear the clicks but she glanced toward the kitchen and saw the phones pointed at them.

"Glad to hear it." Constance flashed one of her light-up-the-room smiles. "So how do you tell them apart?"

Renee watched the girls cross the room carrying desserts to the table. "Cara is more reserved than Chloe. She has the same stillness you have when you're thinking through something. Chloe is like you when you're being playful and teasing. They both have both elements but I think that's one thing that differentiates them."

"Correct." Constance nodded. "You know, Renee, I'm exhausted. Would you mind if the girls and I go home after they eat dessert? Let's get together over the weekend to talk about the show and arrange a time for the four of us to do something together."

Renee worried all day Saturday that once Constance had time to think about her taking on a parental role last night, she might pull away. She was pleasantly surprised when late in the afternoon her phone rang and it was Constance. "Well, Renee, you certainly did a fabulous job of seducing my innocent girls. They want to make you pancakes tomorrow so I'm charged with inviting you to brunch."

Her lighthearted tone made Renee smile. "You are so wrong. Those two little Constance dolls seduced me. And the little devils already know the way to a woman's heart is through her stomach. I'd be delighted to come for pancakes."

"See you at noon. Don't worry, I'll protect you." Constance was laughing as she cut the connection.

An image of the four of them as a family flashed through her mind, leaving her with a stupid grin on her face, feeling giddy. She stared at the phone in her hand. Suddenly she wanted to see Constance, and she was surprised to realize, the twins, immediately. Should she call back and invite them to her apartment for dinner tonight?

Her feelings for Chloe and Cara astonished her. Just a few days ago she was sure they would be a problem for her having any kind of a relationship with Constance. Now after one evening spent together, she was smitten. But was it them or Constance she was smitten with? Chloe and Cara had touched something inside of her, bringing up feelings about herself as a child, her loneliness, her awkwardness. She felt a strong impulse to help them through the minefield of teenage angst, an impulse to protect them, an impulse to make them happy. And, if she was honest, to take on some of the burden Constance was carrying.

Was she in love with Constance? She could only compare it to falling in love with Darcy. With Darcy, she was so young and naïve, unformed really, and she felt like she was in a freefall from an airplane, tumbling through the air, unable to do anything to stop the inevitable crash to earth. It was thrilling but the total loss of control terrified her.

Renee took a deep breath. Her feelings for Constance were different. Though the fireworks were there and the sexual attraction and the desire to make love to Constance were as strong as they had been with Darcy, her impulse was to run toward her, not away. The only frightening thing was that she might screw it up. She would follow the plan and go slowly.

CHAPTER SEVENTEEN

Renee arrived at noon with flowers and chocolates for the three of them. Constance opened the door. She kissed Renee's cheek and thanked her, then led her to the kitchen where the girls were prepping the pancakes. Chloe and Cara were thrilled with the gifts and shyly hugged Renee. Constance watched with a sweet smile.

After the flowers were taken care of, Constance showed Renee around the apartment. The living room, Constance's bedroom with a private bath and shower, the bedroom the girls shared and a third bedroom with a private bathroom between them, all overlooked Riverside Park and had beautiful views of the Hudson River. The kitchen, the dining room, a maid's room that served as an office, a fourth bedroom and a bathroom all faced an interior courtyard.

Constance led her into the comfortably but nicely furnished living room and moved some books off the couch so she and Renee could sit. Renee thumbed through a nearby book. "I noticed these sketchbooks, pencils, and charcoals everywhere in the house."

Constance laughed. "The girls are always complaining that I'm messy, but I often have the impulse to sketch something I see or something that flits into my imagination, so I like to have a pad handy to capture the image."

"Do you paint here or just in your studio? How often do you paint?"

"I have an easel and paints in a closet in the office but I only use it if the girls are sick and need me at home during the day or if I'm inspired in the middle of the night, which doesn't happen that often since I paint in my studio just about every weekday and occasionally on the weekend."

"Is your studio near here?"

"It's in a converted industrial building owned by a really lovely lesbian NYPD detective. It's in the Meat Packing District."

Renee felt a sharp pang of jealousy. She hadn't realized that Constance knew any other lesbians in New York City. "So how did you meet this…*lovely* lesbian landlord?"

"Ooh, Renee, do I hear a trace of jealousy in your voice?"

"No." She felt bad lying. Constance already knew she cared so what was the harm. "Yes. I'm surprised you know another lesbian. How did you meet her?"

Constance put her hand on Renee's thigh and leaned into her. "You have nothing to worry about, dear girl. She's lovely, but not my type at all. The art teacher at the girls' school knew I was looking for a studio when we first arrived, so when she heard this studio was available, she passed the information on to me. So I called and the super's wife, another lesbian artist, showed me the studio. I didn't meet the owner until after I'd signed the lease. You might have read about her. Chiara was shot when she and her partner captured the killer of a couple of gay guys and a lesbian. She was at home rehabbing and the super introduced us in the lobby one day."

"A damned hero, no less." Renee couldn't help feeling outclassed.

Constance elbowed Renee. "Don't be so grumpy. I don't expect you to run around capturing bad guys and getting yourself shot."

"Are you sure?" Renee elbowed her back. "Because I would, though I'd rather not." She needed to change the subject. "So tell me about the studio."

"It's the top floor of the building, one wall of windows faces south toward the World Financial Center and the other wall of windows faces west and has a view of New Jersey and the Hudson River, plus there's a skylight. The light is incredible and it was empty so I was able to move in and start painting right away."

Constance was describing how she'd set up the studio when Chloe came to escort them to the table. She served them orange juice and coffee while Cara cooked the cottage cheese pancakes they'd prepped.

Cara proudly carried a huge platter of pancakes to the table and put three on each of their plates. Chloe handed Renee a large bowl of strawberries, mango, and blueberries then poured more coffee, tea, and juice for everyone.

Three sets of green eyes were on Renee as she lifted her fork. Damn, she hadn't thought this through. What if the pancakes were awful? Was she risking damaging her fragile connection with the girls? Her mother's advice about Constance's paintings popped into her head, find something you like and mention that, tell the truth gently. She took the first bite of pancake and chewed slowly. Thank heavens they were delicious. "Yum. Am I being too piggy to ask for seconds before I've even finished my firsts?"

The girls giggled and reassured her she could have as many as she wanted. Chloe passed the platter to Renee. "Thank you for inviting me for brunch. Do you both enjoy cooking?"

Chloe put her orange juice down. "We both cook. Cara's better at eggs and pancakes and breakfast things than I am, so she usually does them, but we both like to do dinners."

"Where did you learn to cook?"

The girls giggled again. "We learned from our fabulous live-in cook, a very lovely woman named Lady Constance Worthington. She taught us everything we know."

Renee turned to Constance. "No live-in cook? You actually cook?"

"Yes. To both questions." Constance blushed. "It's not so outlandish, you know."

"I knew you were a woman of many talents but somehow I pictured you the lady of the manor eating chocolates while the cook and the butler and—"

The laughter of the three blond beauties stopped Renee short. "What? No chocolates?"

Chloe was the first to gain control. "No, Renee, no servants. We were so embarrassed…" The three of them went off again, obviously a family joke. "We were the only ones in our posh school without tons of servants." She cracked up again.

Constance put her hand on top of Renee's. "Sorry, we're being so silly. Nigel and I didn't want a house full of servants. We decided we could open our own doors, dress ourselves and drive our own car but neither of us liked to clean house or garden so we had people come in to do those things. We both loved to cook, though I did most of it since he worked, and I was at home caring for the girls and painting. The girls helped Nigel and me cook and clean up from a very early age. As I remember, you cook as well."

Constance's hand was warm and Renee kept her hand still to prolong the contact. "I do cook, though not as often as I would like. And I too learned by working with my mom."

Chloe clapped her hands. "Ooh, tell us about growing up in Paris."

Renee kept them laughing with stories, some of which seemed hilarious in retrospect but were far from funny at the time. They, even Constance, were intrigued to hear about growing up with four siblings so much older than her, that some of her nieces and nephews were around her age, about the number of nieces and nephews and grandnieces and grandnephews she had, and how hard it was to keep them all straight since she only saw them a few times a year.

With somewhat anxious glances at Constance, Chloe and Cara volunteered some funny stories about their adventures with their dad. Constance laughed along with them and added a comment or two, but she mostly listened, though she seemed to enjoy their easy camaraderie.

Chloe and Cara exchanged a look, then Cara spoke. "Why do you wear men's clothing, Renee?" She glanced at Constance as if expecting to be scolded.

Chloe jumped in before Renee could answer. "We mean it looks very wonderful on you but we just wondered why."

Renee wasn't surprised at the question. She was surprised at the directness of it. "I guess the most obvious answer is I feel good dressing this way. The day I started wearing men's clothing, I felt comfortable with myself in a way that I never had before. I can't really explain it any better than that." She smiled to signal she wasn't upset by the question.

"But do you want to be a man?" Chloe asked.

Renee didn't hesitate. "No. The clothing expresses a part of me but I'm very happy to be a woman."

The twins did that silent communication thing again. This time Cara asked the question. "Are you a lesbian?"

Constance opened her mouth but Renee put a hand up to stop her before she could say anything. "Yes, I am. Does that upset you?"

"No." The girls answered immediately. "We just wanted to know for sure," Chloe said. "Is it all right that we asked?" Cara said.

"Yes," Renee said. "Feel free to ask me anything you want. And if it's something I don't want to discuss, I'll let you know. Is that fair?"

They nodded. "So we have another question." Chloe once again looked at Constance. "You're very beautiful. Given your height, your high cheekbones, gorgeous eyes and beautiful lips, we were wondering whether you ever thought about modeling? Do you look like your mum?"

Constance stood abruptly. "All right, I think that's enough personal questions for today. Why don't you clear the table and clean up the kitchen. Then maybe we can all take a walk in Riverside Park."

Renee took hold of Constance's arm. "It's all right, Constance. Please sit." She tugged Constance back down. "It's natural to be curious. And I meant what I said about wanting you all to feel free to ask me anything." Her gaze moved from one to the other of them.

"I modeled when I was in graduate school to pick up some extra money. I even got to model men's clothing twice which was unusual at the time, but being prodded and posed, and standing around waiting between shots bored me. I wanted to do something that interested me with my life so I stopped after I graduated.

"As for my looks, I do look like my African-American mom. We have the same high cheekbones, same shaped eyes and full lips plus the same body type."

Cara frowned. "But you're white."

"I'm biracial, Cara. My blue eyes, skin color and height come from my dad, who is a white French guy. I look white, but in reality, I'm as much black, as I am white."

"Oh, like Prince Harry's Meghan?"

"Yes, exactly. Do you have any black or mixed-race friends?"

"Our friend Radha in London has an Indian mom and English dad," Chloe said. "And, here in the States, our friends Nora and Sarah are twins like us, and they're mixed something or other but we don't know what. They all have darker complexions than you, though."

The twins had another silent consultation. "So you pass as white?" Chloe said. She seemed almost afraid to ask.

"That's a hard question. As Cara said, I look white so most people assume I am. I don't run around making announcements to the general world about my race or my sexuality, but anyone who knows me, knows I'm biracial, like they know I'm a lesbian." Renee met Constance's eyes.

Constance nodded. "That is correct. And now I really think that's enough questions for today. Go clean up. Give me and Renee some privacy, please."

The twins seemed deflated as they stood and started clearing the table. Renee did not want the day to end on a down note so she stood, put an arm over each girl, and pulled them both close. "Thank you, Chloe and Cara, for a delicious breakfast. I had a lot of fun. Remember what I said. You can ask me anything about anything whenever you want. Can I get a hug?"

They had a three-way hug. "Before you go, I'm looking into getting reservations for us to go ice skating in Rockefeller Center, but I was thinking we could go to the rink in Central Park first, just to practice so we don't look foolish in such a public place. Is that all right with the three of you?"

"Yes," Then, coordinated as usual, the girls hugged her again and bubbling with excitement about ice skating, carried the dishes into the kitchen.

Renee locked eyes with Constance, not sure what to expect. Was Constance upset? Was it because she was forthcoming about being biracial?

Constance broke the contact. "I'd like to get some air. Take a walk with me."

"Sure." Shit. She was in trouble. Well, she wouldn't lie to the girls or to anyone who asked a direct question. Constance would just have to deal with it.

Constance moved into the doorway of the kitchen. "Chloe and Cara, after you clean up please finish your homework. Renee and I are going out for about a half hour."

"Is Renee coming back, Mums?" Renee couldn't tell which twin asked because they sounded the same but it was most likely Chloe.

"We'll see." Constance led Renee to the hall closet and pulled out both their coats.

They were silent in the elevator. Once on the street, Constance put her arm through Renee's and led her across the street to walk on the park side of Riverside Drive. Renee clutched Constance's arm close to her body. If she was ever going to ask this question, now was the time. "When you made the decision to leave Stanford, to leave me, was it because I'm biracial?"

Constance stopped and turned, pulling her arm away from Renee. She glared at Renee. "It never entered my mind. The fact that you are a woman, the fact I was committed to marry a man, the pressure to be a good daughter, the training from birth to be a good royal, loyalty to my country, those were the things that fueled my running away from you."

"Why didn't you tell the girls I'm biracial?"

Constance moved closer and grabbed both of Renee's biceps. "God, Renee, it's not the first thing that comes to mind. I might say you're a tall, beautiful butch who wears men's clothing, or that you have compelling blue bedroom eyes, or that you're sexy and good in bed. I might also add you're intelligent and charming. Or I might say I thought about you every single day after I ran away from you. Somehow the fact that you're biracial has never seemed that important to me." She dropped her hands. "I'm sorry." She walked away.

"Oh." Renee stared after her then followed. When she caught up, she took Constance's arm. "No. I'm sorry. I didn't mean to accuse you of hiding it. It's...I've just become aware in therapy that I use being biracial to explain being rejected. In my mind, that was why you left me."

Constance didn't respond, just kept walking. Renee waited. Finally, Constance broke the silence. "Of course I knew you were biracial since practically the first thing you told me after your name, was that your mother was African-American and your father was a white Frenchman. And you did it again with Chloe and Cara. But I promise it wasn't an issue then and isn't now. I left for all the reasons I mentioned earlier. You seem so confident and make no attempt to pass even though you could. I'm surprised to hear it's an issue for you."

"I was surprised too." Renee laughed. "I think I declare I'm biracial to head off anyone thinking I'm trying to pass. But I'm still exploring the issue in therapy so maybe we should leave it until I have more clarity."

Constance looked up at Renee. "I'm happy to talk whenever you're ready. I appreciate your willingness to be honest with me and your willingness to answer the twins' questions fully and truthfully." She laughed. "By the way, you looked like I was asking you to go outside so I could dump you. I only wanted some alone time with you and I wanted to ask how you felt about their curiosity. They like you and want to know who you are." Constance entwined their fingers. "And so do I, my lovely biracial girl. I'm not running so fast this time. Trust that I'm with you because I want to be. I'm here, unless you clearly state a desire for me to go."

Wow, she had totally misread Constance. Then. And now. "Their questions seem to come from a positive place and I want them to know who I am. You know, I thought I would have a problem with you having two almost-grown daughters but they're wonderful and I really enjoy interacting with them. I'm impressed that their noses aren't always in their phones. You and Nigel did a wonderful job. You should be proud."

"They are wonderful, aren't they? Although there are plenty of times I'm ready to kill them. They weren't allowed to have phones at their school in London. Right before we came here I bought the phones with the understanding they could use the camera and make an occasional phone call. So far they've been good. We'll see how long that lasts." Constance squeezed Renee's fingers as they continued to stroll along Riverside Drive. "You are spot-on with them. In your two times together you've managed to get them to talk about Nigel, to remember the good times with him. And you get them to laugh and be the teenagers they are instead of the worrywarts afraid to mention his name in front of me. Just for that I would want us to spend time with you. But the real reason is you make me feel good too."

Renee stopped abruptly and spun Constance around to face her. "I'm glad I make you feel good. You do the same for me. And so do Chloe and Cara. In a million years I never would have thought that could be true." She dragged her fingers over Constance's cheek, thought about kissing her, but slow seemed to be working so why screw with the formula? "I'm working as hard as I can to be worthy of you, Lady Constance."

Constance stood on her toes and kissed her cheek. "You've always been worthy of me, Renee. That was never the issue."

Renee sighed. "Maybe it's not an issue for you but I've learned in therapy that it's an issue for me. My being worthy of love, that is. I'm still trying to unravel the threads of who I am but I'm getting close."

Constance shivered. "It's kind of cold out here with the wind off the river. Let's head back. It's early. Will you come upstairs for a cup of tea or coffee?"

Renee pivoted them in the direction of Constance's building. "I'd love to give you some feedback on your show, if you're open to hearing it?"

"Oh, yes, please do."

Constance slipped her arm through Renee's and steered them toward her building.

In the apartment, Constance went in the kitchen to prep the tea while Renee sat in the living room ordering her thoughts. Ten minutes later, Constance deposited two mugs, a pot of tea, and a dish of cookies on the coffee table. She poured tea for both of them and handed Renee a mug before sitting on the sofa with her own mug. "So."

Renee cleared her throat. "First, showing the range of paintings, from Stanford to now, highlighted your incredible growth from a good artist to a brilliant one."

Constance put her mug down and shifted on the sofa so they were face-to-face. "Thank you."

Renee took Constance's hands. "Even the earliest ones conveyed your emotions. I could see your youthful vigor and joy, then anger and a period of sadness, then a different kind of joy, more soft and pastel than vivid. I assume that was after Chloe and Cara were born."

Constance nodded. Her eyes were wide and luminous in the late afternoon sunlight streaming through the windows. The intensity of her gaze warmed Renee. "Your paintings are so expressive. Your emotions come through and evoke the viewer's emotions. I could trace your changing moods—happy, sad, angry, and then devastated. I love the totally representational earlier works and the evolution to abstracts but I adored the later works where you combined both. Every single painting is beautiful. But the last three, bold statements of freedom, joy, and love, blew me away. The brilliance of the colors, the freedom of the brush, and the intensity of the feelings pulled me right in. I don't know how you did it, but in the last three I could make out the figures at certain angles, but then they were hidden in the abstract. You are a wonderful artist, Constance. Did the show sell out?"

"Thank you so much, Renee. I knew you would understand. And, yes, every painting sold except the last three, which were not for sale. I want them for myself. What did you see in the last three?"

"That you were working out Nigel's death." Renee closed her eyes seeing images of the paintings. "In the first of the three, I saw the back of a man with a briefcase, walking away. In the middle one, I think it was a man sitting on a cloud with a woman reaching up. And in the last one, a woman and two smaller figures with their arms open wide, flying. But as I said, depending on how I looked at the paintings, I saw glimpses of these vague figures hidden in the abstract of the overall canvases."

"I lot of people didn't see the figures at all. The *New York Times* art critic also saw them. Did you see her review of the show in today's arts section of *The New York Times*? She loved my work."

Renee moved closer and put an arm over Constance's shoulder. "No, I was busy this morning buying flowers and chocolates for two beautiful young ladies and one not-so-young lady."

Constance gently punched Renee's arm. "Just so you know, reminding me that I'm not so young is not the way to ingratiate yourself with me."

"Maybe telling you that my mom and dad are not only familiar with your work but think highly of it without even having seen your latest efforts, will help with that."

Constance flushed and leaned into Renee. "Consider yourself ingratiated."

CHAPTER EIGHTEEN

Chloe and Cara bounced back and forth for a couple of days, first deciding they'd like to go to the Wollman Rink in Central Park in the evening to skate under the stars, then reconsidering in favor of the beauty of the park and the daytime view of the New York City skyline.

So on a crisp, sunny, November Saturday morning under a crystal blue sky dotted with occasional puffs of clouds, the four of them made their way across the park, crunchy red, yellow, and green leaves underfoot, the smell of burning leaves drifting in the air. Each of them carried their ice skates. Renee had owned hers for years but since the three Worthingtons had never skated she'd suggested they rent them at the rink. However, the girls were absolutely sure they would love skating and their school had some winter skiing and skating trips planned, so Constance gave in and bought skates for them and herself.

As Renee laced up Cara's skates, she glanced at Chloe struggling with hers and Constance trying to figure how tight to make the laces and wondered whether Beth and Gina would show up. Last night it had dawned on her that keeping three neophytes on their feet and teaching them to skate was probably not possible for one person. And, duh, she should have recruited experienced skaters to assist her. So she called and left messages for Gina and Beth. Neither had gotten back to her this morning.

As she shifted to Chloe, a hand clasped her shoulder. "Need some help?"

She looked up, thrilled to see Gina and Beth with skates over their shoulders. "Wow, I'm really happy to see you two."

Gina leaned over and hugged Renee. "We're happy to see you too and happy to assist. We stopped for a drink with Tori and Elle at the restaurant last night so it was too late to call when we got home. And this morning we slept late. But we're here, skates in hand, ready to go."

"Let me do that." The always energetic Beth elbowed Renee and knelt in front of Chloe. "Hi, I'm Beth, is it okay for me to lace your skates?"

Constance cleared her throat. "An introduction would be nice, Renee."

Renee flushed. "Sorry. Constance, Chloe, and Cara," she said pointing at each, "I'd like you to meet my good friends, Beth, the one on her knees, and Gina. I invited them to join us and help me teach you to skate." Looking alarmed, the girls glanced at each other, then at Constance. Renee hastened to assure them and Constance. "It will be faster and easier with three of us. Gina was a champion skater in high school and college. And Beth is good at all sports."

Chloe responded immediately. "Really, Gina? How old were you when you started? How long will it take?" And they were off and running. Renee laced up Constance and whispered, "Which of you should I work with?"

Constance whispered back, "I think you're stuck with me." She tilted her head toward the girls who were in deep conversation with Gina and Beth. Renee grinned. Chloe and Cara were holding hands, the only sign of nervousness she could detect, but they engaged with Gina and Beth as two adults might. She was constantly surprised by their maturity and their flexibility. Cara caught her watching and smiled as if to reassure her.

When everyone was laced up, Renee opened the bag she'd carried and handed the three of them the helmets she'd brought with her.

Gina stepped back. "We should practice a few things before we go on the ice. Are you all right with that, Renee?"

"I'm fine with whatever you suggest, Gina. You're the professional."

"Okay, so the first thing we're going to do is march in small steps instead of walk." Gina demonstrated. "This will help you learn to transfer your weight." She watched the three of them practice. When she was satisfied, she held up a hand. "Although I'm sure none of you will ever fall on the ice, I'd like to practice falling and getting up before we get there. So watch me and Beth and try to follow along.

"First, bend your knees and squat into a dip position, like this." Gina corrected Constance. "Okay, fall to the side and lean a bit forward as you fall down." Renee had Chloe repeat the fall. "Now, turn onto your hands and knees." When everyone was in the proper position, Gina demonstrated. "Place your feet between your hands." She checked that everyone was in position. "Now, push yourself up." She looked the small crew over. "Perfect. You guys are terrific. Now let's do it again, starting with small steps, then falling and getting up."

After the fourth repetition, Gina clapped. "You three are going to be terrific skaters so let's get on to the ice."

Chloe and Cara grinned. Renee could feel their confidence soar. Gina was a natural teacher, positive, confident, and inspiring. And Beth was so energetic and encouraging, it was no wonder she was such a successful business owner and personal trainer.

Reminding them to take small steps, Renee, Gina, and Beth helped their chosen skater to the ice. They claimed a piece of the wall as their own and had the three novices hold on to the wall to acclimate to the ice while the teachers removed their skate guards.

When it seemed they were ready, Gina demonstrated falling down and getting up on the ice. Each of the three did that several times before Gina announced, "Almost ready to skate. But first, let's learn to stop." She led them through stopping, then marching, then gliding. Soon Constance, Chloe, and Cara were skating, slowly, haltingly, but skating. After an hour the girls had the hang of it and were in high spirits, high-fiving Beth and Gina and each other. Renee could tell they would be spending a lot of time here in the future. Constance was slower getting it, but she eventually caught on and as the two of them circled the rink, Renee glanced at the girls, not surprised to see their phones pointed at them. She pulled Constance closer and instructed her to smile for the camera as they glided across the ice with the New York City skyline in the background.

When Beth and Gina had to leave to drive to New Jersey to visit Gina's parents, Renee and Constance decided it was a good time to end the lesson for the day. With high fives, and lots of hugs and kisses, Beth and Gina left and the four of them made their way out of the park in search of hot chocolate.

Renee suggested they walk back to the West Side but the girls moaned that their legs were weak from skating and a look at Constance confirmed the truth of the complaint so she waved down a cab and ferried them all to Café Lalo on West Eighty-third Street.

They were seated at a round table in front of the windows and given menus. While Renee ordered hot chocolate for all and the girls decided to share a warmed-up scone, Constance eyed the twinkling lights on the trees outside the wall of windows. Then she swiveled to take in the brick wall lined with brightly colored posters, the delicious-looking pastries in the glass case, and Renee sitting across the table from her. Her sweet, gentle smile warmed Renee. "A lovely place to end a lovely day, Renee."

"Yes, Renee," Cara said. "This café is very pretty."

The waitress arrived with their hot chocolates and the warmed-up scone for the girls. The moans of pleasure after the first sip warmed her heart. She was batting a thousand today.

"Gina and Beth are fun," Chloe said.

"And good teachers," Cara added. "Are you really, really old friends?"

"Gina and I have been close since freshman year in college. In fact, she taught me to ice skate. She got together with Beth a few years ago."

Constance sipped her hot chocolate. "They were wonderful."

"Yes, they were. And it was a good thing they showed up. I don't think we would have made nearly the same progress without them. Speaking of progress, we should go to the rink again sooner rather than later so you don't forget what you learned today."

"Can we go after school this week? Please, Renee." Chloe put a hand on Renee's arm.

"I'll work out something with your mum later, Chloe."

Constance put her arm through Renee's. "Come home with us and stay for dinner. We'll order in later."

Renee quickly accepted the offer. As they strolled to the Riverside Drive apartment, Renee suggested to Constance that the four of them go to the rink early one evening, skate for a while, then go out to dinner. Constance was silent.

"Am I going too fast?"

"I'm just flabbergasted that you want to spend so much time with the girls." Constance laughed. "Figure out what night works best for you and we'll fit your schedule." She checked that the girls were far enough ahead so they wouldn't overhear their conversation. "Is Gina an ex?"

Renee wondered where that question was coming from. "Yes. We were casual sex partners off and on starting freshman year and then in a committed relationship our senior year of college but not after. How did you know?"

"There's a level of intimacy that old lovers have that shows in small ways. For instance, you and she touched a lot but not you and Beth. And you had shared references. Really good old friends can have the same kind of intimacy but knowing your history, I assumed lovers."

"Does it bother you?"

"Not at all. I want to know everything about you. At Stanford and even now, except for the girls, we shut out the world. It was fun to see you with your friends."

At the Riverside apartment, the girls immediately headed to their room to call their friends to brag about the skating expedition and Constance and Renee settled on the sofa with glasses of wine.

"Since you like seeing me with me friends and ex-lovers, would you and the girls like to join me at the Inner Circle's Songfest next week?"

"Songfest?" Constance said. "What is that?"

"Just one of my favorite things in the world. It's a way I connect with my closest friends. When we were in college, a group of us used to get together Sunday nights to sing. Everyone would bring their instruments and some food and beer and we'd hang out together. It was a great way to relax and connect. We all enjoyed it so much we've been doing it ever since, every couple of months. We've opened it up to other friends since college, but we're very careful to preserve the intimacy."

Constance brushed Renee's cheek. "You were singing and playing that magical night when I... The first time I really saw you. So you still sing and play?"

"I do." Renee covered Constance's hand. "And I probably always will. Music is one way I express my feelings, sometimes feelings I'm not even aware of when I start. I'm my true self at Songfest. It's relaxed and fun. And, if I must say so myself, we make pretty good music. I've never invited anyone to come with me, but I think you and the girls would enjoy it. I'd love for you all to come."

Constance gazed into Renee's eyes. "Will Darcy be there?"

"No."

Constance reached for Renee's hand. "You're still in love with her, aren't you?" Her voice was soft.

Renee thought she heard regret and sadness in Constance's question. Was she still in love with Darcy? Maybe. But she was definitely feeling something stronger for Constance or she wouldn't have invited her to songfest to meet her friends. "Yes. No." She lifted her shoulders. "I don't know."

Constance squeezed her hand. "Well, that covers it."

Renee got to her feet. She needed to get away from the intensity of her feelings, from talking about this, trying to explain what she didn't understand herself. Constance must have sensed her panic because she held on to Renee's hand, gently stroking her, calming her. She sat again. And took a deep breath. She had promised to be honest and honest she would be. "For twenty years I thought I was in love with Darcy, but recently I realized I might have been using her as a shield to keep me from loving and being loved. Anyway, that's why I'm in therapy. If you're interested, I'll tell you about it."

Constance loosened her grip on Renee's hand but she didn't stop caressing it. She chewed her lower lip, then blew out a breath. "I'm definitely interested."

Renee started at the beginning and spoke about meeting and falling in love with Darcy, about abandoning her but expecting her to be there when she was ready, about them both wanting to get back together at various points but neither trying to make it happen. She talked about her feelings at the wedding and her brunch with Darcy just before she left for her honeymoon. And then she discussed her therapy. By the time she had brought Constance up to date, she was on her third glass of wine.

They sat in silence for a few minutes. "Thank you for sharing that, Renee. I'm glad you're trying to work it out. It seems we've both given up years of our lives needlessly."

Renee couldn't keep the regret out of her voice. "Yes, but you have Chloe and Cara to show for it. And though you weren't in love with Nigel, it sounds like you at least were in a loving relationship while I deprived myself of loving and being loved."

Constance cupped Renee's cheek. "It's true, my life wasn't what I'd hoped for, but I was mostly happy. Weren't you happy at all?"

Renee considered the question. "I thought I was until almost a year ago when I started to feel like something was missing and I pretty much stopped dating."

"Was that when Darcy met her wife?"

"It was months before that. And I couldn't tell you what brought it on. But suddenly my life felt empty. Midlife crisis, I guess."

Constance dropped her hands into her lap. "You said Tori, Elle, and Darcy knew you were still in love with Darcy. Will any of your other friends at this music thing know about it?"

Renee sensed Constance's insecurity and realized she was probably feeling like she was second best. That was definitely not the case. "I talked to Gina recently about some issues between us and it came up, but to my knowledge, no one else suspects. Have I told you, Constance, you're the only woman besides Darcy and Gina I've ever wanted a future with? It scared the stuffing out of me and I was ready to run, but you saved me the trouble and ran first. Since we've found each other again, I've barely given Darcy a thought and I still want a future with you." Renee cleared her throat. "Let me remind you that I said I had things to work through before I could make any commitment. That's still true. But my therapy is not focused on my love for Darcy but why I used her as a shield to keep myself from loving anyone, including her. And you. I hope you trust me enough and care enough to give me the time I need."

Constance glanced at her phone. She stood. "It's late. We should order dinner."

Disappointment flooded Renee. Had being truthful cost her Constance? And the girls. Now she really wanted to run. She steeled herself to end the evening as friends and then go home and let herself feel the loss.

After what seemed like hours but was a minute, Constance pulled Renee up. "Take all the time you need." She entwined their fingers and smiled. "I think the girls and I will love Songfest."

Disappointment was replaced by joy. Renee pulled Constance around to face her. "I thought I'd lost you." Renee couldn't keep the smile from her face. "Are we all right, then?"

She kissed the tip of Renee's nose. "We're more than all right." Constance hugged her. "Trust me. I'm not running and neither should you."

CHAPTER NINETEEN

The following Monday evening Renee entered the private room of Tori and Elle's restaurant with Constance, Cara, and Chloe in tow. She carried her guitar and would alternate playing it and the piano. Constance carried the stew she'd made and the girls carried Renee's contribution, wine and soda. When they entered, all eyes shifted to them and the buzz in the room died out. She'd warned Constance to expect jaws to drop when her friends saw her walk into Songfest with a beautiful woman and two beautiful teenagers. She put her arm over Constance's shoulder. "Hello, everyone, I'd like you to meet my friends Constance, Chloe, and Cara." She pointed at each as she said their names. "And now go back to your conversations and I'll bring them around to meet you individually." Conversations resumed. Gina and Beth met them at the table and hugged the three newcomers. Gina winked at Renee as she embraced Constance. The girls were excited to see their skating teachers and anxious to share their latest escapades on the ice, but Renee waved her friends off and herded her guests along.

"Don't worry, we'll catch up with Gina and Beth later. There are some girls I want you to meet." After they dropped their food and drink offerings on the appropriate tables and hung their coats, she led them to Joel and Erik and their teenagers. Fifteen-year-old Moira and thirteen-year-old Megan were happy to have some teenage company and quickly dragged the girls into a corner. Once they seemed comfortable, Renee turned Constance toward Tori and Elle, but before she could introduce them, Constance gasped. Her eyes widened. "Aren't you models? I can't remember the product, but I'm sure I saw you two in a magazine ad." She waved her hand as if trying to cool down. "And you sizzled on the page. I looked at those pictures often reminding myself about how good a connection between women could be. I'm sure I still have a copy of that magazine in my house in London."

Renee snorted. "Are you sure you only looked and didn't—"

"Of course." Constance elbowed Renee. "It was you I fantasized about all those years."

The warmth moved up from her toes, quickly reached her neck and hit her face. She wasn't sure if Constance was teasing but the pleasure in hearing she was in Constance's thoughts outweighed the embarrassment of her saying it in front of Tori and Elle.

"You deserved that, Renee." Tori laughed. "Yes, it was us." The look she shared with Elle made clear that the sizzle hadn't left their relationship. "We'd just met and the sparks between us lit up the set. You're very observant. It wasn't obvious to everyone." Tori glanced at Renee. "You must be Constance. Welcome to Songfest." She hugged Constance. "I'm Tori and this gorgeous woman is my wife, Elle."

"Renee said you own this restaurant."

"We do." Elle took Constance's hand. "We gave up modeling before it could dump us and followed another dream. Tori is the chef and I manage the place. We'd love for you and Renee to join us for dinner some weeknight when we'll have time to sit and chat with you. In the meantime, I hope you enjoy Songfest." She glanced around. "I think just about everyone is here. Excuse me.

I need to make sure the staff brought all the food Tori prepped. You should get something to eat now."

Constance punched Renee's arm. "Oh, my God, Renee, you let me bring a stew I cooked to a restaurant?"

"Don't be hard on Renee," Tori said. "We just supplement what you all bring, Constance, so don't worry about it. I'm always looking for new recipes so I'm going to grab some of that stew. See you later. Oh, hi, Maya, glad you made it."

Renee sucked in her breath and spun around. Constance turned to see what had her attention.

Maya flashed a smile, the one Renee thought of as her "spider inviting the fly into her web" smile. Renee snaked her arm around Constance's waist, staking her claim and hopefully warning Maya off.

"Hello there, I don't believe we've met," Maya said in her mellifluous voice. "Aren't you going to introduce us, Renee?"

Renee flushed. "Of course. Constance, this is my friend, Maya. Maya, this is Constance, a good friend from Stanford whom I recently had the good fortune to find again."

Constance's smile was just as brilliant as Maya's. She extended her hand. "Very nice to meet you, Maya." Renee prayed she wasn't going to be the odd girl out here. Seeing Chloe and Cara approaching she removed her arm from Constance.

Maya took Constance's hand. "And I'm thrilled to meet you. Renee has been holding out on me. Such a lovely accent." Maya laughed. Her gaze shifted to Chloe and Cara who appeared next to Constance. "Oh my God, am I seeing triple or are these two beauties yours?" The girls giggled. The stab of jealousy surprised Renee almost more than the image of her hands around Maya's throat. She and Maya had often competed for women. Until now it had been a game. But it was a game she no longer wanted to play, especially with Constance as the prize.

Maya's sexy laugh and thousand-watt smile were intended to seduce. "So, are you all ready to sing?"

Constance wrapped an arm around Cara, leaned into Renee and put her other arm around Renee's waist. "Cara and Chloe are wonderful singers. I'm hoping I don't embarrass Renee."

Renee was warmed by Constance's display of affection. But was she just sending Maya a message? Or did she mean it? Trust me, she'd said. Renee relaxed. Constance tickled Renee's side. Renee covered Constance's hand and smiled at her.

Maya met Renee's eyes. Apparently she'd gotten the message. She cleared her throat. "Well, I'd better get some food before we start. Nice meeting you Constance, Chloe, and Cara. I hope you enjoy our little get-together."

Maya had backed off and Renee relaxed. "Ready to get something to eat? And drink?"

"We're starving," Chloe said. "Do we just serve ourselves?"

"Yes. And sit anywhere," Renee said.

"I'm hungry too." Constance tucked her arm under Renee's. "Maya is quite the flirt, isn't she?"

So Constance had seen the flirting and had used her to fend Maya off. The all-too familiar feelings of disappointment and sadness filled her. She led Constance to the food table. While they filled their plates, she realized she was doing it again. Constance had given her absolutely no reason to doubt she was where she wanted to be, with Renee. Why couldn't she trust her? Why did she always choose to feel the rejection? Questions for Olivia but right now she was here with her people, with Constance and the twins, and she wanted to reclaim the happiness and pleasure she felt before she allowed Maya to take it away from her. No, not Maya, she'd done it to herself.

Constance interrupted her internal monologue by taking her hand. "Hey, where did you go?"

Renee squeezed Constance's hand. "Sorry, I drifted off. I'm right here with you." She scanned the room for a place to sit and led Constance to a corner sofa already occupied by two women. "Constance Worthington let me introduce Doctors Julie Castillo and Karin Simons."

Julie stood and extended her hand. "Pleased to meet you. Just Julie and Karin will be fine."

Constance shook the offered hand. "And please call me Constance."

While Renee and Julie dragged two chairs over, Karin waved Constance onto the sofa next to her. "Do I hear London in your voice?"

"You do." Constance settled and swiveled toward Karin. "You've been?"

"As a matter of fact, I was born in London," Karin said. "My dad was a diplomat stationed in London and we lived there until he was assigned to New York City when I was twelve. I loved London and went back after graduating from Columbia University to get my doctorate in clinical psychology at Kings College. Where in London do you live?"

Constance hesitated. "I have a home in Kensington but I actually live in New York City. My daughters and I moved here in late August."

Karin's eyes widened. "Kensington is beautiful. If I might ask, what brought you to the States?"

"I went to college in California. That's where I met Renee. I've always loved the US and when my daughters and I needed a change, I decided to move back."

"Ignore me if I'm asking too many questions. Why New York City and not California?"

Renee sat in the chair she'd pulled over. "Constance is too modest to tell you she's an artist, a really fine one, and she came here for the art scene. She recently had a very successful, very well reviewed show at the Fine Gallery in Chelsea."

"You're Constance Martindale?" Karin brightened. "I read a review of the show and it sounded wonderful."

Constance blushed but was clearly pleased. "Yes, I started painting under my maiden name and I didn't want to lose the little name recognition that I had at the time so I never changed it."

The *New York Times* review had mentioned that Constance's husband had recently been murdered so Karin knew Constance had been married, but Renee could see the question in Karin's eyes about Constance's sexuality. She decided it wasn't her place to discuss Constance's personal life. Besides, the Inner Circle grapevine was alive and well, and she hadn't attempted to keep her interest in Constance a secret. Judging by the looks and smiles it seemed most everyone got the picture. Since Karin and Julie were new additions to the group, their access to news was probably slower with Andrea on her honeymoon. Renee's gaze went to Chloe and Cara laughing with the other teenagers. She'd always made a point of not dating women with children so her friends would find her involvement with Constance and the girls surprising. And bringing them to Songfest where she'd never brought a date, must be shocking.

After dinner, conversation was cut short by Maya hitting a chord on the piano. "All right everyone, get your instruments and tune your voices, it's time. We'll start with 'Amazing Grace' then move down the list our teenage singers are handing out." Everyone quieted down. Maya hummed the tune then belted out the song in her deep, rich voice. When she completed the first verse, Renee joined in and the others followed one by one. Renee looked down at Constance as her pure soprano joined the harmony. Chloe and Cara settled at Constance's feet and sang as well. When the group had sung all the verses a cheer went up.

Constance was glowing. "That was beautiful. I haven't sung in…" her eyes met Renee's, "…almost a year." She leaned down to speak to her daughters. "It was brilliant, wasn't it?"

Renee picked up her guitar and started the next song. Over the course of the evening Renee shifted between her guitar and the piano. Constance and Maya also took turns at the piano. Lead singers varied according to the song and the voice needed. Renee led the last song, Leonard Cohen's "Hallelujah," while Constance and other voices joined in spontaneous harmonizing. The last note was followed by an awed silence as the group contemplated the gorgeousness of their unrehearsed rendition.

"Wow, we are good," Maya shouted. Everyone laughed and started talking as they gathered their belongings and said their goodbyes.

In the taxi driving across the park, Chloe leaned forward to talk to Renee, who was sitting in the front seat with the driver. "We didn't know you could sing so beautifully, Renee. You were wonderful. Would you teach us to play the guitar?"

"If you're serious, I will."

Cara harrumphed. "Of course we're serious or we wouldn't have asked."

"Well, all right then. We'll start over the weekend."

The girls' high-fived each other and became even more hyped than they'd been after the songfest, giggling, talking fast, asking a thousand questions.

Constance tapped on the plastic separating the driver in front from the passengers in back. "Renee, what would you think about getting out on Central Park West and walking the rest of the way so the girls can decompress?"

"Excellent idea. Please pull over on Central Park West. We're going to walk." She paid and they got out. The girls barely missed a beat and strode ahead for several blocks chattering about the evening. Renee and Constance followed at a more sedate pace. They caught up when the twins stopped at a red light.

Chloe, of course, was ready with a question. "So Megan and Moira have two dads and they thought we had two mums, because you two look like lovers. Are you?"

Renee stiffened. She waited for Constance to reply. "Not at this time."

"But soon?" Cara asked.

Constance glanced at Renee. "We'll see."

The girls grumbled. "Sod it, Mum. Why do adults always say 'we'll see?'" It was Chloe again.

"Language, Chloe. We say we'll see because we can't predict the future." Constance put an arm over each of her daughter's shoulders and pulled them close. "Would it be all right with you if we were a couple?"

The girls exchanged one of those looks, glanced at Renee then moved closer to Constance. Renee could barely hear Cara's whispered response. "Um, we like Renee an awful lot, but you won't forget Daddy, will you, Mum?" The pain and despair in the child's voice brought tears to Renee's eyes.

"Your dad will always be in my heart." Constance kissed both their cheeks. "He gave me you two, my most precious possessions. I see him every time I look at you. And nothing or no one will ever be more important to me than you." Constance's emotion-filled response punctured Renee's heart. She wanted a relationship with Constance, but she now understood she would always be the outsider, an intruder in their family.

"Promise you'll never forget him." The girls were crying, and as they often did, spoke in unison.

"I promise." Constance's voice was strong enough to reassure her daughters.

The very last thing Renee wanted was to hurt Cara and Chloe. Or Constance. And, to be honest, herself. It would be easier to go now than later. She cleared her throat. "I'm kind of tired so I'll leave you ladies here. I hope you enjoyed Songfest. Goodnight."

Constance turned and reached for her, presumably to stop her but she moved away quickly and didn't look back for fear of the three of them seeing the tears leaving her eyes without permission. She thought she heard Constance call her name but it could have been wishful thinking.

CHAPTER TWENTY

"Really, Olivia, I'm confused. I thought the three of them liked me and wanted me in their lives. But Chloe and Cara don't want me to replace their dad, and Constance says no one will ever be more important to her than them. I'm so embarrassed by the whole thing I've avoided my friends." Renee hesitated and then plunged ahead. "And I canceled my Monday therapy session because I didn't even want to discuss Chloe and Cara's rejection with you."

"I imagine the rejection touched feelings deep inside you."

"What?" Renee had expected sympathy and support, but instead, Olivia had tossed it back to her. Renee's stomach clenched. "Of course not. What feelings?"

Not at all disturbed by Renee's snarky reply, Olivia's gaze was compassionate and caring. Renee bit her lip, reminded herself Olivia was on her side, and if she wanted to change, she needed to be truthful and take risks. She took a deep breath and thought about it. In the serene safety of this place, secure that

Olivia would catch her if she fell, she allowed the feelings to well up. But she couldn't go there.

She was surprised when Olivia jumped in to give her a hand. Or maybe it was to kick her ass. "Your feelings about not being lovable, not good enough? Have you discussed being biracial with your friends yet?"

This was why she didn't want to talk about it. Now Olivia was mad at her for not doing what she told her to do. "No. I haven't felt ready. And I don't want to talk about it today."

They stared at each other for a few minutes. Renee knew Olivia would stare at her the rest of the hour if she didn't speak and another therapy session would be down the tubes. She looked away, breaking the stalemate. "Constance has texted and called but I don't know what to say and I'm afraid I'll break down when I talk to her."

"Would it be so awful for her to know you're human?"

Renee flushed. "I don't want her to think I'm weak."

Olivia responded immediately. "So you would think she's weak if she cried in front of you? If she showed you her pain?"

Renee felt cornered. "No, of course not. It's just...I'm afraid I'll fall apart in front of her, you know, like I do in here sometimes." She waited for Olivia to respond but she remained quiet. "I guess I want to be strong for her, to prove I can take care of her."

"Does running from her at the first sign of a potential problem show her your strength?"

Damn, she'd fallen right into that trap. She stared out the window. Would Constance think any less of her if she showed her feelings, her fears, her pain? No. As she'd reminded herself several times, what you see is what you get with Constance. She's a warm, caring woman who would likely open her arms and offer support. It was all her. Her fear and expectation of rejection. Olivia was right, the biracial issue. She turned at the sound of Olivia's voice.

"Tell me what you were thinking and feeling right before and then after you heard Constance and...her daughters reject you."

"Chloe and Cara are their names." Renee closed her eyes and tried to put herself back on that street corner. "Before is easy. We were on our way home from Songfest and we were all feeling good. I felt happy."

"What else? Go deep. What were your thoughts?"

Renee closed her eyes again, thinking about Songfest. "I was singing a solo and when I looked up from my guitar, Constance's gaze was so intense I could feel her across the room. I glanced at Chloe and Cara and they looked proud and loving. I was sure Chloe, Cara, and Constance wanted me in their lives and I felt, I don't know, happy, elated. And then it occurred to me that we really could be a family." She gazed at Olivia. "I guess I was wrong."

"What was it you felt from Constance?"

Renee loosened her tie. "I could be wrong, I mean, she didn't say anything and it was quite a distance." She met Olivia's eyes but her voice was almost a whisper. "I felt she loved me." Saying it out loud even in this safe place made her anxious.

Olivia gave her space to continue and, when she didn't respond, helped her out with a question. "How did that make you feel?"

Renee thought back to Songfest again. She was flying high and she'd brushed them away, but she'd heard the voices. "I heard the voices and I felt frightened."

Olivia let her sit with that before asking another question. "Do you think you were wrong about being a family because Chloe and Cara expressed fear that their mom might forget their dad, who's been dead less than a year, and she reassured them?"

Renee took a deep breath. "I guess."

"Did it occur to you that they might have been feeling the same thing as you? That they might have felt love for you and imagined being a family, and that scared them? That maybe they were afraid *they* were forgetting their dad or letting him down by loving you?"

"But Constance said she would never love anyone more than them." Renee looked at Olivia, but she could see this was one of those times when it was up to her to process what she'd said. "I see what you mean about the girls. They were close to their dad and I imagine wanting me to be with their mom would make them feel disloyal to him. And Constance loves her daughters more than life. She didn't say she'd never love anyone else, just not more than them. What an ass I am."

Renee mulled over those thoughts. She hadn't considered their feelings, only her own. What a selfish bitch. Olivia's question interrupted her self-flagellation. "What do you feel for Constance?"

Olivia was being unusually active today. Renee tried not to let her annoyance show, but her voice gave her away. "What do you mean? I just told you."

As always, Olivia ignored the rebuke and gently but firmly pushed Renee to go deeper. "You just told me how you reacted to what you thought Constance was feeling for you. Since you're the one in the room with me, I'm interested in your feelings."

Renee sat up straighter. What did she feel? "Uh, I'm not sure. I enjoy being with her. She's warm and intelligent and witty, and I think she wants to be with me." She hesitated, feeling foolish. "I guess I'm doing it again. Focusing on Constance and not me."

Silence. Olivia was doing her imitation of a sphinx. Renee ran her fingers through her hair. How was she supposed to know what she was feeling for Constance? She laughed at herself. "Okay, I get it. You can't tell me what I'm feeling. But I'll be damned if I know." Well what did she know? She leaned toward Olivia as if proximity to the therapist would enlighten her. "Unless I'm anxious that she might be dumping me, which is about fifty percent of the time, I'm happy when I'm with her. I never thought I'd want to be with a woman who had children, but I adore Chloe and Cara. I fantasize about spending the rest of my life with the three of them. Constance turns me on and she's the first woman in nearly a year that I've wanted to have sex with." Renee caught herself. No, that wasn't it at all. "Correction. I don't want to have sex. I want to make love to her. But I'm holding back until I figure out my life because I don't want to screw with Chloe and Cara or do anything to screw up my relationship with Constance, whatever it turns out to be. Constance and I can talk about everything and anything. I told her about Darcy and she understands I need to work it through. But the reality is, I've hardly thought about Darcy recently. Mostly, I'm totally in the present with Constance. And when I'm not with her, I think about her, I dream about her. I'm in love with her."

Olivia had listened intently and she took her usual minute to process what she'd just heard. "Does Constance do anything that makes you feel she'll reject you?"

Renee's gaze went to the windows. Did Constance make her feel insecure? "I don't think so. She's honest and direct. She's tried to reassure me that she isn't going anywhere, but sometimes when we're talking, she'll hesitate to answer or maybe she'll interrupt to respond to the girls or tell them to stop something they're doing, and in the seconds or minutes I'm waiting for her, I'm suddenly terrified she's stalling and is going to reject me."

"You said you believe Constance wants to be with you, that she loves you, yet you also think she's going to dump you." Olivia sipped her tea. "Renee." Olivia waited until Renee looked at her. "What are you feeling right now?"

"Sad."

"Do you know why?"

Renee nodded. "I think she loves me. And I'm afraid she'll leave. She's done it before."

"Her circumstances are different now. But are you feeling like running?"

"Not this time. I just picture myself watching them walk away like they did the other night, and feeling alone and broken."

"You need to dig deep on this Renee. Is it only the biracial issue or is it something more?" Olivia sipped her tea. "Tell me about Darcy."

Renee glanced at her phone hoping the session was over. No such luck. "What about her? I've told you everything." *Well not everything.* "Except that she called me the other day from Sicily where she and Andrea are visiting Andrea's parents and

Darcy's aunt and uncle. She's still on her honeymoon, but she was checking in with me to see how I'm doing and to remind me that she expects to see me in Paris New Year's week."

Olivia looked surprised. "You say Darcy encouraged you to free yourself of her so doesn't it seem counterintuitive for her to call you from her honeymoon?"

Was Olivia suggesting that Darcy was playing her? Telling her to move on but trying to hold her back? Nothing could be further from the truth. "She's looking out for me. That's who Darcy is. Once you're in her orbit she feels responsible. Besides, despite hiding my love for her all these years, she's one of my closest friends and I'm one of hers. Though she's not in love with me, she cares a lot about my happiness. And now that my feelings for her are finally out in the open, she will do everything she can to encourage me to move on. This was actually the second time she called to check that I was in therapy as I'd promised. She knows if I don't show up in Paris New Year's Eve, I'll be making a statement about my feelings for her. I have no doubt she wants me to be happy."

"How did you feel talking to her?"

Renee stared out the window, replaying the conversation and trying to recall her feelings. "I enjoyed it." She turned to Olivia. "I could feel her happiness over the phone and…I was glad for her. Usually I feel sad, kind of sorry for myself, but not this time. I told her about Constance—"

Olivia's eyebrows shot up.

Renee laughed. "I told you she's my best friend. She was excited for me. And said she hoped I'd bring Constance and the girls to Paris."

Olivia took the cover off her tea and sipped. "So you feel free of Darcy?"

Renee hadn't let herself analyze the conversation or her feelings for Darcy or what sharing Constance with her meant. "I'm afraid to say it but I'm pretty sure I am. Free of Darcy." She threw her arms up in the air. "Mission accomplished." She lowered her arms. "Maybe."

"So will you be going to Paris with Constance and the girls?"

Would she? It had seemed so far off but Thursday was Thanksgiving and the business class flight she'd reserved months ago was just a few weeks later. Olivia had just let the air out of her. She expelled her breath. "I haven't let myself think about it and I haven't broached the subject with Constance because I'm afraid she'll say no." Renee's smile did not reach her eyes. "I guess I do need to think about why I expect her to reject me."

"So maybe only part of the mission is accomplished." Olivia shifted forward in her seat, a sure sign the session was over.

CHAPTER TWENTY-ONE

Working in her office the next afternoon, Renee looked up when Jenna, her assistant, cleared her throat. She hadn't heard her enter. "I'm sorry to interrupt, Renee, but there are two beautiful women in the waiting room and they are extremely anxious to see you."

Damn, this had happened before. Two women she dumped getting together to beat on her. But why now? It had been almost a year since she'd been with someone. She really wasn't in the mood to deal with old stuff now. She'd promised herself she'd call Constance tonight, and not knowing what kind of shape she'd be in tomorrow, she wanted to finish reading this report before she went home. "Two? Did you get their names?"

Jenna grinned. "Well, they were kind of giggly but I believe they said Chloe and Cara."

Renee shot out of her seat. "Here? They're in the office?"

"Sorry, should I have said you weren't in?" Jenna looked upset.

Were they here to dump her? To ask her to leave Constance alone? "No, no. It's fine. I'm just surprised. Show them in. No wait, I'll come out and get them." Jenna turned. "Wait, you show them in." Jenna came back and clasped Renee's biceps. "Geez, Renee, I've never seen you so flustered. Take a deep breath and tell me about these girls. They look so young, I hope you're not fooling around with them."

Renee took the recommended breath. "They're Constance's daughters. If you'd come to Songfest you would have met them."

"And are they somehow responsible for you looking unhappy lately?"

Renee stepped back. "No, I'm responsible. But they're sort of involved." Whatever they wanted, she'd have to deal with it. "Please bring them in, Jenna."

Chloe and Cara looked nervous but determined when the door closed behind them. Renee smiled and moved toward them. They flew into her arms, both talking at the same time. So they weren't angry. She kissed each of them on the forehead and led them to the sofa. Her office door opened and Jenna walked in with a large bottle of sparkling water. After pouring three glasses, she left, closing the door softly behind her. Renee sat opposite them on a club chair. "I'm surprised to see you here. Is everything all right?" She held her breath.

Chloe spoke. "We want to apologize for hurting your feelings after Songfest the other night."

Cara picked up. "We didn't mean we don't want you to be with Mummy if that's what you both want, we just... Do you think it's possible to be happy and sad at the same time, Renee?"

Renee took a second to regain control. She really did love these girls. "I do, Cara. It's confusing sometimes, isn't it?"

"Yes, it is. We really, really like you, but you know, sometimes we feel a bit sad about our dad not being here. It's not like we want Mummy to be alone or anything. We want her to be happy. And we think you make her happy."

Renee took a deep breath. "I know how important your dad was to the three of you and I would never want to come between you and your memories of him."

Chloe moved forward on the sofa. "Mum's been miserable since that night. We've been begging her to call you but she says she can't, that you have to choose us or it won't work."

Renee sat on the coffee table in front of the girls and took their hands. "Remember your mum said we both had some problems we need to work out?" Seeing their nods, she continued. "That's what I've been doing."

"But you can come back to us while you work on it, right? You were doing that before we messed everything up." Cara spoke but both girls were looking at her with such hope. "Mummy is such a wreck. She's not even painting."

Chloe jumped in. "We want to cook dinner for you and Mummy tomorrow night. Will you come?"

"Does your mum know?"

They exchanged that twins' glance. "We'll tell her later if you say yes. Say yes, please."

Renee didn't have to think about it. "Yes, please."

Giggling, the girls hugged and kissed her. She offered to get them a taxi but they refused, so she walked them to the elevator.

"We'll see you tomorrow."

The doorman called up to the apartment and was told to send her up. Clutching the flowers she brought for all of them and a bottle of wine in one arm, she straightened her tie, ran her fingers through her hair and pulled her jacket down as she rode up in the elevator. The girls hadn't called to cancel, so either they hadn't told Constance or she was all right with seeing Renee again. She hoped it was the latter and prayed she was able to talk coherently when she saw her.

The elevator door slid open slowly and Renee stepped out into the hall, surprised to see a smiling Constance standing in the open door to her apartment. She was so beautiful Renee would have been happy to stand and stare at her all night. Instead she walked over, bowed, and handed her the largest bouquet. "Hi, I've missed you."

Constance accepted the flowers, sniffed them, and kissed Renee lightly on the lips. "I've missed you too. A lot. Come in. Our cupid chefs are busy cooking dinner." She leaned close. "Rumor has it they bought a love potion from a wizened old woman they found somewhere in the city, and they'll be dosing us with it tonight." She hugged Renee and whispered, "They don't realize it isn't necessary."

Renee was dizzy with the smell of her and the feel of her body pressing against her. Maybe she was more ready for this than she thought. But how do you manage with two nosy teenagers in the house? "Did you send them to me?"

Constance laughed. "The little buggers took it upon themselves to make things right with you. They felt they'd hurt you and they could see I was distressed by your absence."

Renee felt bad about feeling happy to hear that Constance had missed her but it didn't dampen her happiness. "Let me poke my head in the kitchen and present my flowers. Then I'd like to talk."

They sat close on the sofa. "I did it again," Renee said. "I'm sorry."

Constance put her hand on Renee's thigh. "You're here now so we're all right."

"But I'm tired of being scared. I'm tired of running. And I'm tired of expecting to be discarded." Constance squeezed Renee's thigh sending butterflies zipping through her body, making it difficult to concentrate. As much as she wanted to go where her body was beckoning, she knew with only "part of the mission completed," she wasn't totally ready to move wholeheartedly into a relationship. She covered Constance's hand with her own and intertwined their fingers. "Just so you know, when the girls arrived yesterday afternoon, I was working to clear my desk so I could call you last night and have time to recover at home this morning, if necessary."

"You thought you'd need time to recover?"

"I did. I wasn't sure whether you'd be hurt or angry at the way I dealt with the whole thing, and I was afraid you'd tell me you didn't want to see me again. That would have devastated me."

Constance leaned in close. "So what do you think of your reception so far?"

"I'm loving it." Renee leaned in for a gentle kiss.

CHAPTER TWENTY-TWO

The girls were sleepy and uncharacteristically grumpy. The four of then had gone to Central Park West and 80th Street last night to watch the Macy's Thanksgiving Parade balloons blown up. It was thrilling to see all the familiar parade characters grow from limp piles to giant floating figures, but it was late when they got home and the girls were so excited they were awake until almost two in the morning.

Though Renee arrived early to help bake the three apple and three pecan pies they were contributing to Tori and Elle's Thanksgiving dinner, she and Constance were not much better off than the twins. Coffee helped. And eggs, fresh fruit, and toast revived them all. After they'd cleared the breakfast dishes, they got to work. Laughing and teasing, the four of them worked together easily, as if they'd done it many times before. Renee and Chloe peeled and sliced the apples while Cara and Constance mixed the dough and rolled out the pie shells. Constance seasoned the apples with lemon juice, cinnamon, nutmeg, and brown sugar, then she and Cara filled the shells, put the top layer of pastry in place, crimped the edges, and slit steam vents in each. When the three apple pies were in the oven, they moved on to the pecan pies.

The baking pies filled the kitchen with the heavenly fragrance of cinnamon and nutmeg and pried loose Renee's memories of cooking with her mother and feelings she hadn't experienced since she left home for college. Comfort. Home. Family. This was what she wanted. To be with Constance. To be with Chloe and Cara. To be a family.

Once the pies were baked and the kitchen cleaned, the girls decided naps were in order and scampered to their bedroom. Renee had brought clothes to wear to the dinner later but she considered leaving so Constance could nap. Constance seemed to sense her discomfort and put a hand on her arm. "Stay. You can nap in the guest bedroom or you can nap with me. I have a king-size bed. We'll leave the door open so we don't go astray and the girls don't get the wrong idea."

How could she turn down an offer like that? They stretched out, facing each other, one on each side of the bed with considerable space between them. Though they didn't touch or speak, their eyes locked and erotic tension sparked between them. Constance extended her hand and Renee reached out. When their fingers touched, Constance's eyebrows shot up, but she maintained the eye contact. Renee watched Constance's eyelids drift closed, then closed her own eyes. As she dropped off to sleep Renee imagined she heard Constance whisper sweet words.

When Renee opened her eyes, she was alone in the bed. She listened to the shower and wondered whether she'd dreamed that connection. Then the girls ran in and it was all up and at 'em. It didn't take long for the four of them to shower and dress, pack the pies and head crosstown to Buonasola, which Tori and Elle had closed for the day.

As usual, Tori and Elle had rearranged the room so long tables with food lined the sides of the dining room. Renee counted eight turkeys and five hams, a couple of roast beefs, some dishes labeled vegetarian and dishes piled high with various rice stuffing and bread stuffing and sausage stuffing and apple cranberry walnut stuffing. The guests provided most of the rest of the food, usually a dish that was a family favorite like the trays of lasagna, eggplant parmesan, and moussaka, and the sides tables were loaded with sweet potatoes, mashed potatoes, sautéed mushrooms, Brussels sprouts, broccoli di rape, creamed oysters, smothered string beans, collard greens, various cranberry concoctions, and a couple of veggie grain salads and green salads. Of course, there were lots of desserts in addition to their pies.

Constance and the twins stared gaped-mouth at the food-laden tables. "Wow, this is definitely a Thanksgiving feast." Constance made no attempt to tamp down the awe in her voice.

Chloe poked Renee. "Do gourds and mead and dancing girls accompany this feast?" Renee poked smart-mouth Chloe back. "Only after the knights and gladiators finish their business."

Chloe put her pie on the nearest table before doubling over with laughter but Constance had to put a hand out to steady Cara who was laughing so hard she looked to be in danger of dropping her pie. Renee used her phone to take pictures of the girls doubled over and texted them to their phones. Finally back in control, Chloe picked up her pie. "Very good, Renee. Now where do we put these pies?"

Renee led them in the direction of the dessert tables and after the four of them deposited their pies, Chloe and Cara made a beeline for Moira and Megan, the friends they'd made at Songfest.

Renee scanned the crowd. It seemed to get bigger each year as the members of the Inner Circle had children and brought friends and lovers, just as she had brought Constance and the girls. She estimated sixty including Gregg and some bus and wait staff with no family and no place to have Thanksgiving dinner who volunteered to help, then join them for dinner.

People were milling about talking to each other, greeting friends and introducing themselves. Renee waltzed Constance around the room introducing her to friends who hadn't been at Songfest, like Francine and Jennifer. Although she was sure word about her and Constance had spread, Renee expected and got lots of raised eyebrows, gentle elbows in the side, and whispered questions. Constance took it all with good grace and even teased her about it.

Gina and Beth found them helping themselves to wine. While Beth engaged Constance with questions about their latest ice-skating expedition, Gina hugged Renee and asked quietly. "How's it going? The three beauties are still with you, I see."

"Yes, they're still with me." Renee laughed. "For the most part it goes well, but I seem to be a master of screwing myself up." She gazed at Constance talking animatedly with Beth. "And I really don't want to screw this one up."

Gina squeezed her arm. "I'm here if you need me."

Olivia's idea of talking with her friends about being biracial popped into Renee's mind. Constance had picked up on their strong connection when she met Gina at the ice skating rink. It wasn't just that they'd had a year-long relationship in college. But their connection had continued after their breakup and beyond the occasional sex they'd shared since and deepened over the years into a strong, loving, and supportive friendship. She would trust Gina with her life, and had, over the years, trusted her with all of her inner feelings. Well, most of them. Though she and Gina had already talked about race in the context of their relationship, she would definitely contribute to a more general discussion. As would Beth.

Renee's gaze fell on Elle escorting additional guests to the food tables. She trusted Elle as well. And there were others. Could she do it? Could she bare her soul? Would it help? "You know Gina, there might just be. I'll get back to you later." As Gina turned away, Renee gazed into space, weighing the idea of a gathering at her house.

"Hey, bub. Have you abandoned me?" Constance appeared at her side, jolting Renee out of her reverie. "What? Of course not, I was lost in thought."

"Hey Renee. Nice to see you and the girls again, Constance." They greeted Joel and Erik, Megan and Moira's dads. Joel cleared his throat. "Um, Renee, you know Megan and Moira are mixed race, right?"

"I do." Renee glanced at the girls huddled with Chloe and Cara and all seemed well. Funny, she'd never noticed how Moira presented white while Megan was darker, definitely not white. "Are they having problems?"

"Not exactly problems but the issue of how they deal with it out in the world has come up recently. You know, they get things like you can't really be sisters and it hurts." Joel waved a finger between Erik and himself. "Since we're two black guys we thought maybe talking with a mixed-race woman would be helpful."

Renee was stunned. She glanced at Constance for support but all she got was slightly raised eyebrows, which she took to mean she was on her own. "Truthfully guys, I don't know how helpful I can be." She scanned the room, her gaze bouncing from Gina to Elle to the two teenagers, and back to the two gay guys trying to do right by their adopted daughters. She decided she could trust them. She took a deep breath. "Actually, I'm dealing with this issue in therapy right now so I may not be the best person until I get my own head on straight, so to speak."

Erik nodded. "It could probably wait a little while."

No, it probably shouldn't wait. The sooner the girls figure out what they feel about it the better. "Listen, I'm planning a dinner Monday night to discuss the issue. I'm asking Gina and Beth and Elle and Tori." She glanced at Constance. "And I hope you'll come, Constance. It would be great if you guys could make it. It might help you with the girls as much as I hope it will help me."

Erik shook his head. "I'll be out of town Monday."

"I'm a definite yes, Renee," Joel said. "Elle is calling us to dinner. I'll get the details later."

Chloe sidled over to Renee. "Is it all right if we sit with our friends?" She pointed to a table where Cara was sitting with Moira and Megan, two other girls and three boys.

"Sure." Renee waved to Cara who was watching them. "Have fun."

Renee and Constance took seats at a table for twelve and

Gina and Beth, Francine and Jennifer, Elle and Tori, Karin and Julie, and Maya filled the other seats. Renee glanced up at the tap on her shoulder. She jumped up and hugged Lucia who she hadn't seen since Darcy's wedding. "Lucia, it's good to see you. We missed you at Songfest." She looked around. "Is Candace with you?" She hoped not. Many members of their circle were still angry with Candace for keeping Darcy's accident, which left her helpless, a secret from all her friends, causing her to feel isolated and abandoned and to become angry and volatile.

Lucia clung to Renee. "She decided it would be better for everyone if she skipped it this year. She's going to a couple of AA meetings and in between she's serving dinner at a homeless shelter. But I'm glad to be here. I miss you all." Tears filled her eyes as she hugged one after another of the women who crowded around her.

When Lucia was free, Renee introduced her. "Lucia, this is Constance, my, um, an old friend. Constance, Lucia, a member of the Inner Circle from college."

Constance took Lucia's hand and smiled. "Nice to meet you, Lucia. I love your pantsuit."

"Thank you. It's one of my own," Lucia said.

At Constance's look of confusion, Renee explained. "Lucia is a designer and she has her own fashion line. She's in all the better department stores and boutiques."

Lucia planted a quick kiss on Renee's lips. "Thank you, my love, it's still hard for me to toot my own horn."

Constance placed an arm around Renee's waist. "Well if that suit is any indication, I'll have to get a list of where to find you."

Dared she hope Constance was feeling jealous? Renee patted Constance's hand.

Lucia eyed Constance. "I have some pieces that would look lovely on you. I'd love to show you my entire line." Lucia turned to Renee. "Bring her to my workshop, Renee."

"I will. Will you join us for dinner?" Renee indicated the empty chair near Maya.

Elle called for quiet. "Welcome everyone. Tori and are so

grateful you're able to share this Thanksgiving with us and with each other. The food you all brought looks fabulous and I can't wait to dig in. I'm sure many of you feel the same. Tori and I are truly thankful to have such wonderful friends and we appreciate all you do for us throughout the year.

"After dinner we'll have a time for anyone who would like to share something they're grateful for, and maybe Renee and Maya would lead us in a song or two. Now I won't delay any longer but to keep things orderly let's serve ourselves one table at a time starting with the youth table and moving toward the door. We've put sparkling water and soda on every table and there's plenty more near the bar. There's red and white wine on every table except for the teenage and children's tables and plenty more behind the bar. There's also tap water if you prefer. Helpers please raise your hand. If you need anything grab me, Tori, or one of the helpers, and we'll do what we can. Enjoy."

Later that night, with the girls in their bedroom, they were on the sofa talking about the day and Constance was full of questions. "So how many of the women there were your lovers in college and after?"

Renee laughed. "Honestly, I never counted." She blushed. "But a lot of them."

"How long were you with Lucia?"

"A few weeks, maybe a month, my junior year." So she was right earlier. Constance was insecure about Lucia. "But as usual I moved on as soon as someone else interested me. Remember, I told you the two months you and I were together was my longest relationship other than Darcy and Gina?"

Constance was a woman on a mission. "And casual was how it was for you until now? Were we casual?"

"I've been celibate about a year but up to that time it was casual sex." Renee took Constance's hand. "I wouldn't characterize us as casual. With hindsight, I think I fell in love with you the first time we locked eyes as I sang love songs to you at that party. You were different. I was turned on by you, but rather than rushing to get you into bed I wanted to get to know you, to spend time with you. I think I told myself we were casual in the beginning, but by the end, I knew I was in love with you. That was why I started to pull away."

Constance kissed Renee, no tongue, but the kiss was intense, filled with feeling. She squeezed Renee's hand. "There was a lot of talk about going to Paris for New Year's Eve. What's that about?"

Renee blanched. Damn, was she ready to risk bringing this up now? "Darcy and her wife are throwing a New Year's Eve party in Paris. She's reserved a hotel and many of their friends are going for a long weekend, or more, to celebrate with them."

"And you?" Constance asked, her voice reflecting her uncertainty.

Renee felt bad. This wasn't how she'd pictured this going. The last thing she wanted was for Constance to feel uncomfortable. Yet, instead of presenting it as an exciting opportunity, a trip to Paris to meet her family and ring in the New Year, she was making Constance drag the invitation out of her. "I committed to spend two weeks around the holidays with my family in Paris." She cleared her throat. "And I was thinking of asking if you and the girls would accompany me as my guests."

"Thinking?"

"Yes. No. I'm inviting you. I would love for you and the girls to be my guests in Paris for New Year's Eve and as much of the two weeks you can stay with me."

"This sounds like a big deal. Can I think about it?"

Nice going, Renee. Constance isn't sure she believes you want her to come. Now Renee was the one feeling uncertain.

CHAPTER TWENTY-THREE

It had taken a while, but Renee had finally acknowledged that Olivia was right, that being biracial was a fundamental issue in her life. In the last two sessions, Olivia had encouraged her to dig deep to expose the fears and the self-hate that kept her from committing to love and being loved. It was painful and scary but cathartic. Together they'd isolated three emotions stemming from being biracial that had influenced her life negatively—self-hate, guilt, and anger.

Olivia agreed it wasn't necessary or appropriate for Renee to discuss her self-hate and the relationship issues it caused in a random group of friends, so tonight she would bring up her guilt, and though it hadn't been a big issue for her, the anger that seemed to bubble up frequently these days.

Renee surveyed her little focus group. One black and white couple, one black couple, a black gay man and the uninvited white man he'd inexplicably brought. Last but not least, her and Constance who didn't look like a mixed-race couple but were. And that was the issue.

Renee was pissed at Joel. Thinking the conversation would help him and Erik deal with their mixed-race daughters, she'd invited him even though they weren't as close friends as the women who were here, and he'd invited Ed, a white friend, without consulting her. Talking about something so personal with a stranger in the room made her uncomfortable. She couldn't throw him out so she'd proceed as planned and hope he didn't put a pall on the discussion.

She'd decided on a buffet to keep things informal, so they could sit around in the living room and talk while they ate. When everyone was seated with food and drink, Renee cleared her throat. "Thank you for coming tonight. You know I asked you here to discuss being biracial. I've recently discovered in therapy that being mixed race is more basic to who I am and how I live my life than I allowed myself to know. This is a very personal subject for me and I invited only people I felt I could trust enough to open up with." She met Ed's eyes. "And to be frank Ed, I'm not sure why you're here." She hadn't intended to show her anger but there it was out in the open. "I apologize. I don't mean to be rude."

Joel glanced at Ed, then shifted his gaze to Renee. "No, I'm sorry. I should have cleared his coming with you, but I only learned he was in town an hour or so ago. Ed and I grew up together. We lost touch years ago and since he was coming to New York City he got my number from my mom in Chicago. When he called me from his hotel earlier, it seemed like fate had sent him."

Ed smiled. "Like you, Renee, I'm biracial."

Renee flushed. "Wow, am I an ass or what? I'm sorry for assuming you're white, Ed. Please excuse my racism." She shook her head. "But, damn, if I haven't just illustrated exactly the issue I want to address." The group erupted in laughter. "I'm trying to figure out what it means to be a biracial woman who presents as white, and how to deal with the guilt and anger I feel."

She smiled at her friends. "No, I didn't stage this but it is a perfect introduction." She took a deep breath. "Your mission, should you choose to accept it, is to help me figure out how to be two things at once." Her gaze moved from person to person, holding Ed's for a moment longer than the others. "Most of you know my mom is black and my dad is white. Growing up in France with my artist parents I was surrounded by a wide range of people, many black but mostly white, and except for some early family things and an incident in the fourth grade, color has never been an issue for me. I thought." She waited for the nods. "Recently, I realized I'm conflicted. That I feel if I don't declare that I'm half black, I'm denying my mom, lying to people and enjoying white privilege. And, if I claim to be black, I'm being inauthentic because I don't have to deal with the slings and arrows that people who present as black deal with every single day. Thoughts, anyone?"

Tori leaned over and patted Renee's knee. "I would never have guessed being biracial was an issue for you. You've always seemed so comfortable in your skin."

"I am. France certainly has its race problems but the slavery issue in the US engendered systemic racism and race is a cultural hot button here in a way that it isn't in France. So when I arrived at college, being multiracial wasn't a big deal for me; it was my latent lesbianism that consumed me. But I've become aware that I announce I'm biracial immediately upon meeting someone, almost like a warning, and my therapist pointed out that it's more of an issue for me than I realized."

Gina slid to the edge of her seat, as if needing to be close to Renee. "As we've discussed Renee, I no longer believe I can tell you how to be biracial and I apologize again for any of the guilt and anger I caused." She reached for Renee's hand. "It's pretty obvious I'm black so I don't have to decide or declare who I am. Her gaze settled on Joel and Ed. "To give you some background, in college I was a militant black activist in love with Renee, a biracial woman, who lived a white life because of her skin color. We fought constantly because I wanted her to experience and understand the world the way I did. With maturity and a good deal of therapy, I came to see that while Renee was able to understand and react to my world intellectually, it was impossible for her to experience it in the gut level way I and other dark-skinned people do. But I also realized that some part of my anger was resentment because she was able to enjoy white privilege, and to this scholarship kid from Newark, class privilege." She turned to Renee. "I no longer see simple solutions. I see you, Renee. All your friends, the people you care about and those who care about you know you're biracial and it's not an issue for us. The world sees you as white and as you just demonstrated with Ed, that's just the way it is. While you don't hide that you're half black, I get that trying to be black and white at the same time is impossible. You need to just be you. Love yourself like we all love you."

Renee hugged Gina. "Thank you, I love you too." She sat next to Constance again, feeling uncomfortable about putting her friends on the hot seat. Should she change the subject? Constance must have sensed her discomfort because she put a hand on her thigh and smiled warmly.

Elle's majestic voice pulled her back into the room. "Gina and Beth obviously have some white blood back somewhere in their families, so like you Renee, they are mixed race, but because of their darker skin color they're considered black. I, on the other hand, am so dark it would never enter anyone's mind that I might be half white, which, of course, I could be. That said, if one of my parents were white, would I feel it necessary to explain that I'm biracial? Or try to figure out how to be white? I don't think so. The world sees me as black. Regardless of my blood, when I look in the mirror, I see a black woman. It's the opposite for you, Renee. The world sees you as white. And, I presume, regardless of your blood, when you look in the mirror you see a damned attractive white woman, as does anyone who looks at you. From what I know of you, you've experienced life as a white woman. Trying to be black and white means you're neither. Suppose I did have a white parent. How ridiculous would I be if I claimed I was a white woman? Your skin color has chosen for you. You are white. It doesn't mean you should hide your black family or your black blood. And I know you don't. It doesn't mean you shouldn't stand up to fight against discrimination and oppression. And I know you do. It means you should live your life fully without feeling like you're living a lie. I agree with Gina. In my not-so-humble opinion, the work for you is not trying to figure out whether you're black or white. It's learning to love yourself, it's learning to accept that you are loveable just as you are, and it's learning to let love into your life."

Renee hugged Elle. "Thank you, Elle. You are wonderful." Elle kissed her forehead. "So are you, babe."

"If I may?" Ed spoke up.

"Please do, Ed."

"I also have a black mother and a white father. He left my mother right before I was born and I grew up in a totally black environment in Chicago, as did Joel. Though I have light brown hair and blue eyes, I have always felt black. And, even though I present as white, I was mostly accepted as just another kid on the wide continuum of colors in the neighborhood. I only thought about my color occasionally." He sipped his wine. "Until I went to college. There I was welcomed by whites and rejected by blacks. But after a while, my white friends thought I was crazy for insisting I was black and rejected me, and the blacks I tried to socialize with rejected me for the same reason as Renee was rejected, because I could never understand what it is to be black. I did manage to have a couple of friends, both black and white, but I spent a lot of time during those four years reading and thinking about race, about myself. No matter how I look to the world, culturally I'm black. My experience is the same as my two darker-skinned half-brothers and the friends I grew up with. I define who I am. And I don't let anyone tell me different."

"Have you encountered problems working and living that way?" Constance asked.

Ed smiled. "Of course. But I live in a black neighborhood surrounded by black friends and family, and I work in an organization fighting to improve black lives. I occasionally get stared at when I'm with my darker-skinned wife and children, but it's not a big issue. Do I still get weird looks and questions outside my community when I say I'm black? Yes. But I patiently explain and if they don't understand, so be it." He picked up his glass but it was empty.

Grateful for a minute to process what Ed said, Renee leaped up for the wine bottle and filled his glass. "Anyone else?" Ed grew up in a predominantly black world so he feels black and identifies with the black part of him. But she grew up in a mostly white world and never gave much thought to her color. When she moved to the US, her whiteness was assumed and she broadcast that she was mixed race. He was at peace with choosing but she felt she didn't have a choice. Was she lying to herself? Was that why she was still wondering whether she could be both? She met Ed's eyes. "You and I both have blue eyes and white skin yet you feel black and I feel white. So does that mean that how you identify depends on the environment in which you grow up?"

Joel spoke up. "I've been reading any articles I can find on the issue to help us with the girls, and I believe there are studies that show that."

Renee made a mental note to ask Joel about the articles. "So, Ed, am I right in thinking you feel we have to go with who we feel we are?"

He leaned forward. "I hope I'm not overstepping here. But you wear men's clothes and have short hair like a man. Do you experience any conflict about presenting as a man rather than a woman?"

Renee thought about that for a second. "Not at all. It's who I am. Although I might be mistaken for a man, I know I'm a woman. I'm not pretending to be a man. I'm making a choice to be myself." Interesting. "Good point, Ed. But to get back to race, can I ask if you feel disloyal to your white side because you identify as black?"

Ed tapped his fingers on his glass as he considered the question. "Not at all. Neither my father nor any of his family has ever been in my life, so I'm not in conflict about maybe hurting their feelings or having to be both. You, I gather, have both parents still in your life?"

Renee nodded. "I do. And four much older siblings with a range of skin colors, none with blue eyes or skin as white as mine, though some of my many nieces and nephews look like me. I remember talking about race and about skin color with my parents, but it wasn't a big issue for me, or them. Unlike you, except for my immediate family and some family friends, I grew up in a mainly white society. I was only eighteen when I moved to America so maybe race got lost for me in the swirl of moving to a new country, finding my inner male, acting on my lesbianism, and switching to English as my predominant language. It may be time for a family discussion when I go back to France for the holidays."

"Do you feel disloyal to your mother for living as white?" Joel asked.

Renee frowned. "There was a brief period when I was ashamed to be seen with my mom. Maybe that's why I feel I have to be black and white at the same time because being white means choosing my dad over her. I believe announcing I'm biracial almost as soon as I meet someone is an unconscious attempt to prevent being accused of trying to pass, of hiding or lying about my black blood."

Elle leaned forward. "Speaking of lying. What do you all think about that woman, Rachel something, who was living as a black woman until she was exposed as being white?"

Renee had read the articles about the "scandal" but she didn't feel strongly one way or the other, maybe because she herself wasn't black enough. "It's complex. She looks more black than either me or Ed, yet I've read she has no black blood. I've heard the cultural appropriation argument but in a way, I understand. If she truly feels black, as she says she does, who am I to tell her otherwise? It's not like black people get a free ride in our society. There's no black privilege. So I'm not sure what she gains except feeling like she's living her life. The race issue is complex and confusing. Trying to figure it out for myself gives me a headache. And trying to figure it out for anyone else is way beyond me. Any thoughts, Ed?"

Ed tugged on a lock of hair falling in his face, seeming to formulate an answer. "We can get into the psychology, or is it sociology, and have a discussion of race as a social construct, but I think it suffices to say, as you did, that this is not a simple issue and there are no simple societal solutions right now. Only personal solutions. You and I, Renee, facing similar decisions about how we choose to live as mixed-race people, have made different choices based on our personal history. In my opinion, the important thing is that we make the right decisions for ourselves, decisions that enable us to live happy, fulfilled lives, while fighting for racial equality and justice."

Tori waved her hand. "Hey, can I say one thing?"

"Be my guest." Renee laughed. "Oh, wait, you are my guest. You sort of started me on this journey, Tori, so please say whatever you want."

"I don't think of Elle as a black woman or my black wife. She's just Elle. And, in all the years I've known you, Renee, I've heard people refer to you as the beautiful, sexy butch or the brilliant butch or the butch with the great singing voice or the one who dresses like a man. I've never heard anyone say Renee the biracial butch."

Beth piped up. "I second all of that. I too have heard you called a lot of things in the years since Gina introduced us, some not so flattering by women you've dumped, but I don't ever remember biracial being applied to you. You may announce it to everyone you meet, but people don't see you through that filter."

Constance spoke into the silence that followed Beth's statement. "I said the exact same thing to Renee. Though I might describe her in many different ways, biracial is not something that has ever come to mind." She smiled and squeezed Renee's hand.

Renee looked around the group, making a point again to meet everyone's eyes.

"Thank you all. I asked and you responded. You've given me a lot to think about. Now, how about more wine?" She grabbed the bottle and filled the glasses thrust at her. "So what will you tell Moira and Megan, Joel?"

He took a sip of the wine she'd just poured for him. "I can see it's not a one-time discussion. We need to have an ongoing dialogue about the issue, about their feelings, and maybe we need to find them a therapist to help them work through their feelings. I'll share some of what we discussed here about the different choices you and Ed have made and why. Is that okay, Renee?"

"That sounds good."

"I can talk with them some while I'm here," Ed said. "It may help them to speak to both of us separately, but whatever you do, I suggest you don't make a big deal of it."

"I agree with Ed, Joel. I think you can talk to them, then maybe he can share his thoughts. And when they're ready, I'll spend some time with them." Renee sat again. "Ed, would it be all right if I call you to talk sometime?"

He removed a card from his wallet, jotted a number on the back and handed it to her. "That's my personal cell on the back. Please call anytime and I hope I may do the same."

She tucked the card into her jacket pocket. "I'd love to hear from you. I'll give you my card before you leave." She felt so close to these people. She was so lucky. Why did she even doubt herself? She'd have to discuss that and the rest of this with Olivia. "I knew talking to you all would help. Well, actually, Olivia, my therapist, knew it and I just obeyed her orders."

Everyone laughed.

CHAPTER TWENTY-FOUR

Renee arrived at Constance's door at five thirty though she'd been invited for dinner at seven. She'd been feeling light-headed all afternoon and thought a nap before dinner would steady her. She hoped Constance wouldn't mind.

Constance opened the door and raised her eyebrows. "You usually dash in at the last moment. Are you really hungry? Or desperate to see me?"

"Always desperate to see you." Renee swayed in the doorway. "But the truth is I'm feeling a little off so I thought maybe you wouldn't mind if I arrived early and took a nap."

"Of course I don't mind." Constance narrowed her eyes. "You look awful. Come let's get you to bed." Renee headed for the guest bedroom. "No, my sketchbooks are strewn all over the bed in there, you can use my bedroom." She sat Renee on the bed, helped her remove her coat, jacket, and tie, unbuttoned the top few buttons of her shirt, pulled off her shoes, and eased her onto the bed. "Would you like some tea, or water or some toast to settle your stomach?"

Renee looked up at Constance, who seemed to be swaying. Her stomach flipped and she quickly closed her eyes. "No, no. I just need rest. Wake me for dinner." She rolled over and was filled with the scent of Constance as her face met the pillow. She smiled. No matter the reason, it was nice to be in Constance's bed.

She woke to moans and someone pulling her pants down. "It's okay, my girl, I'm not trying to take advantage of you so don't fight me." It was Constance. "You have a high fever and I need all your clothes off so I can get you under the covers." Renee tried to open her eyes and make a joke, but she couldn't pull herself back from the darkness of sleep.

It was so hot. Her body was slick with sweat. And she hurt all over. Was she the one moaning? She coughed and couldn't stop. Someone lifted her into a half-sitting position and she caught her breath. Damn, breathing hurt. Actually, everything hurt. Voices. Constance and...Laurie. What was her doctor doing here? Had they had a threesome? She giggled at the thought. The cool thing on her forehead felt wonderful. Strong arms held her. Cool hands gently touched her back, her breasts. Not her breasts her chest. "Open your mouth, love, you need to drink to get better." Why was Constance in her bedroom? She drank the water and swallowed the pills, then gratefully drank more. Moans again. No, not sex, someone in pain.

"She's fine naked, but keep her covered with a sheet and or a light blanket. Her fever is one hundred and three point four and rising. Keep sponging her with warm water, make sure she drinks lots of water, and give her extra strength Tylenol every six hours. If her temperature continues to go up, call me immediately and I'll admit her to the hospital."

Naked? She tried to say no hospital but she couldn't get the words out. Constance and Laurie discussing her, touching her? She didn't feel turned on so why was her body on fire? Had she swallowed sand? Why was her tongue suddenly too big for her mouth? And how did she get naked? Cool hands on her shoulders and lips on her forehead. Maman? "I've got you, Renee, just relax and sleep." Constance.

Damn, they keep telling her to sleep, then they wake her up to force pills into her mouth and drink. Why don't they leave her alone? Who was touching her all over? Ah, it was Constance's gentle voice and her gentle hands soothing and cooling her burning skin. She wanted to touch Constance but she couldn't lift her arm. Her body ached. The voice faded away as she slipped back into the darkness.

Renee opened her eyes. She was lying on her back in a strange room. Where the hell was she? She turned her head. And gazed into the emerald eyes of the woman lying next to her. Constance. She blinked. Was she hallucinating? She tried to sit up but didn't have the strength. She was naked under a sheet. And she smelled of sweat. Really smelled, like she'd been jogging for days. Or had had days of sex without a shower. Shit. What had she done?

Constance put a hand on her cheek. "Hey, you're awake. Welcome back."

Back? What did she mean? Had they had sex and she had no memory of it? Her breath caught. She was having trouble taking in air. She opened her mouth but it was so dry she was unable to get a word out. Constance jumped out of bed, helped her to sit up and held a glass of water to her lips. "It's okay. You've been sick."

The water wasn't cold but it felt wonderful going down. She emptied the glass. Suddenly aware the sheet was pooled around her waist, she jerked it up.

Constance laughed. "I wouldn't worry about that, Renee. Not only have I seen it all before but I sponged your lovely naked body for a day and half to bring your fever down."

Renee flushed. "Fever? How did I get in your bed?"

Constance sat next to her on the bed and put an arm over her shoulder. "Do you remember the girls and I had invited you to dinner?"

"No." Renee rubbed her forehead and tried to recall the dinner. "Yes. I was feeling light-headed so I came early to take a nap."

"That's right. Well, when I came in to wake you, you were tossing and turning, burning with fever and hallucinating. Your fever was much too high so I called Tori and asked for the name of your doctor. She sent Laurie Feldman. I hope it was all right that I called her. I gather she's an ex."

"She is but she's also a friend and my doctor. I thought I dreamed she was here."

"She was real. Apparently you had a very bad case of the flu, high fever, achy muscles, vomiting. She was worried about pneumonia but your fever came down and your breathing cleared so she never tested you for it."

Renee placed her head in her hands and groaned. "Shit Constance, I'm so sorry. Did I vomit all over?"

Constance patted her shoulder. "You were very neat, darling. The first time you were able to stumble to the bathroom and we spent quite a bit of time there, you hugging the toilet, me hugging you while you shivered. The other times you were too weak to walk but I was able to get the wastebasket under you in time."

Just picturing the vomit was enough to make her want to throw up. "Oh, damn. I'm so sorry to put you through that."

Constance waved the apology away. "Don't forget. I'm a mother. I've been through worse than that."

Oh, no. Had she infected Chloe and Cara? The stab of panic she felt at the thought of the girls being so sick surprised Renee. "Did I make the girls sick? And what about you?"

"We're all fine. As soon as I realized you were burning with fever, I shipped Chloe and Cara off to their friend's house. And for some reason, I'm fine."

"I don't know how to thank you. But if you help me find my clothes I'll get dressed and get out of your hair." Renee tried to swing her feet off the bed, but she didn't have the strength. She flopped back.

Constance stood over her, glaring. "You will do no such thing. Laurie said you need at least a week of bed rest, maybe two. And I'm not letting you out of my sight until she says you're okay."

Constance's fierce protectiveness warmed Renee. It had been a very long time since anyone cared enough to take care of her. Was the last time really when Darcy nursed her after a particularly bad stomach virus their sophomore year in college? "How long have I been here?"

"You came Friday evening and today is Thursday. Tori let your assistant Jenna know you were deathly ill and she took care of getting your work covered by your partners and letting your therapist know. Tori and Jenna called every day to see how you were. I don't know whether Tori or Laurie called Francine but she offered to come over and help bathe you to bring down your fever and made me promise to call if I needed her. A number of other women called as well. I have a list when you're ready to see it. Tori sent food for me, and last night she and Elle dropped by with a pot of terrific-smelling chicken soup. Since you're staying, would you like some soup?"

Renee started to object but realized she was so weak she really didn't have a choice. Besides, it would be nice to spend time with Constance. Some time when she was awake. "Now that you mention it, I'm starving." She took Constance's hand. "Are you sure? It's a lot to ask since you've already been waiting on me for a week. I can get someone to help me back to my apartment."

"I'm sure." Constance tapped Renee's nose. "Now let me get you that soup."

After a few tablespoons of soup, she was exhausted. Constance insisted she sleep. That was how the day went—eat a little soup, then sleep. She was able to stay awake and even talk a little while Constance had dinner but soon after she slept again.

The next day Renee was sitting up in bed trying to read something Jenna had sent for her to review. She was feeling stronger but she couldn't really concentrate. She'd have to tell Jenna to have someone else look at it. Constance was sitting in bed next to her sketching. Renee sighed.

"You're still weak. One of your sexy romances would be a better choice of reading matter right now." Constance put her pad down. "The girls will be moving back home after school today. Would you like to take a shower and put on pajamas before they get here?"

Renee raised her eyebrows. "Are you insinuating that I smell or that I shouldn't greet them in my birthday suit?"

"I never insinuate. I'm stating both. Loudly and clearly. If you want them to come into this room, I insist on a shower and clothes. Laurie says if we're careful and I go in with you, you can get out of bed and into the shower."

Renee attempted to look lascivious but the last thing on her mind was sex. "Now that's a picture I can't get out of my mind and an offer I can't refuse. But what will I wear? Your pj's will be too small."

"Don't worry that pretty head of yours. I arranged for Maya to drop off a couple pairs of your pj's."

Damn. "Maya was here?" Her voice went up an octave. Had Maya made a move on Constance while she was out of it?

"Sort of. She called to see how you were and asked if I needed anything. When I mentioned the pj's, she volunteered to retrieve them from your apartment and drop them off with my doorman on her way to some event." Suddenly Constance looked uncomfortable. "Uh, I was wondering. Are you? I mean she has the key to your apartment—"

"We're friends. I have her key too." She loved it when Constance was jealous but she hated seeing her uncomfortable so she tried to introduce a little humor. "Can I trust you won't molest me if we shower together?"

Constance frowned. "Are you ready?" She sounded annoyed.

What an ass. Constance was being so caring and putting herself out to make her comfortable and she was being childish. "I'm sorry. I'm stalling. Even though you've seen me naked before I'm uncomfortable with the idea since we're..." She averted her eyes.

"I understand, Renee. But remember you've been naked in my bed for almost a week and for some of that time I was bathing your naked body every hour to bring your temperature down."

"The fact that you've already seen it doesn't make me feel any better."

Constance sat next to her and took her hand. "You really do need a shower and it's not going to happen without assistance. Do you want me to call someone to help? Maybe Francine would come?"

Renee knew she was being ridiculous. Instead of appreciating everything Constance was doing for her, she was giving the poor woman a hard time. She would just think of Constance as her nurse not…Not what? Not ready to go there Renee sighed. "No. One of my friends is already here offering to help and I'm being a jerk. I'm ready if you are."

Constance eyed her for a second before smiling. "Good girl. Give me a minute to get the bathroom ready." Renee tried not to stare when Constance returned to the bedroom wearing only a tan lace bra and matching bikini panties, or knickers, as she would have said. But she couldn't seem to control her eyes.

Age and motherhood had padded her breasts and hips but with the added pounds she was more curvaceous, even more lovely than Renee remembered.

Constance stood with her hands on her hips. "Come on, bub. Are you going to stare all day or are we going into the shower?"

"Well, you put a luscious fruit in front of a starving woman, what do you expect?" Renee raised her eyes to Constance's face and was happy to see her lips twitch as she tried to hold back a smile.

"Luscious fruit, huh. What woman could resist being described as a luscious fruit? I hope you aren't comparing me to a pear."

Renee pretended to be horrified. "No, no, not a pear. More like a ripe mango, very sweet and juicy, you know how the juices get all over your face when you eat it."

Constance patted Renee's cheek. "Feeling better, are we?"

Renee captured the hand on her cheek. "I could have called you a delicate rose." She kissed Constance's knuckles. "But that doesn't capture the essence of you the way luscious fruit does."

"I'm definitely not a delicate rose but I've never seen myself as a mango either." Constance sniffed the air. "But you smell more like a dozen rotten mangos than a flower of any sort. Shower time." She wrapped her arms around Renee and pulled her up. "Let's stand for a second to steady you."

Renee was all for standing in Constance's arms. It felt natural. And necessary, since her legs were as floppy as cooked spaghetti. "It's not fair that I'm naked and you're covered."

"No pouting." Constance looked up into Renee's eyes. "Pay attention. As weak as you are, I could easily drown you. Now, I'm going to swing around so we're facing the bathroom. Lean on me and we'll slowly walk to the shower."

Renee tried to avoid putting weight on Constance but she needed the support. When they arrived in the bathroom, after what seemed like hours, Constance eased her onto the toilet seat. "Catch your breath before we get in."

Gasping, Renee dropped her head onto the two bath towels on the counter and closed her eyes. She'd never felt so weak, so helpless. And dependent. She used a piece of toilet paper to dab at the tears filling her eyes. "This is harder than I thought. I'm sorry I'm putting you to so much trouble."

Constance put one hand on Renee's shoulder and the other on her cheek. She looked into Renee's teary eyes and leaned in and kissed her. It was sweet, not passionate, and the tenderness did Renee in. A sob escaped. Constance pulled Renee's head to her breasts and ran her fingers through Renee's hair while she sobbed. "It's all right my sweet girl, let it out, you've had a rough time, and you're so used to being on your own that I imagine it's hard for you to accept someone caring for you." As the sobs receded, Constance kissed Renee's hair, then put a finger under her chin and raised her head so they were face-to-face. "Feel better?"

Renee flushed. She reached for more toilet paper, dried her eyes then blew her nose. "I'm sorr—"

Constance spoke over her. "Don't you dare apologize for showing me your feelings. You don't have to be Wonder Woman, always cool and together and in control. It's okay to be needy sometimes. You've been really, really sick. You could have died. Your body needs time to heal. And I'm here, ready, willing, and able to help. I really want to take care of you, Renee. Will you let me?"

Renee was silent, trying to sort through her feelings. Except for therapy, she hadn't sobbed like that since she realized Darcy was committed to Tori and she'd lost her. Or was it after Constance abandoned her. In any case, since Darcy she'd cut off her feelings and run from anyone who cared for her. Now she was drowning in feelings and she wasn't sure what to do with them. But it was clear she couldn't take care of herself, and even clearer that taking care of her made Constance happy. And what was clearest was, though it made her emotional she was enjoying being cared for. The cherry on top was she would get to spend time with Constance. She sighed. Why fight it? "I will. Thank you, my little luscious fruit."

Constance beamed. "Call me whatever you'd like." She handed Renee a toothbrush with toothpaste on it. "Brush." When Renee signaled she was done brushing, Constance put a cup of water on the counter. "Can you stand?" She leaned over. "Put your hands on my shoulders and pull yourself up." She held Renee in front of the sink. "Rinse."

Weak as she was, Renee enjoyed the press of Constance's breasts against her back, the comfort of her arms wrapped around her body and the warmth of her breath on her neck. She took the cup of water Constance had placed on the sink and took her time rinsing her mouth.

Constance loosened her grip. "Okay, let's get on with this shower before you get chilled." She helped Renee turn.

Constance propped her up against the tiles and leaned into her to keep her on her feet. Under other circumstances this position would be a turn-on, but today Renee focused on staying upright. The hot water was restorative and after a minute or two she was able to take on more of her own weight. Constance seemed to sense what she needed. "Can you wash yourself?"

She nodded. Constance handed her a washcloth and soap then stepped back just enough to allow Renee to soap herself, then rinse off. Again Constance seemed to sense that she was tiring. "Give me the washcloth and I'll wash your back." She

pushed Renee against the wall again and leaning in to keep her
upright scrubbed her back then reached for the shampoo. "I'll
do your hair." She quickly shampooed and rinsed Renee's hair,
turned off the water, wrapped Renee in a bath towel, then eased
her back onto the toilet seat. She rubbed Renee's hair with a
smaller towel, used the large towel to dry her and maneuvered
her into her pajamas. By the time Constance dried herself
and dried Renee's hair with the hair dryer, Renee's eyes were
drooping and she could barely sit up. "You're exhausted. You
need to nap but I want to change the sheets. Can you sit here
another few minutes?"

Renee yawned. "Okay. You don't look so energetic yourself.
You've been up taking care of me. Why don't you nap too?"

"Maybe I will." Constance left Renee sitting on the toilet
while she changed the sheets and pillowcases and arranged the
blanket. When the bed was ready, she settled Renee under the
sheets and went back into the bathroom to put on dry clothing
and clean up.

"Oh, oh, hanky-panky."

Renee opened her eyes. Constance was curled around her
holding her close with an arm around her waist and Chloe and
Cara were giggling in the doorway. Damn, Constance must have
decided to leave the bedroom door open. Renee raised herself
onto her elbows and glared. "Shush. You'll wake your mom."

Constance groaned. "Don't worry, I'm awake now. Believe
me girls, there's no hanky-panky here."

"Yeah, Yeah." Chloe and Cara giggled again. "We aren't
blind."

Constance sat up. "And what do you two know about hanky-
panky? Huh? Renee has been very sick and I've hardly slept all
week taking care of her."

"A likely story." More giggles. "Is spooning part of the
treatment?"

"Likely because it's true. And the spooning was an accident.
Renee is weak and tires easily. After her shower she was cold so
I moved close to warm her up and fell asleep. Anyway, if it was

hanky-panky, the door would have been closed to keep you two twerps out."

Renee whispered in Constance's ear. "You should drop it. I have a feeling you can't win this argument."

Constance got out of bed. "Okay, say hello to Renee, then into your room for homework. We'll all have dinner together later."

When they left, Constance muttered. "I hope seeing that I'm fully clothed puts an end to this conversation." She turned and straightened the covers on the bed. "Try to get back to sleep. I'm going to start dinner. We'll eat in here with you, unless you feel up to moving to the kitchen."

"Yes, Maman."

Constance kissed Renee's forehead. She started to straighten, but seeming to have second thoughts, pressed a tender kiss to Renee's lips, then turned with a smug smile, hips swinging gently, and sashayed out of the room. Renee grinned and closed her eyes, enjoying the warmth spreading through her. She could get used to this.

CHAPTER TWENTY-FIVE

It had been exactly two weeks since she'd agreed to let Constance take care of her while she was recuperating, and Renee was feeling terrific. On her own in her apartment she would probably have not eaten or slept as well, and most likely would have gone right back to work instead of taking the time to regain her strength. Besides being good for her health, she'd enjoyed living like a family for the two weeks, the periods of intense connection with Constance, the days when Constance sketched at home or went to her studio to paint while Renee napped, did some work, or, this last week, went to therapy. And, she enjoyed the four of them having dinner together every night, hearing about the girls' day, discussing art and politics and world events. It was wonderful living with her three girls.

Today was the last day of school before the holiday break for Chloe and Cara and Moira and Megan. Erik and Joel had picked the four of them up after school to spend a weekend at their cabin in the Catskill Mountains. Renee and Constance would have the entire weekend to themselves, and Sunday night Renee would go back to her apartment. And she'd be alone again.

They were quiet at dinner. Renee was feeling melancholy about leaving, and Constance was distant, maybe feeling the same.

After they finished eating, Constance, still in caretaker mode, insisted Renee relax in the living room while she cleaned up the meal. Renee stretched out on the sofa with the book she'd started earlier in the week. When Constance came in she settled next to Renee, lifted Renee's head onto her lap and began to run her fingers through Renee's hair. Renee closed her eyes, enjoying the sweet warmth gushing through her. This had been happening more and more. Being touched by Constance, a casual meeting of eyes, the whisper of her sexy English accent, spooning in bed with her at night, and sometimes just watching her sketch or read or cook or talk to the girls turned Renee on. As much as she enjoyed living here, it was getting more difficult each day. They still hadn't crossed the line from friends to lovers, but the better she felt, the more active her libido had become. She was horny day and night, and this week, she'd been having vivid sexual dreams and had taken a lot of cold showers. The last time she'd felt so inflamed with desire she was a college freshman lusting for Darcy. That passion, realizing she was in love with Darcy, had scared the hell out of her and not understanding what she was giving up, she'd rationalized a reason to walk away. That wasn't going to happen this time.

Constance slipped off the sofa. Missing the contact, Renee opened her eyes and was surprised to see Constance kneeling next to her. She kissed Renee's forehead, then her eyes, her nose, her chin, then brushed her lips. Constance's gentle kisses, her sweet breath and the purr of her ragged breathing stoked Renee's already heightened arousal and her eyes fluttered closed again. The next kiss was more insistent. Constance's tongue teased, Renee parted her lips and Constance deepened the kiss. Renee's brain fogged, her body heated and softened, melding with the sofa cushions. Her fever was back.

When Constance's mouth deserted her again, Renee lifted to follow but not finding her, opened dreamy eyes. Constance's gaze was tender as she caressed Renee's face, traced her eyebrows, her cheeks, her lips, her jaw. She kissed Renee's nose. "Renee sweetheart, I'm so very fond of you. I don't want to wait any longer."

Become lovers? Renee hesitated, waiting for the fear and the impulse to run to bubble up. Instead, she felt a rush of anticipation. She swung her legs off the sofa and shifted to face Constance. She was in love with her and wanted desperately to make love to her. But these last few weeks had solidified her feelings, she was certain she wanted the whole family thing with Constance and the girls, not just sex. What did she mean to Constance? What did *she* want? "Um, how fond?"

"Very, very fond." Constance framed Renee's face with her hands. "Will it freak you out if I say, I'm in love with you?"

Renee swallowed. Was she freaked? No. During the two weeks she'd been recuperating, Constance constantly touched her, kissed her frequently, and though she left the bedroom door open, she continued to sleep in the same bed and spoon with her. A few mornings they'd gazed at each other in bed with such intensity, that Renee had almost come. She'd been hesitant to let herself know that Constance was in love with her but she'd felt it.

Constance kissed Renee's lips lightly. "It's all right if you want to wait some more." She gazed over Renee's shoulder. "Or if you still want Darcy."

The pain in Constance's face surprised Renee. But of course she would be insecure about Darcy. "I want you, Constance. I don't want Darcy. I've been in love with you since the night we met, but I was too afraid to let myself know before you disappeared and too afraid to admit it to myself since. I'm madly in love with you. And, I don't want to wait either. I—"

"Are you sure, Renee? I don't want to cock this up."

Suddenly confident, ready to love and let herself be loved, Renee lifted Constance's hands one at a time and kissed each of her palms. "Absolutely sure. I love you and I want to make love with you. I want us to be together. The four of us."

Constance kissed her softly. Renee closed her eyes. Constance held Renee's face between her hands and deepened the kiss.

Renee pulled away. "Bedroom."

Constance moaned as Renee helped her off her knees. "Being on my knees on a hard floor in front of you was a lot easier the last time we did this."

Renee laughed. "We're two smart ladies. I'll bet we can come up with a way to accomplish the same thing on the bed with no pain." She took Constance's hand and led her to the bedroom.

It was strange. They'd had sex and had even made love before. And, more recently, during Renee's illness, Constance had bathed her and touched her intimately. They'd slept and cuddled together for three weeks, and yet Renee felt shy. And from the look on Constance's face, she was feeling the same. Renee sat on the edge of the bed and pulled Constance onto her lap. She kissed each of Constance's knuckles, then her sensitive palm. Constance shivered. Renee tumbled them both onto the bed and side by side they gazed into each other's eyes. Renee brushed Constance's hair away and caressed her face. "I love you." She stroked Constance's lips and inched closer kissing her gently at first then more fervidly, while her hands played Constance's body like an instrument, building their passion so all resistance, all fear, all shyness was forgotten.

Renee pulled away and whispered. "I'd like to undress you, if that's all right."

Hooded eyes popped open, then closed. Constance turned away.

Confused by Constance's apparent change of mind, Renee sat up. "Did I misunderstand, Constance?"

Constance shook her head. She turned to look at Renee. "No. It's just..."

"It's just what?" Renee maneuvered Constance into her lap again. "Talk to me, please. Is it too soon."

"No." Constance shook her head. "I hadn't even realized I was worried about this but I need to tell you that my body is not the same body you had sex with before."

Renee laughed. "You mean you're not twenty-two years old anymore?" She tickled her. "If I wanted a twenty-two year old, we would have said goodbye at the Metropolitan Gala and I would have continued to have meaningless sexual encounters for the rest of my life." She tightened her arms around Constance. "I thought you understood I've been working in therapy to free myself to love you, not some twenty-two-year-old. It's you I want. And you forget I saw you in your bra and bikini panties when you showered me. They were as wet as I was after our shower, and let me tell you if I had been capable of holding my head up, or standing, I probably would have ravished you then and there. It's you I'm in love with."

"You don't mind the stretch marks and the additional weight?"

"Remember, *mon amour*, we French don't have a skinny fetish. I adore your body just as it is."

"I should have known." Constance dried her eyes on her sleeve. "I would love for you to undress me, if you still want to." Her smile was shy as she tucked her face into Renee's armpit.

Renee swiveled, stretched Constance out on the bed, and knelt over her. "I do." She reverently undid each button on Constance's blouse, kissing and caressing the newly exposed area of skin from her neck to her waistband, lavishing considerable attention on the mound of her breasts above the line of the lace of her bra and spending time on her bellybutton. As she tossed the blouse aside Renee fastened her mouth on one of Constance's breasts through her bra and moved her hand under Constance's skirt, running her fingers over the crotch of her bikini panties, then stroking her inner thighs. Constance moaned.

Renee unzipped the skirt, sat back on her knees, pulled the skirt over Constance's hips and threw it aside. Her gaze swept over Constance, the low-cut red lace bra and matching bikini panties, the soft curves, and, yes, a few faded stretch marks. "I may have been too weak to do anything about the feelings you inspired, but I wasn't too weak to be turned on. You are as beautiful as I remembered from our shower, even more beautiful than before." She deposited kisses along the stretch marks, then easing off the red bikinis she dropped them on the floor and buried her face in the patch of glistening golden hair now exposed. Constance smelled and tasted like the spices in the curry she'd prepared for dinner, but now the tang of her arousal filled Renee's senses, fueling her already flaming desire.

Renee hesitated, drawn to Constance's breasts but unable to resist the glistening opening before her. But before she could decide, Constance pulled her up, rolled her over and lay on top of her. "No, let me." She breathed hot breath into Renee's ear then slipped her tongue in. Renee writhed in pleasure. "I see you still like that."

"Oh, God, I do." Renee was breathless. "No one else has ever done that. Did you remember or is it something you always do?"

Constance turned Renee's face so they were eye to eye. "Oh, my lovely girl, I've never done that to anyone else. I remember everything about you, everything about our time together, everything about making love with you. I won't say I thought about you every day but except for a couple of aborted attempts with women early on and the one drunken quickie with Nigel, you've been the only one in my bed, the only one in my heart for the past sixteen years. Our lovemaking, especially the last few times when I knew I was in love with you, replayed in my mind like a favorite movie."

Constance blew in Renee's ear and whispered. "Now that you're really in my bed I want you naked so I can show you what I remember, what I've been imagining. Do it fast or I'll be forced to rip your clothes to shreds." She rolled off Renee.

Renee got to her knees and as she threw her clothes off, she remembered what differentiated Constance, Darcy, and Gina from all the other women with whom she'd had sex. With them she felt free. She could be herself rather than playing the role of the cool, giving, expert lover. With other women, Renee was the giver of orgasms but rarely had been the receiver. But with the three women she loved, multiple orgasms were normal. Also, all three liked to take charge, they gave as good as they got, and making love with them was always passionate, playful, and fun.

Constance toppled Renee and began to explore Renee's body with fingers like butterflies, followed by teeth nipping gently followed by lips kissing softly.

"I forgot you were a biter," Renee panted.

Constance looked up, grinning. "Nipper, not biter, there is a difference. Want me to stop?"

"Oh, god, no, don't stop but I'm close to—"

Constance's head popped up. "Oh no you don't. I haven't even started."

While Constance was distracted, Renee rolled them over so she was on top, quickly unhooked Constance's bra and took a breast in her mouth. She shifted slightly, used her weight to part Constance's thighs and eased her fingers between them.

Constance gasped. "No, wait. Renee. I want...What I've dreamed about is making love to each other at the same time. Do you remember what I liked? I want that for our first time. Please."

Renee grinned. Something else she'd never done with anyone since their last time. "I remember." She kissed Constance, then shifted on the bed so her face was at Constance's crotch, her crotch at Constance's face. She gripped Constance's ass, pulled her close and buried her head in the golden triangle.

Constance sighed as she placed her head between Renee's thighs. "Thank you." Constance's warm breath was followed immediately by her tongue. Renee moaned enjoying the delicious sensations but a pinch to her buttock and a muffled, "no daydreaming," reminded her this was supposed to be a duet, not a solo. She buried her head and put her tongue and lips to work pleasuring Constance. The vigorous pressure of licking tongues and sucking mouths exploded their already burning passion. As the moans from both sides of the intimate sculpture increased in frequency and volume, their bodies slickened with sweat, their breaths came in gasps, and Renee's body tensed on the brink of orgasm waiting for Constance.

As Constance desired, the first time they came, they came together. Then sated, sweaty, and smelling of sex, Renee crawled around until they were face-to-face. Holding each other, they kissed, each tasting herself on the other's lips, then dozed.

Constance woke Renee with kisses and made love to her again, then again, as if she couldn't satisfy her deep need for Renee. With more sleep, Renee roused to make love to Constance. This time they slept wrapped in each other until late morning.

They spent Saturday, day and night, in bed talking about their lives, making love, and snacking or eating light meals. After they'd made love again Sunday morning, Constance faced Renee and traced her features. "I wish we could stay here forever, but I need to shift into mum mode before the girls get home this afternoon and I won't be able to do that with you here. How about we shower and go out for brunch, then you go home?"

"It's not what I want to do but I know I won't be able to keep my hands off you, so let's do it."

They showered and dressed, then spent a long time kissing. Finally, Renee broke away. "If we don't stop now, I'm going to throw you on the bed and make love to you again. And I don't want to do that to the girls, so let's go."

"Okay." Constance kissed Renee. "But before we leave, I have something for you." She went into her closet and came out with a package wrapped in brown mailing paper and tied with string. She handed it to Renee. "I've waited a long time to give this to you. I hope you like it."

Renee sat on the bed. "What is it?"

Constance laughed. "I guess you'll have to unwrap it." She sat next to Renee.

Renee hefted the package. It was two feet by two feet and fairly heavy. She undid the string and slowly peeled the paper off. She was looking at the back of a framed painting. She turned it slowly. It was a remarkable likeness of the two of them at Stanford, sitting up in bed, hair tousled, sheet covering their breasts, obviously having just made love. They gazed at each other with eyes filled with love. Renee was overwhelmed. The tears rushed to her eyes. It took a few minutes for her to be able to speak. "This is gorgeous, Constance. When did you paint it?"

Constance caressed Renee's face. "I sketched it the morning after we last made love. It was how I knew I needed to leave immediately or I'd never let you go. That sketch and the canvas

I'd started were just about the only things I took with me when I flew to London that night. One of my friends packed and shipped everything else later. When I arrived in London I was distraught but I couldn't tell anyone why. I locked myself in my room and worked feverishly to finish it, as if capturing that moment would tie me to you. And in a way, it did. I can't tell you how much time I spent staring at it in the last sixteen years. And not just when I was masturbating. Do you really like it?"

Renee ran her fingers over the images. "I love it. And I love you. Are you sure you want me to have it?"

"Yes, though I hope one day soon it will hang in our bedroom."

Renee laughed. "Did you just propose to me, Lady Constance?"

Constance gazed at the painting. "Yes. Yes, I guess I did. Is that all right? I don't want us to be separated again."

Renee grinned. "It's more than all right. It's fantastic. I accept."

Constance wrapped her arm around Renee's shoulder. "But I'd like to take some time before we tell the girls or anyone else, if that's all right?"

"Yes. But let's not wait too long because I want you and the girls to come to Paris with me for New Year's Eve. Will you?"

"Yes."

"We leave Saturday night. I thought we'd spend Christmas with my family as well as New Year's Eve and Day. But if you want to pop over to London for Christmas or in between, that would be fine too."

Constance seemed shocked. "You made reservations not knowing?"

She'd paid extra for refundable seats but she wanted to be sure they could be together if they wanted to be. "I made them weeks ago, just in case. Does that freak you out?"

Constance caressed her face. "And you're ready, Renee?"

"I am so ready, my love."

CHAPTER TWENTY-SIX

"So I'm here to say, mission accomplished."

Olivia looked amused.

"I haven't given Darcy a thought in weeks. And I'm head over heels in love with Constance."

"And Constance returns your feelings?"

Renee leaned forward. "Constance definitely feels the same. She gave me a gorgeous painting of the two of us based on a sketch she did the morning after we made love, the day she ran back to London. It was the sketch that made her realize she had to leave immediately or she'd never be able to go. Oh, and, she proposed to me."

Olivia was silent for a moment. "Interesting. The proposal sounded to me like an, oh by the way, rather than an excited engagement announcement. How did you respond?"

Renee was surprised at the questions. "I'm really excited about the painting and I said yes of course."

Olivia pressed. "No second thoughts? No fear of commitment?"

Renee was annoyed. Was Olivia trying to put a damper on her news? "No. I love her. This is what I want."

"Have you set a date?"

"It happened so fast that we really didn't discuss it. And actually, at first I thought she was kidding."

"And her daughters are okay with your relationship?"

"I'm sure Chloe and Cara will approve but we, uh, haven't told them yet."

Olivia nodded. "Why not?"

"I knew you'd ask that. It just happened yesterday." Renee ran her fingers through her hair. "I don't know why Constance asked if we could wait but she agreed to go to Paris with me, the three of them, so we'll have to tell them before we leave Saturday night."

"Don't you think it's strange that she asked you to marry her but she doesn't want her daughters to know?"

Renee raised her hands in front of her. "Stop it, Olivia. I'm sure. She's sure. We'll tell the girls this week."

"And what about being biracial and not feeling part of your family, are those issues resolved?"

Renee listened closely for any condemnation in Olivia's voice but didn't find any. She gave it some thought. "I've explored being biracial with you and talking about it with friends helped me clarify my feelings, but I know it's still a crucial issue for me. I think allowing myself to love and be loved is an indication that in some ways I'm no longer crippled by those things, but I feel there's additional work to do on both issues. And I hope you're willing to let me come back to work on them."

"Congratulations." Olivia smiled. "I'll be happy to see you in January. And, I want to hear all about New Year's Eve."

CHAPTER TWENTY-SEVEN

Renee had been busy trying to wrap up things before she left work for two weeks. But she was worried. She hadn't spoken to Constance since they parted early Sunday evening, almost four days. Each time she called, Constance said, 'I love you' then rushed her off the phone with a promise to call later but she hadn't followed through. If they were going to speak to the girls together, they should do it soon to give them time to work out their feelings before leaving for Paris in two days.

She tried to contact Constance on her cell and her landline to invite them all for dinner, not necessarily to speak to the girls but to make sure everything was all right. When she couldn't get through all day, she left work and went to Constance's apartment to see what was going on.

She greeted the doorman when she arrived at Constance's apartment building.

"Hi, please ring Ms. Martindale's apartment to let her know I'm on the way up."

The doorman frowned. "I'm sorry, Ms. Rousseau, the Martindales left for England last night and I was told Ms. Martindale wasn't sure whether they'd be back."

Renee felt as if she'd been sucker punched. Her blood drained and she started to collapse. Strong arms caught her and dragged her to a chair in the lobby. Someone handed her a cup of water. Her head was spinning. This is exactly what happened the last time they got close.

"Are you okay, Ms. Rousseau?"

She sipped the water. "Yes, sorry, I haven't had much to eat today. I guess I got faint. If I can just sit here I'll be fine in a few minutes. Please get me a taxi."

How could Constance do this again? She thought she might vomit.

"Your taxi is here. Can I help you out?" The doorman looked worried.

"Thank you but I think I'm okay. Did I hear you correctly? Ms. Martindale left last night?"

"Yes. Apparently it was a last-minute thing so they were rushing to the airport."

She stood. He took her elbow, escorted her to the cab and helped her in. The sound of a throat being cleared caught her attention. She looked up. The driver was glaring at her in the rearview mirror, obviously waiting for instructions but she couldn't think of what to do. After a few minutes, the driver turned and yelled, "Hey lady, the meter is up to ten dollars. You wanna go someplace or what?"

Her head shot up, suddenly clear. She needed to talk. "East Side, Buonasola Restaurant, please."

By the time the taxi pulled up to the restaurant, she was starting to feel angry.

It was still early so Tori and Elle were able to sit with her and listen. Talking about it dissipated her anger and she ended up feeling helpless again.

Tori broke the silence. "Wow. I get why you're upset, Renee, but think about it. You know she's in love with you. She gave you that painting showing her love. And she pretty much proposed. She must be scared shitless."

Renee glared at her. She hadn't expected Tori to take Constance's part.

Elle took Renee's hand as the waiter arrived with their wine so they were silent as she poured.

"Tori isn't abandoning you, Renee, I think she's trying to tell you maybe you don't have to worry, that it's a natural reaction for someone like Constance who has loved you and dreamed about being with you for years, to panic when it becomes real."

Renee sipped her wine. "I don't understand. This is the same thing she did at Stanford. If she wanted it so badly, why run?"

Tori laughed. "Why did you run from Darcy?"

Renee pushed back from the table. "What does that have to do with Constance?"

Her two friends didn't respond. Renee considered Tori's question. The depth of her love for Darcy, the intensity of their passion, had scared her. And, saying she was too young to be tied down, she'd run. And had kept running for twenty plus years. The only difference between her and Constance, was that Constance didn't give her an excuse. She'd just run from their love and the intensity of their passion. She nodded slowly. "I get it."

Tori patted her hand. "The question, Renee, is what are you going to do about it?"

"What choice do I have?"

Tori squeezed her hand. "Really, that's all you've got? Poor me, I'm helpless. She doesn't want me?"

Renee pulled her hand back and started to stand. "Fuck you, Tori. I thought you'd understand."

Elle took both their hands. "Ladies, this is not the time for dramatics. Tori, you need to stop being provocative. And, Renee, are you going to let the woman you love, the family you love, just walk away?"

Tori jumped in. "And waste another twenty years passively sitting around waiting for her?"

"Tori." Elle's voice was a command to shut up.

Renee rubbed her forehead. "It's okay, Elle. Tori's right. I need to fight for her, to make her come to her senses."

Tori grinned. She raised her glass to Renee. "That's my girl. Go get her. We want to see you all in Paris."

The three of them drank to that, then while the restaurant owners tended to their business Renee ate dinner and thought about what she needed to do to get Constance back. After she paid for dinner and the wine they'd shared, she hugged Tori and Elle. "You two are the best. I can't thank you enough for helping me with this. I hope to see you in Paris with my three girls in tow. Wish me luck."

CHAPTER TWENTY-EIGHT

Renee decided to give Constance some time to think about things, and hopefully, realize she'd made a mistake, so she canceled the three tickets to Paris, but feeling optimistic held on to the three returns with her the week after New Year's. She went to Paris as planned and spent a few days before and after Christmas with her family, renewing her bonds with her brothers and sister and her nieces and nephews. Observing the family dynamic with new eyes, she saw how she was the one who acted as if she didn't belong, not the other way as she'd imagined. Of course. She was the baby and as she interacted with them, she remembered how they'd all doted on her, at least until she turned into a bratty, withdrawn teenager who batted everyone away. For the first time since she was eighteen, she connected with her brothers and sisters, who seemed happy to have her with them.

Christmas Day, sitting around after dinner with her parents and brothers and sister and their spouses, she grabbed a framed photograph off the wall and cleared her throat. All eyes turned to her. "Mom, Dad, Miriam, Alexandre, Auguste, and Nicholas, we all refer to this photograph as the family picture." She displayed it so everyone could see. "Have you ever noticed that I'm not in it?" There was a burst of laughter and then excited conversation as one of her sisters-in-law took the picture, examined it, then passed it around.

Maman answered the unasked question. "That's true, Renee, you weren't born when it was taken. Dad and I discussed taking another when you were about five but by then your sister and brothers were spread out over the world and it was impossible. It wasn't because we didn't love you."

Renee hugged her mom. "I know that logically, but I think somewhere inside of me I've always felt that not being in the photo considered the family picture was symbolic, that I'm not really part of the family." She put her hand up to hold off the protests. "The adult me knows that's not true. I feel very loved and close to all of you, especially this Christmas, but I hope you'll humor me. I would like to have a new family picture taken of just the seven of us. And then I would like for us to have a photograph of the entire family taken each year."

And just like that, a sitting with a photographer was arranged for the next evening. The photographer, a family friend, suggested all seven wear black clothing, and promised she would have framed copies ready before Renee left for the States. They also scheduled a sitting for the entire family New Year's Day when everyone would be in Paris.

Later Christmas night, after her brothers, sister and their families had left, Renee and her mom sat in front of the fire having a nightcap. Feeling her mom's eyes on her, Renee grinned. She'd wondered when the inquisition would begin. "So, Renee, you look different this trip, and I'm happy to say, you were unusually loving with your sister and brothers. What's up?"

Renee sipped her whiskey. "It's Christmas." Deflection rarely helped but you never knew.

"So it is, baby girl." She patted Renee's knee. "But we both know you're dying to let me in on your secret."

And she was right, of course. Ever since Renee had started talking, she had shared her fears, her hopes, her failures, her triumphs, everything, with Maman. Well everything except the time she hated her for being black. "Since I saw you at Darcy's wedding, my life has changed in several very important ways. One, I'm in therapy. Two, I'm in love."

Maman looked confused. "Darcy?"

"No. She's still my best friend, but it's not her." Seeing her mother's arched eyebrows, Renee went on. "Right after the wedding, I started therapy to work out why I was still clinging to Darcy and I discovered a number of things about myself. First, that I wasn't actually still in love with Darcy but I was using her to keep me from committing to anyone. Second, that I felt like an outsider in our family." She held up a hand. "Please Maman, it wasn't you or anyone else in the family. The last few days confirmed for me that it was all in my head." She hesitated to bring up being biracial, but she trusted her mother to help her process it. "Third, that I have unexplored issues about being biracial."

"I wondered about that, Renee, but you never mentioned it so I didn't bring it up. But I did wonder if you were totally comfortable with yourself."

"I am. Yet, I do have feelings about being mixed race..." Renee took her mother's hands. "...feelings I wasn't conscious of until I started working with Olivia, my therapist. I need to talk about it with you in more detail while I'm here, but there's something else I want to talk about tonight, if that's all right."

"Of course, it's all right. But after you and I have our private talk about being biracial, I'd like to have one with the whole family. As far as I know, it's not an issue for your brothers and sister, but some of your nieces and nephews are lighter-skinned, some as white as you, and it might be healthy for them to express their feelings about it as well."

Overwhelmed with love for her mother, Renee swiveled and hugged her. "I love you, Maman."

"And, I you, baby girl." She kissed Renee's forehead, then leaned away so she could see her face. "So what's more important than the very basic issue of who you are?"

Renee laughed. Maman always got it. Being biracial was the core of her being but they weren't going to solve that problem tonight. "Right after I started therapy to free myself of Darcy, the only woman I've ever had strong feelings for besides Darcy and Gina, serendipitously reappeared in my life."

Maman smiled. "Ah, the universe works in strange ways. Was it the English girl from Stanford, Lady somebody?"

Renee's jaw dropped. "How do you know that?"

"You told me, of course. Don't you remember calling me in the middle of the night from California? You were brokenhearted that you found someone you could love and she walked out on you without saying goodbye."

Renee was flabbergasted. She had no memory of having admitted her feelings for Constance to herself at that time. Or, of talking to her mom, or anyone for that matter, about her feelings for Constance and about being dumped. Had she just shoved it away so she could move on and pretend that she would have dumped Constance if Constance hadn't dumped her first? Maybe that's why she'd rarely thought about Constance in all the years they'd been separated. Maybe the loss after letting herself love again was too hard to bear? Fodder for Olivia.

"Yes, Lady Constance Martindale. She said she was in love with me at Stanford but left because of the obligations of being a royal. But we've been working on being together since we found each other again."

Maman listened as Renee told her the story in detail, how they'd gotten together, the intensity of their lovemaking and their connection, and how Constance had suddenly disappeared again. "I wonder if it's the same problem as before, the royal issue."

Before responding, her mom got up to refill their brandy glasses, then sat next to Renee again. "From what you've told me, I'd say Constance had worked the royal issue through before coming to New York City. You say she and her husband had a loving friendship but do you know whether Constance has ever had a deep, loving relationship, one as passionate as it seems the two of you have?"

Renee rotated her glass in her hand, thinking back over her discussions with Constance. "I think our relationship at Stanford was the strongest she'd ever had and it was no way near what we were feeling the second time around."

"Is it possible Constance was frightened by the intensity of her feelings for you?"

Renee sipped her brandy. "Tori suggested the same thing. You're both right. I'm Constance's first and only love. No wonder she ran."

"Another possibility, Renee, is that Constance felt exposed after giving you the painting, a very personal and raw symbol of her love for you. Did you reciprocate in any way to show her the depth of your feelings for her?"

Renee's stomach plummeted. "Maybe not." She thought about her response to Constance's indirect proposal. She'd almost thought Constance was kidding so she'd probably come across as off-handed and not truly loving. How in the world could she be so thoughtless? She'd told herself she was giving Constance space but was she also frightened? She should have rushed over the next afternoon to reassure Constance, to let her know how much she loved her. Did Constance not trust that Renee really loved her? Is that why she ran? "I got her a beautiful necklace for Christmas. Will that do it?"

Maman thought about it. "Her gift was not obligatory like a Christmas present. It was extremely personal and showed her love for you."

Renee cringed at her thoughtlessness. "Do you think I can make it up to her?"

"I believe you can." Maman chewed her lip. "Are you ready to commit to Constance? I mean really ready? Take a minute to think about it."

"I don't have to think, Maman, she's the one for me."

"Then you have to let her know that by getting down on your knee and proposing."

Proposing. Why hadn't she thought of that? "You are right as usual, Maman. I'll buy a ring and propose. Hopefully, she'll say yes."

"Are you sure, baby girl? You've never shown any interest in marriage. Are you ready to make a lifetime commitment?"

"A lifetime with Constance and the girls is exactly what I want." And it was about time she told Constance. "I want a special ring, not a run of the mill engagement ring or a plain gold band. Will you go shopping with me tomorrow?"

After finding nothing special at three jewelry stores, Renee was ready to give up but Maman suggested they try the studio of one of her artist friends who also made jewelry. And it was there she found a wide beaten gold band with a large emerald surrounded by diamonds and rubies, a ring she felt embodied Constance's beauty, fragility, and strength. She hoped it also conveyed her love and desire for Constance. She couldn't resist the matching earrings. And then to seal the deal she'd bought rings for Chloe and Cara, gold with small rubies, their birthstone.

Now, the third day after Christmas, waiting in the Gare du Nord to board the Eurostar for London, she checked her ticket, confirmed that the paper with the address of Constance's London home was in her pocket, and, at least fifty times, touched the rings to make sure they were still where she'd put them. Once on the train, she stowed her suitcase and the bag with the Christmas presents she'd dragged from New York and tried to relax and formulate what she would say to convince Constance of her love and her desire to be with her. All she could think of was, I love you, I want to be with you forever, which sounded kind of boring. Two and a half hours later she got off the train in St. Pancras station and walked a while trying to steady her nerves. So much was riding on this next conversation and she was afraid she would screw it up. Remembering her mother's advice, "Let Constance know how much you love her and she won't be able to resist," bolstered her courage. She crossed her fingers and hailed a taxi to Kensington.

Standing on the sidewalk, she thought she saw the curtain in an upstairs window move but she might have imagined it.

In fact, other than that slight movement, the house appeared empty. Maybe she'd gotten this wrong. Maybe Constance wasn't in England. Maybe she'd gone to Mexico or Tahiti or Australia. She didn't think it was possible for her heart to beat so fast yet clutch in fear, but it did. What if she never found Constance? Or worse, what if she found her and Constance had realized it was all a fantasy and she didn't really love Renee? It was freezing but sweat was rolling down her back. She started to shiver, not from cold, but from the certainty of rejection. Then she caught herself. She was doing it again, expecting to be rejected even though when she pushed those nasty voices aside, she knew, in her heart, that Constance loved her and wanted to be with her. She also knew that the intensity of Constance's feelings, the desire to merge with the loved one, had panicked her and caused her to run for home. She understood. She was here, and, she would follow the plan. "Let Constance know how much you love her and she won't be able to resist." She prayed Maman was right as usual.

She raised her eyes once more and this time the curtain did move and two blond heads bobbed in the window. With big grins, they waved her in. Her heart flipped. Chloe and Cara were happy to see her and that was half the battle won. What had Constance told them? She took a deep breath. She loved Constance and she loved the twins and she would fight for them. She marched up the steps and stared at the knocker, a coat of arms, most likely Nigel's family crest. What if Constance had decided she really did want the life of a royal? Renee wouldn't fit in with that life plan. Olivia should be happy. This time she knew she wouldn't fit in because she was a woman, not because she was biracial. She heard laughter and raised voices inside. She lifted her hand to knock but the door was opened by a white-faced Constance who looked ready to puke.

Renee smiled at Chloe and Cara, standing a little way back on the staircase in the entry hall behind Constance. When she focused on Constance again she was shivering and appeared to be about to close the door. Not the welcome she'd hoped for. Would Constance actually slam the door in her face? Better safe than sorry, she positioned her foot so the door couldn't totally close. "Hey there." Renee kept her voice soft so she wouldn't frighten Constance.

"Hi." Constance sounded as if she hadn't spoken in a while and now that Renee looked closely her eyes were red and swollen.

"Muuuum, it's cold. Close the door or you'll get sick," one of the girls complained.

Constance glanced over her shoulder at Chloe and Cara, but she stood there shivering. This time it was definitely Chloe and her voice was almost a command. "Close the door, Mum. It's rude to keep Renee standing in the cold."

The call to politeness seemed to wake Constance. "Yes, of course. I'm sorry, would you like to come in?"

Renee nodded and moved quickly into the entryway. The girls rushed down and threw themselves at her, both talking excitedly at the same time so she didn't really get what they were saying. She hugged them and kissed them both on the cheek but her eyes kept returning to Constance. "Do you think we could talk, Constance?"

Constance glanced around seeming to just remember where they were. "I…all right. Let's go into the garden room." She took Renee's arm and started walking but realizing her daughters were following, she stopped. "Please give us a little privacy, girls."

The twins looked from Constance to Renee and back as if trying to gauge what was happening. Maybe Constance hadn't told them anything. Grumbling, they went upstairs. Constance led Renee to the rear of the house into a room with three walls of glass filled with plants and flowers, hence, she supposed, the name.

"I just made a pot of tea. Would you like a cup or I could make coffee?"

She wanted to get this over with but her throat was dry. "Tea would be fine."

So far, Constance had avoided looking directly at Renee so while she poured the tea from the steeping pot, Renee studied her. Thinner than the last time and tired in an exhausted rather than a sated way, she had dark circles under her red and swollen eyes. Her hand trembled as she handed Renee the cup of steaming tea. Renee blew on the tea, sipped, then put it down on a nearby table. "I'm happy to see you, Constance."

"Why are you here?" Constance walked to the window and stared into the barren garden, shoulders humped, her back to Renee.

It hurt Renee to see Constance in so much pain. Maybe she was totally wrong. Maybe Constance wasn't just scared. Maybe their lovemaking had been disappointing for her. Maybe she didn't want to have anything to do with Renee. She should leave. No wait. This wasn't about her. A look at Constance was enough to see it was about Constance, her pain, her issues. She'd come here with a purpose and she wasn't going to leave until she'd at least professed her love and offered the ring.

"I'm here because I'm in love with you." Renee moved behind Constance, gently turned her so they were facing each other. "I believe the relevant question is, what are *you* doing here?" Renee cupped Constance's face. "Does this have to do with being a royal?"

Constance shook her head.

Suddenly aware of noise behind a nearby door, Renee assumed Chloe and Cara were eavesdropping and positioned herself as a shield in front of Constance to keep their conversation private. "Do you love me?" She pitched her voice low and waited for a response that seemed to take forever.

Constance nodded. A tear dribbled down and bounced off her nose, then the tears came full force.

"I'd like to hold you. Would that be all right?"

Constance stepped closer and wrapped her arms around Renee's waist. Renee returned the favor, pulled her close, and rested her head on the top of Constance's head. Progress. Constance sighed and sank into Renee, melding their bodies. Renee was silent, giving Constance time to pull herself together.

A few minutes went by before Constance pulled away and looked up at Renee. "I'm afraid I'll never measure up to Darcy in bed, or anywhere. And I'm sure you'll figure out it's still Darcy you want."

"Did you think I was lying about discovering in therapy that I hadn't been in love with Darcy all those years but used the idea of loving her as a shield?"

Constance shook her head.

"And did you think after confessing that I love you, after spending that glorious weekend in bed with you, I would dump you and go back to meaningless sexual liaisons while I waited another twenty or more years for Darcy to divorce her wife?"

Constance almost smiled. "It does sound kind of dumb."

"It is dumb." She kissed Constance's temple. "Constance, you are one of the smartest women I know, but you couldn't be more wrong about this. It's you I love, not Darcy. It's you I want, not Darcy. I'm hurt that you thought I was thinking about Darcy while making love to you. If you felt I wasn't there with you one hundred and ten percent, I failed as a lover."

"No, you didn't fail as a lover." Constance tightened her hold on Renee. "It's me, Renee. I've never felt so loved as I feel by you. And I've never loved anyone as deeply, as passionately as I love you. I was overwhelmed by the intensity of our lovemaking. I felt what I think a drug addict must feel. All I wanted was you, to be with you to the exclusion of the world, even Chloe and Cara. I had to get away so I could breathe. I'm sorry."

"Our lovemaking was amazing and more intense than any I've ever experienced. It's understandable that it scared you, Constance."

"But why aren't you scared?"

Renee cleared her throat, not sure how honest to be. "Actually, what you're feeling is pretty much what I felt with Darcy, and as you know, I ran too. So loving you as much as I do, the intensity and the depth of our passion didn't surprise me. I wanted to run to you, not away."

Constance took a minute to consider what Renee said. "You think it's because you're my first and only true love?"

"I do." Renee slipped to her knee and took Constance's hand in hers. She kissed her palm. "Lady Constance Elizabeth

Martindale Worthington, I love you more than words can say and I want to be with you, and with Chloe and Cara, forever." As she extracted the ring from her pocket, she wondered if Constance had heard the gasps and the rustling from the door to the room behind her. "The painting you gave me is the most extraordinary gift I've ever received. It showed me how deep your love is and I apologize for failing to communicate how in love with you I am and how much I want us to be together as a family but I hope you can hear me now." Renee held the ring out. "Will you marry me?" Constance's eyes widened but she didn't pull her hand away so Renee slipped the ring on her finger.

Constance burst into tears again. The girls burst into the room. "Say yes, Mummy, say yes." Nearly knocking Renee over, they embraced her and Constance.

Constance seemed to be stunned. She held the hand with the ring in front of her, reached out to touch Renee's face as if to confirm she was real, really there. Renee ached in the silence, afraid she'd misunderstood.

After what seemed like hours, Constance breathed, "Yes." She smiled. "Yes I will marry you." She leaned down and kissed Renee. "Of course, I can't speak for Chloe and Cara."

Constance was joking. The tension drained from Renee.

"We will, we will." The girls pulled Constance toward them and the four of them toppled onto the floor. Renee struggled under them and finally was able to get the other two rings out of her pocket. She got to her knee again. "Cara and Chloe, will you accept my proposal?"

For once the girls didn't check in with each other. "Yes," they said simultaneously. She put a ring on each of their fingers and kissed their cheeks.

Constance beamed from the floor. "Can I get a kiss, bub?"

"Always happy to accommodate you, Lady Constance."

CHAPTER TWENTY-NINE

"Are we going to Paris then?" The girls stood with their hands on their hips, and the same expectant expression on their faces. Would she ever get used to how they mirrored each other without a word of discussion or how like Constance they looked and acted?

"If we're still invited." Constance flushed. "Are we, Renee?"

"Absolutely. I won't go without you."

"But Mum didn't tell us about New Year's Eve so we don't have anything to wear," Chloe moaned.

Renee put a hand up to prevent Constance from answering. "Please get the shopping bag I left in the hall."

Chloe ran out and returned with the bag.

Renee handed a large box to each of the girls. "Merry Christmas."

"Thank you."

Constance looked stricken. "We left yours in New York City."

"No, we didn't, Mum," Cara said. "When you said to pack all our presents, we didn't know what was happening so we included the ones we bought for Renee." Chloe put her box down. "I'll go get them." She ran from the room again.

When Chloe returned she placed the bag next to Constance and picked up her box. "Can we open our presents now?"

Renee answered. "Yes, I'd like to see if you like what I bought you."

Wrapping paper flew as the twins raced to open their gifts. "Ooh, a pretty dress," Chloe pulled the lavender garment out of the bag.

"Not dress, Chloe. Renee bought us gowns." Cara's voice shook with excitement. "Let's try them on."

Constance reached for Renee's hand. "The gowns are beautiful. How did you figure out their size?"

"I peeked in their closet in New York one day when you were all out. I wanted to be sure of the size and confirm they always wear the same thing in the same color."

"How do we look?" The girls walked in front of them, twirling as if on a fashion runway.

"You're both gorgeous," Renee said. "We can shop for shoes and bags in Paris."

"What do you think, Mum?" Cara asked.

Constance walked around the girls. "I think the dresses fit you perfectly and you both look lovely. Maybe you should thank Renee?" She gave them both a gentle push.

"We love them, Renee. They're so pretty and so grown up. Thank you, thank you." They spoke at the same time as they often did when excited and rewarded her with hugs and kisses.

Renee was thrilled they liked the gowns. She'd spent a lot of time shopping for them. She pulled a small box out of the bag and handed it to Constance. "Merry Christmas."

Chloe elbowed her sister. "We recognize that blue paper, don't we Cara?"

"Thank you." Constance shook the box. "I guess it's not a matching gown. And it's not a ring since you've already given me one. Doesn't look like shoes. Hmm."

"Muuum." The girls stood in front of her in their gowns. "Please open it."

She slowly unwrapped the box and lifted the cover. She gasped. "This is beautiful." She turned. "Please put it on me." Renee draped the emerald necklace over Constance's neck and hooked the catch and the safety.

"That's beautiful, Renee. It matches our eyes," Chloe said, with a mischievous grin.

"Don't be getting any ideas about borrowing it, Chloe," Constance teased as she went to the mirror to see for herself. "Oh, it's absolutely gorgeous, Renee, thank you." She pulled Renee up and kissed her.

"Yuk, Mum, save it for later. Can we give Renee her presents now?" Cheeky Chloe again.

Constance pulled back, but kept her arm around Renee's waist. "Go on."

Renee slowly unwrapped the first gift the girls handed her. "I love this color blue." She fingered the silk tie. "And the shirt and matching tie are beautiful." She unwrapped another. "Hmm, three thousand pieces. You're all going to have to help me with this jigsaw puzzle. It looks really difficult." She reached for a small package and tore the paper. "Personalized guitar picks. Oh boy, I'm always losing my picks. Thank you." She picked up another present. "Does this mean you like doing the Sunday *New York Times* crossword puzzle with me? Now we have a whole book of them. I love it." The last package was large and looked like a framed print. She tore the paper and stared at the framed collage of pictures of the four of them in various configurations in various places. She was so moved, her eyes filled and she couldn't speak for a few seconds. She stood and kissed them. "You don't know how much this means to me. I love you both."

"We love you too, Renee," the girls said.

Constance cleared her throat. "Hello. Can I join this party?" She handed Renee a box. It could have been another shirt or perhaps pajamas but it was pretty light.

Renee took a deep breath. She looked at Constance. Their eyes locked.

"Go on, Renee, we want to see if you like it." The girls had taken off their gowns and were looking at her expectantly.

Her gaze shifted to the box in her hand. She slowly removed the wrapping paper and opened it. Inside was a handwritten letter and a very small box, obviously a ring box, wrapped in the same blue Tiffany paper as the necklace she'd given Constance. "Should I open the box first or read the letter?"

"The box." Constance's voice was soft and shaky.

Good, they were both nervous. She removed the paper and opened the black leather box. A ring. An emerald surrounded by three small diamonds set in a wide gold band, winked at her. It was a perfect match for her, for her style, for her essence. She immediately put it on and leaned over to embrace Constance. "I love you. Thank you."

"Do you like it? I designed the band and the setting."

"It's perfect." She extended her hand, admiring the ring.

"Read the letter, Renee." Cara handed it to her.

My dearest Renee,

I give you this emerald ring as a symbol of my deep love for you.

Many properties attributed to the emerald through the centuries seem appropriate for us. It is considered the stone of love. It is thought to be protective of the heart and to give the wearer the courage to love and be loved. It opens and activates the heart and the heart chakra, giving the wearer the strength to share her love with those who understand and appreciate her. It also helps the wearer express love, devotion, and adoration.

Other properties attributed to this lovely green stone are the support of truthfulness, which means living your life according to the truth in your heart, thereby earning the trust of others and enjoying the blessings of domestic bliss and a long-lasting relationship.

These are all the things I wish for us.

Renee, my love, I have never felt for anyone what I feel for you. That is the truth in my heart and I hope to live it every day. It is both exhilarating and terrifying.

All my love,
Constance

Renee was overwhelmed. Obviously this had been written before Constance ran. She pulled Constance into a hug and kissed her deeply. "Are you sure?" she whispered in Constance's ear.

"I am now. I'm sorry I panicked but I was terrified. I didn't know what to do with those feelings."

"All right. Enough mushy stuff," Chloe said. "Are we going to Paris tomorrow? Should we pack?"

"Oh, fuck." Constance jumped up.

"Language, Mum." Chloe again.

"Sorry. I just remembered we're supposed to have dinner with the Grandees tomorrow night." She glanced at Renee. "My parents and Nigel's didn't expect us for the holidays so they've been in Scotland and we haven't seen them yet. They're coming back tonight."

The blood drained from Renee. "Yes, the Grandees, I remember."

She hadn't thought about Constance's coming out. Though Constance had told her parents she was a lesbian before she left for New York, it hadn't been a real issue because she was still mourning Nigel's death and wasn't with a woman. Now that had changed. Would Constance want to pretend she was just a friend and hide their relationship? She'd been out forever and she wouldn't hide now. Besides, what would the twins think? Rather than deny who she is by denying their relationship, she'd go to Paris and Constance and the girls could join her later, but she wouldn't feel good about it.

"Can you come with us, Renee?" Cara asked.

With the clarity of youth and the openness of their generation, Chloe and Cara had no idea how difficult it would be for Constance to confront her parents and in-laws. Constance looked ready to throw up. Renee waited for Constance to explain but she remained silent. "I don't think I can, Cara. I'll go to Paris tomorrow. The three of you can follow whenever you can get away."

"No, you…" Cara stopped midsentence. She touched Chloe's arm. Perhaps one of their silent communications. The two of them turned to Constance.

Renee stared out the window trying to hold on to the fact that Constance loved her, had exchanged rings, and would, hopefully, not cave to family pressure. The silence was excruciating.

"Renee, please stay and join us for dinner tomorrow evening. I'd like to introduce you to your future in-laws."

Renee turned to Constance. She didn't have to ask whether she was sure. Given that dazzling smile and judging by the strength of her voice, her royal straight posture, and the determined lift of her chin, Lady Constance Martindale Worthington was ready to take on the world, her royal world. "I'd love to." *Just as much as I'd enjoy chewing on some broken glass.*

"My brave girl." Constance embraced her. "But springing you and our relationship on them wouldn't be fair to them. And, no fun for you. Or, the rest of us. I'll call them to let them know you're coming and explain who you are to me and to Cara and Chloe."

"Will they be upset because of daddy?" Chloe took Cara's hand.

"It's more likely they'll be upset by my relationship with Renee, my darlings. I told them I was a lesbian before we left England, but knowing it in the abstract is different than seeing me with Renee and learning we're going to marry. It's possible they'll disown me and not want to see me. But if they want me to come to dinner, they'll have to accept Renee and our relationship. Do you understand?"

"We're not babies, Mum. If they don't want Renee, we won't go either." Chloe's determined chin mirrored her mother's.

Renee blinked to block the tears that rushed to her eyes. "I appreciate the sentiment. While this is all hypothetical right now, I would never ask you to give up your grandparents on my behalf."

"But you're our…" Cara looked at Chloe as she sought the word to express who Renee was to them. "Um, our second mum?" Cara touched Renee's arm. "So if they're not willing to accept that we're a family we'd be playacting to humor them, and that would feel awful in so many ways."

Renee could only whisper. "Thank you."

Constance hugged Chloe and Cara. "Thank you for your love and support."

"But if we're all invited can Chloe and I still spend the afternoon with all the Grandees? We haven't seen them in so long."

"Of course." Constance took a deep breath. "Wish me luck." She left the room to call her mum.

The phone call turned out to be several phone calls. After her mum, Constance spoke to her dad, then to Nigel's mum and dad. Two hours later they were all invited to dinner the next evening. After some discussion they decided to shop for proper shoes for New Year's Eve and then go out to dinner.

The girls were ready when the Mercedes appeared in front of the house at one p.m. the next day. With quick kisses for Constance and Renee, they dashed out the door, each holding a package.

Renee sat next to Constance on the sofa. "Do you think the girls will be all right?"

Constance laughed. "Don't worry about them. The Grandees adore them and will eat them up." She flashed a wolfish look. "And speaking of eating up, we have a few hours to ourselves so what do you say—"

"What did you have in mind, you dirty girl?"

"Come along, let me show you."

Hours later, they showered and were dressing. Though Renee had brought mostly casual clothing to London, she'd learned from her business travel to always be prepared, so she'd also packed a suit, a dress shirt, a tie, and dress shoes, clothing that would be appropriate to meet the in-laws. Now, looking into the mirror while knotting her tie, Renee watched Constance slip into a slim green dress that brought out the sparkle in her eyes, the soft mounds of her cleavage and the curves in her figure. The glint of the emerald on the ring she'd given Constance reminded her of the matching earrings. She dug into her bag and dangled them in front of Constance. "In the excitement yesterday I forgot to give you these. They would look nice with that dress."

Constance's eyes widened as she reached for the earrings. "Oh my, they match my ring." She held one up to her ear and looked in the mirror. "They're gorgeous. Have I told you lately that I love you?" She tilted her head from side to side as she slipped an earring in each ear then gazed in the mirror admiring them. "They're perfect."

Renee moved behind Constance and whispered into her ear. "You are perfect. So sexy, so beautiful."

Constance leaned back into Renee's arms. "Thank you."

Renee rested her chin on Constance's head. "Are you nervous?"

"A little. But for thirty-eight years I've lived the life they chose for me. Now I'm determined to live the rest of my life my way and I refuse to hide our love. I'll deal with whatever they throw at us. What about you?"

"I was really nervous when I thought you were going to want me to hide. I'm a little nervous about meeting all four at once, but I'll handle them. And be polite about it."

Constance turned in Renee's arms. "I don't want to hide you. I just want to stay home and make love all day and night." She kissed Renee. "We'd better go before I change my mind."

They held hands as they walked up the steps to Nigel's parents' mansion. A butler answered the door and greeted Constance effusively, at least effusively for an English butler. He took their coats and directed them to a drawing room. As they walked through the house, Constance took Renee's hand and whispered, "I love you."

The four grandees and the twins stopped talking when Constance and Renee entered the room. After a few seconds of silence, the grandees converged on Constance. This was the first time they were seeing her since she and the girls had flown to New York. The four of them took turns hugging and kissing Constance and remarking at how wonderful she looked. Renee recalled how thin and pale Constance had been when they'd met at the Metropolitan Gala, and now with a little more weight, some color in her cheeks, and love in her life she seemed to glow from within even as she faced the parents and in-laws she feared might reject her for wanting to live an authentic life.

During the excited greetings, the girls migrated to Renee and stood one on each side of her, with an arm through hers, as if to reassure her of her place. Or, maybe, to protect her? Finally, when Constance had been greeted with more enthusiasm than Renee expected, she moved to Renee's side. "I'd like you all to meet my fiancé, Renee Rousseau. Renee, my parents, Anne and Harry, and my parents-in-law, Elizabeth and George."

Renee extended her hand. "Pleased to meet you." She was shocked when, rather than shaking her hand, each of the Grandees pulled her into a hug. Later, sitting on a sofa between Constance's mother and mother-in-law during pre-dinner drinks, Renee commented that she hadn't expected to be welcomed so warmly. The two women smiled and one of them handed her a photo album that Chloe and Cara had presented each of them with earlier in the day. The pictures started the day Constance, Chloe, and Cara left London for New York City and went through yesterday with the four of them smiling and glowing in London. Each photo was annotated to record what was happening before, during and after it was taken. It was clear that the girls and Constance were all sad, withdrawn, thin, and miserable when they arrived in the US. The photos of the early days, of three of them enrolling in school, in their apartment and Constance in her studio continued to show a depressed and unhappy family. But soon after Renee first appeared in the pictures, they started to smile and eventually laugh. All three gained weight, brightened, and looked happy. Even in the first pictures of Renee at Constance's gallery opening, the connection between them was obvious as was their love as time passed. Photos of the four of them showed a happy family until Constance ran from Renee and took the girls to London, where the three of them looked miserable and depressed again. The pictures, taken yesterday after the reunion, showed Constance and Renee radiating love and Chloe and Cara looking jubilant.

Anne, Constance's mom, patted Renee's hand. "How could we reject you? Chloe and Cara haven't stopped talking about how wonderful you are. And we could see in the photos that when you came into their lives the three of them transformed from shadows of themselves back to who they were before Nigel's death. It's not the life I would have chosen for Constance, but she's a grown woman and you obviously make her happy. Happier than I've ever seen her, if truth be told."

Renee dabbed at the tears filling her eyes. "I adore the three of them and I want to make them happy."

Constance appeared. She frowned at the two women flanking Renee. "What have you said to make her cry?"

Renee laughed as she stood to embrace Constance. "Only nice things, I assure you."

"Oh. Sorry, Mums, I misunderstood. Actually, I was just coming to tell you that dinner is about to be served." She took Renee's hand and led them to the table.

Renee was seated between the dads, facing Constance and the girls. She was not surprised to be politely questioned about her financial situation over the several courses of dinner. After assuring himself she wasn't a fortune hunter, Constance's dad relaxed. But Nigel's dad persisted to gently probe for details of how and when she and Constance met. Was he trying to prove that Constance had been unfaithful? She wasn't sure whether Constance had told the Grandees about their relationship at Stanford but they had nothing to hide so full disclosure was the way to go. "We met at Stanford and had a brief affair before Constance flew back to England."

"I see," George said. "And how often did you see each other after that?"

"Never. Until we met again in New York City."

George shifted in his chair slightly to look directly at her. "Surely you kept in touch. It's so easy these days with things like e-mail, Google, and social media. I assume you planned to meet at that gala in New York City. Surely it wasn't a coincidence."

Renee looked into his eyes. "If you're wondering whether Constance was faithful to Nigel, you'll have to ask her. But I can tell you she wasn't unfaithful with me. We had absolutely no contact after she left Stanford and our meeting earlier this year was a total coincidence. Believe me, when I found out that Constance had been married to a man and had two teenage girls, my instinct was to run as fast as I could."

George smiled for the first time. "What stopped you?"

She hesitated, wondering how transparent to be, but once again she went for honesty. "I was shocked when Constance disappeared from Stanford without saying goodbye. Neither of us acknowledged the intensity of our connection and I think we were both scared by it, she because of her commitment to Nigel, me because I'd never let myself feel what I felt for her. I was so self-protective that I buried my feelings and convinced myself she didn't matter to me, but the minute I saw her at that Gala, all my feelings for her rushed back and I knew I wanted to be with her. And though I hadn't bargained for two teenagers, I fell in love with the girls as soon as I met them."

"Thank you for being honest." George swiped a tear from his eye. Then with a glance across the table at Constance and at his wife to his left, he leaned in and whispered. "I admit I'm not really comfortable with this same-sex thing. Constance told us that she and Nigel loved each other but weren't in love, that theirs was a marriage of convenience forced on them by the four of us parents. She said they were happy but each of them was anxious to be free once the girls turned eighteen. I've struggled with the fact that I forced my son to hide himself from me, that I never knew the real Nigel. I'm so sorry he never got to fully live his life and be truly happy." He pulled a handkerchief out of his pocket, blew his nose and surreptitiously blotted his eyes. "I love Constance like a daughter, and I'm determined to not make the same mistake with her. I can't promise I might not be offensive on occasion, but I can promise I will try and I will do my best to support you both in your new life."

Renee choked up at the acceptance by these very human, down-to-earth people she'd always scoffed at as, "the royals."

"Hey, things are looking very serious on that side of the table." Constance grinned. "Do you need to be rescued, Renee?"

All eyes turned to her. "No, I'm fine. We're just getting to know each other." She looked around the table. These four people, her in-laws, were so much more than she'd expected.

"So how's the painting going, Constance? The four of us were so proud to read the reviews of your New York debut." Constance's dad glowed with pride.

"It's going well. Renee's dad likes the slides I sent him so much he's offered to do a joint show with me in New York or London or Paris, my choice."

The Grandees turned to Renee and not getting an answer to the unspoken question, they looked at Constance.

"Oh, sorry, Renee's dad is Alain Rousseau."

"Oh, how wonderful," Constance's mum said. "We met him and Natalie at his last show in Paris. Such warm and genuine people. We were surprised to learn she's…" She stopped talking while the butler cleared the dishes in front of her. Renee tensed, wondering whether she would comment on her mom's color and her being biracial would come up. As the butler carried the tray out of the dining room, Constance's mum turned to Renee again. "We were surprised to learn she's a professional musician. What a lovely woman."

Renee's tension bled away. Maybe her race wasn't an issue for anyone but her, not, at least, for the people she chose to be with. Her mother's final words when she spoke to her last night after they were invited to dinner with the Grandees popped into her mind. "If you like them and think they'll fit, invite them to stay with us for New Year's Eve."

She glanced at Constance, and as if she saw the question, Constance walked around the table, hugged Renee and whispered in her ear. "It's up to you. Invite them, if you're sure."

Renee cleared her throat. "I know it's kind of short notice, but then I never thought I'd meet the four of you." She smiled. "We'd love for you to join us in Paris for New Year's Eve and day. Friends of mine are hosting a party, dinner and dancing at a hotel to ring in the New Year and my parents are hosting a brunch New Year's Day. You'd have to stay with my mom and dad since all the hotels are booked up, but they have plenty of bedrooms and my mom told me to invite you if you seemed, um, friendly."

Renee was suddenly draped in blond teenagers. "Rennaay, we thought you said we were staying in a hotel."

She put her arms around them. "We are. We have a suite but there are no more rooms to be had."

CHAPTER THIRTY

As planned, the eight of them arrived in Paris in time for a late lunch with Renee's parents. Natalie and Alain greeted their guests warmly and as Alain showed the Grandees to their bedrooms, Natalie welcomed Constance, Chloe, and Cara into the family with hugs and kisses.

Renee introduced Chloe and Cara to Henri and Antoine, the sixteen-year-old nephews she'd recruited to be the twins' New Year's Eve dates, and several other teenage nieces and nephews, all of whom would join them for lunch at the separate teenager table Natalie had set up in another room.

The three sets of parents gelled immediately and conversation flowed easily, filled with laughter and a gentle undertone of love for Renee and Constance and the twins. Art, politics, finance and the lovers responsible for bringing them all together were topics of discussion. After lunch, the Grandees retired to their rooms to rest before the dinner and dancing at Darcy and Andrea's New Year's Eve party. Constance accompanied Alain to his studio and Renee helped Natalie clean the kitchen.

Natalie pulled Renee into a hug as she tried to squeeze behind her to get to the refrigerator. "Constance is lovely, Renee, not just visually, but as far as one can tell in a few hours, as a person and a mother. And she's obviously head over heels in love with you." She turned back to stacking the dishwasher. "Are you happy?"

Renee grinned. "I am. I truly am. Thank you for encouraging me to go after her."

"Are you ready to make a lifelong commitment to her and Chloe and Cara? No second thoughts? No wanting to try other women? No wanting to be free?"

"None of the above. I want to be with Constance and the twins as long as they'll have me, forever, I hope."

Natalie hugged Rene again. "I'm so glad, *mon cher*, I've wanted this for you. You were too immature when you loved Darcy, but you're lucky to have found another love as deep. And, with a beautiful ready-made family. I'd given up having grandchildren from you, so Chloe and Cara are a wonderful surprise."

Renee shoulder bumped her mom. "How many grandchildren does a woman need? You already have thirty, plus five greats."

"Unlike children, you can never have too many grandchildren and thirty-two is definitely better than thirty. Have you and Constance discussed having children?"

"Merde, Mamam, we just got together." Renee grinned. "It might be nice but it will be a while before we get around to that discussion. If ever."

"Your papa is in love with Constance's work so I'm sure we'll be in New York for a joint show in the next year, if not for a wedding. But I'm glad Constance and the girls will be staying for the week so we can get to know each other."

Hearing the excited conversation between Constance and her dad coming down the hall, Renee hugged her mom. "Here they come. Time to drag my family to the hotel so we can all nap before the festivities."

CHAPTER THIRTY-ONE

The girls were excited by the suite, excited to be attending their first New Year's Eve party in an elegant hotel in Paris, excited to be wearing gowns, and excited that they would be accompanied by good-looking boys, even if they weren't real dates. It took a while for them to calm down enough to rest or nap in their room. Happily, the bedrooms were separated by the living room so Renee and Constance had privacy. As she lay on the bed waiting for Constance to return from the girls' room, she wondered at her optimism, upgrading her room at the hotel to a suite the night of Constance's art show, the night she'd met the girls. Thinking back, she didn't think she was so sure things would work out between them. Apparently, the heart knew more about the future than the mind.

When Constance returned they kissed and cuddled and talked about all that had happened in the last few days. Constance dozed off first but Renee was not far behind.

Chloe and Cara were in a tizzy running between their own room and Constance and Renee's trying to hurry their mum along. When the boys arrived, Renee greeted them and called the girls out to wait with them until Constance was ready to go. She took a minute to admire them, the boys handsome in their suits and the girls pretty in matching lavender gowns, and brushed at the tears prickling her eyes. She couldn't have been prouder if she'd birthed the four of them. "You all look so beautiful. Let me take a few pictures. First Cara and Chloe alone, then with Henri and Antoine."

Constance, as always, was gorgeous in an iridescent green gown that hid none of her many charms. As Renee slipped into the jacket of her black tux, Constance wrapped her arms around her. "Can I be your date tonight, gorgeous?"

Renee kissed the top of her head. "Tonight and forever. Shall we?"

Constance pulled back and looked at Renee. "I'm nervous."

"You've met most of the important ones already at Songfest or Thanksgiving."

"True, but I haven't met the most important one."

Renee was puzzled for a second. "Darcy? You'll love her. Everyone does."

Constance ran a finger along Renee's jaw. "She's so important to you. What if she hates me?"

Renee kissed her lightly on the lips. "You're the only one I love, the only one I've loved for more than sixteen years. She's just the one I thought I loved. I'm confident Darcy will love you. Come, the troops in the living room are getting restless. Even though I told them Darcy would probably have a professional photographer, the girls want to take some pictures of you and me and the four of us."

They were all quiet as the elevator slowly rose up to the rooftop ballroom, each nervous for their own reasons. The elevator opened to a crowded room with floor-to-ceiling windows and exquisite views of nighttime Paris. Waiters circulated amongst the groups of guests with trays of drinks and hors d'oeuvres. Renee took a deep breath. She took Constance's hand and asked the girls and her nephews to stay close so she could introduce them to their hosts. As they moved through the crowd, Renee was stopped by members of the Inner Circle and the many others she knew. She felt prouder and prouder each time she introduced Constance as her fiancé and the girls as our girls. When they encountered Tori and Elle and Beth and Gina, she pulled Tori into her arms and whispered, "Thank you for pushing me to look for happiness."

Tori pulled away. "It looks like you found her."

"I did."

Renee grinned and put her arm over Constance's shoulders. Maya joined them as Renee spoke to the small group. "You all know Constance and Chloe and Cara. These are my nephews Henri and Antoine. What you don't know is that Constance and I are engaged." She couldn't keep the stupid grin off her face as her friends crowded in to congratulate her and Constance.

Then the crowd shifted slightly and she was face-to-face with Darcy. Darcy stared for a second, as if not believing her eyes, then grinned. "Renee, you made it."

Renee pulled Constance closer. "Yes. And let me introduce you to my fiancé, Constance, and our daughters Chloe and Cara, and my nephews Henri and Antoine. Our hostess and my friend, Darcy Silver."

"My, my, not one but three lovely ladies." Darcy laughed. She kissed Renee then Constance. "Congratulations and welcome to our New Year's Eve party." She turned. "I seem to have lost my wife."

Just then Andrea drifted into the group. She appeared puzzled. "Constance, how did you get here?"

Constance frowned. "I'm sorry, who…oh, Andrea, I didn't recognize you in a tuxedo and out of your apartment. I'm here with my fiancé, Renee."

Renee looked between the two women. "You know each other?"

Constance leaned into Renee. "Andrea is my landlady."

Renee started laughing. "I can't believe this. Andrea is Darcy's wife."

Chloe tugged on Constance's arm. "Can we walk around or do we have to stay with you old folks?"

Renee turned to Darcy. "What are the arrangements for dinner?"

"No assigned seats. I'd love for you and Constance to sit at our table with Tori and Elle so I can grill you. I want to know how this came about." She glanced at the four kids. "Have the girls met Erik and Joel's girls, Moira and Megan? Maybe they could sit together?"

Constance turned to the four youngsters. "You can wander but absolutely no alcohol. As you heard, you can sit anywhere for dinner. I'm sure Henri and Antoine would enjoy meeting Moira and Megan, so why don't you look for them."

"Yes, Mum," Chloe said, rolling her eyes.

Renee punched her shoulder. "Smartypants. Come find us if you need anything." She put her hands on Antoine's shoulders. "I'm depending on you boys to take care of them. No leaving the party and no crazy stuff, please." The boys grinned and saluted then the four of them melted into the crowd.

Renee was overcome by the reception she and Constance received. The Inner Circle and other friends, including women she'd slept with along the way, came to congratulate them, and of course, to meet the woman who had snagged the elusive Renee. She was so proud of Constance she could hardly keep from shouting about her good luck, and, of course, Constance charmed everyone she met. Renee's parents arrived with the Grandees in tow. Renee waved them over and introduced the grandees to Darcy and Andrea. Darcy suggested they sit with her aunt and uncle and Andrea's parents at a table she'd reserved for them in the dining room. Last Renee saw, they were all happily chatting like old friends.

Dinner was announced and the crowd flowed into another room where round tables for twelve were set up. As she tried to figure out which table was Darcy's, a waitress arrived. "Renee and Constance?"

"Yes. How did you know?" Renee asked.

The waitress grinned. "Sexy butch in a tux and beautiful blond in a shimmering green gown. Please follow me." She led them through the crowd to Darcy's table.

At the table, Renee hugged Darcy again and whispered. "Still think I'm sexy though you're married and I'm committed?"

Darcy planted a quick kiss on Renee's lips. "Some things in life are permanent, sweetie." Seeing Constance's frown, she took Constance's hand and kissed her knuckles. "No need to worry. That was an old friend's kiss. You are a lucky woman, Constance. There are lots of broken hearts in this room tonight."

Constance laughed. "I'm prepared to defend my woman."

Dinner was fun, with lots of joking and teasing. Darcy and Andrea wanted the whole story so Renee and Constance recounted meeting again and picking up where they'd left off more than sixteen years ago. At one point, Renee got up to check on the girls and found them happily seated at a table with other teenagers, all wearing paper hats and blowing toy horns in preparation for midnight. She found her parents and the Grandees and they too were having a wonderful time.

When she sat back down next to Constance, she whispered, "I can't remember ever feeling this happy and this alive. Thank you."

Constance kissed her and everyone at the table tapped their water glasses with a piece of silverware, so they kissed again.

"Good practice for the wedding," Tori said. "Have you set the date?"

Constance glanced at Renee before answering. "Not yet, but we will soon."

After dessert they moved back to the glass-enclosed room for dancing. Renee was surprised to see The Tessa DeLong Band playing. She looked at Darcy. "You brought Tessa and her band over for tonight?"

"Actually, she's paying them for the whole week," Andrea said.

Renee shook her head. "You are something else, my wonderful friend."

This was the first time Renee and Constance had been out as a couple and they danced for hours, switching partners but always coming back together, stopping for drinks but always moving onto the dance floor again. Somewhere along the way, Renee danced with each of the girls and Constance with each of the boys, then they all danced a fast dance together and the kids left to search out their friends. As midnight approached, shoes were kicked off, silly hats were donned and champagne was poured. At midnight the band switched to "Auld Lange Syne." Renee and Constance kissed and wished each other a happy New Year. They found the girls with the Grandees, which now included Renee's parents, standing at the windows watching the fireworks and wished everyone a happy new year.

Cara's eyes were wide and luminous. "It so beautiful." She pointed out the window. "Watch with us."

"Come here." Renee pulled Constance, Chloe, and Cara in front of her, draped her arms over her three girls and the four of them with the Grandees and Renee's nephews marveled at the gorgeous explosions of color over the Eiffel Tower. Her heart bursting with love and pride and joy, Renee felt Paris was rejoicing with her. She hadn't known such happiness was possible. When the fireworks ended, the six Grandees said goodnight, taking Renee's nephews with them and escorting the girls to the suite.

The party was in full force. The laughing, talking and dancing went on.

It was early morning when Tessa announced the next song would be the last of the evening. As Tessa and The Tessa DeLong Band eased into "At Last," Darcy and Andrea glided onto the floor. Holding Constance close, Renee watched them for a few seconds trying to remember her feelings that night months ago but only able to feel her incredible love for Constance. She swung them onto the dance floor, Constance melted into her and they kissed. Renee smiled. You really could get drunk on love. The words she sang softly in Constance's ear were different from the lyrics, but they expressed her thoughts and feelings exactly. "At last we found each other, at last you are mine, at last I am yours forever."

Bella Books, Inc.

Women. Books. Even Better Together.

P.O. Box 10543
Tallahassee, FL 32302

Phone: 800-729-4992
www.bellabooks.com

CPSIA information can be obtained
at www.ICGtesting.com
Printed in the USA
LVHW040738120120
643151LV00001B/2/P